Mossy Creek Home

"Delightful."   — *Marie Barnes, former First Lady of Georgia*

"Mitford meets Mayberry in the first book of this innovative and warmhearted new series from BelleBooks."
— Cleveland Daily Banner, *Cleveland, Tennessee*

"MOSSY CREEK is as much fun as a cousin reunion; like sipping ice cold lemonade on a hot summer's afternoon. Hire me a moving van, it's the kind of town where everyone wishes they could live."
— *Debbie Macomber,* NYT *bestselling author*

"A fast, funny, and folksy read. Enjoy!"
— *Lois Battle, acclaimed author of S*toryville, Bed & Breakfast, *and* The Florabama Ladies' Auxiliary & Sewing Circle

"SUMMER IN MOSSY CREEK takes you to a land that time has not forgotten, but has embraced."
— *Jackie K. Cooper, WMAC-AM, Macon, GA*

"Colorfully and cleverly portrayed. A wholesome story."
— *Harriet Klausner, Amazon.com's top reviewer*

"The characters and kinships of MOSSY CREEK are quirky, hilarious and all too human. This story reads like a delicious, meringue-covered slice of home. I couldn't get enough."
— *Pamela Morsi,* USA Today *bestselling author*

"[MOSSY CREEK] is a book you will not lend for fear you won't get it back."
— *Chloe LeMay,* The Herald, *Rock Hill, SC*

"These southern belle authors have done it again, even better this time."
— *Bob Spear, Heartland Reviews*

"In the best tradition of women's fiction, MOSSY CREEK points to a genuine spirit of love and community that is our best hope for the future."
— *Betina Krahn,* NYT *bestselling author of* The Last Bachelor

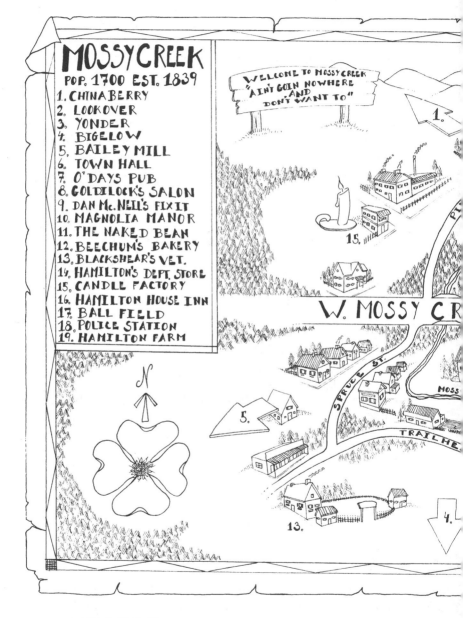

MOSSY CREEK

POP. 1700 EST. 1839

1. CHINA BERRY
2. LOOK OVER
3. YONDER
4. BIGELOW
5. BAILEY MILL
6. TOWN HALL
7. O'DAYS PUB
8. GOLDILOCK'S SALON
9. DAN Mc. NEIL'S FIX IT
10. MAGNOLIA MANOR
11. THE NAKED BEAN
12. BEECHUM'S BAKERY
13. BLACKSHEAR'S VET.
14. HAMILTON'S DEPT. STORE
15. CANDLE FACTORY
16. HAMILTON HOUSE INN
17. BALL FIELD
18. POLICE STATION
19. HAMILTON FARM

WELCOME TO MOSSY CREEK
"AIN'T GOIN NOWHERE
AND
DON'T WANT TO"

W. MOSSY CR

SPRUCE ST.

MOSS

TRAILHE

N

DEDICATION

This book is dedicated to our dear friend and partner, Virginia "Gin" Ellis. We'll say a toast in her honor at O'Day's Pub. We'll ask Jasmine Beleau for a bit of worldly wisdom. We'll make sure young Linda Polk never forgets to believe in herself. We'll always hear Gin's kind voice and cherish her gentle strength in Mossy Creek.

A Day in Mossy Creek

A collective novel featuring the voices of

Deborah Smith, Sandra Chastain
Virginia Ellis and Debra Dixon

with

Susan Goggins, Maureen Hardegree,
Carolyn McSparren, Dee Sterling, Carmen Green,
and Sabrina Jeffries

Smyrna, Georgia

BelleBooks, Inc.

ISBN 978-0-9768760-4-5

A Day in Mossy Creek

This is a work of fiction. Names, characters, places and incidents are either the product of the authors' imaginations or are used ficticiously. Any resemblance to actual persons (living or dead), events or locations is entirely coincidental.

Published by:
BelleBooks, Inc. · P.O. Box 67 · Smyrna, GA 30081
We at BelleBooks enjoy hearing from readers. You can contact us at the address above or at BelleBooks@BelleBooks.com

Visit our website— **www.BelleBooks.com**

First Edition February 2006

10 9 8 7 6 5 4 3

Cover art: © J D Grant | Dreamstime.com"
Cover design: Martha Crockett
Mossy Creek map: Dino Fritz

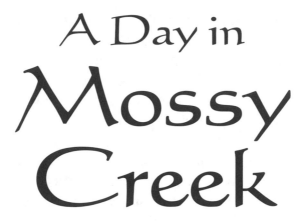

A Day in
Mossy
Creek

Odd Places & Beautiful Spaces
A Guide to the Towns & Attractions of the South

Mossy Creek, Georgia

Don't miss this quirky, historic Southern village on your drive through the Appalachian mountains! Located in a breathtaking valley two hours north of Atlanta, the town (1,700 residents, established 1839) is completely encircled by its lovely namesake creek. Picturesque bridges span the creek around the turn-of-the-century town square like charms on a bracelet. Be sure to arrive via the scenic route along South Bigelow Road, the main two-lane from Bigelow, Mossy Creek's big-sister city, hometown of Georgia governor Ham Bigelow. (Don't be surprised if you overhear "Creekites" in heated debate about Ham, who's the nephew of longtime Mossy Creek mayor, Ida Walker.) You'll know when you reach the Mossy Creek town limits — just look for the charming, whitewashed grain silo by the road at Mayor Walker's farm. Painted with the town's pioneer motto — *Ain't goin' nowhere, and don't want to* — the silo makes a great photo opportunity. The motto perfectly sums up the stubborn (but not unfriendly) free spirits you'll find everywhere in what the chamber of commerce calls "Greater Mossy Creek," which includes the outlying mountain communities of Bailey Mill, Over, Yonder, and Chinaberry.

Lodging, Dining, and Attractions: Shop and eat to your heart's delight around the town's shady square. Don't miss *Mama's All You Can Eat Café*, *Beechum's Bakery* (be sure to say hello to Bob, the "flying" Chihuahua), *The Naked Bean* coffee shop, *O'Day's Pub*, the *Bubba Rice Diner*, *Hamilton's Department Store* (featuring the origami napkin work of local beauty queen Josie McClure), *Hamilton House Inn*, the *I Probably Got It* store, *Moonheart's Natural Living*, and *Mossy Creek Books and What-Nots*. Drop by town hall for a look at the notorious Ten-Cent Gypsy (a carnival booth at the heart of a dramatic Creekite mystery). Stop by the town jail for an update on local shenanigans courtesy of Officer Sandy Crane, who calls herself "the gal in front of the man behind the badge," Mossy Creek Police Chief Amos Royden (recently featured in *Georgia Today Magazine* as the sexiest bachelor police chief in the state). And don't forget to pop into the newspaper offices of the *Mossy Creek Gazette*, where you can get the latest event news from Katie Bell, local gossip columnist *extraordinaire*.

As Katie Bell likes to say, "In Mossy Creek, I can't make up better stories than the truth."

A Who's Who of Mossy Creek

Ida Hamilton Walker — Mayor. Devoted to her town. Menopausal. Gorgeous. Trouble.

Amos Royden — Ida's much-younger police chief. Trying hard not to be irresistible.

Katie Bell — Gossip columnist and town sleuth. Watch out!

Sue Ora Salter Bigelow — Newspaper publisher. Fighting the Salter romance curse.

Jasmine Beleau — Fashion consultant. Her secret past is a shocker.

Josie McClure — Failed beauty queen. Budding interior designer. Talent: origami napkin folding.

Harry Rutherford — Josie's mountain man and fiance. PhD and local version of Bigfoot.

Hamilton Bigelow — Governor of Georgia. Ida's nephew. A typical politician. 'Nuff said?

Win Allen — *aka* Chef Bubba Rice — the *Emeril* of Mossy Creek.

Ingrid Beechum — Baker. Doting surrogate grandma. Owns Bob, the famous "flying" Chihuahua.

Hank and Casey Blackshear — Run the veterinary clinic. Most inspirational local love story.

Sandy Crane — Amos's scrappy dispatcher. If Dolly Parton and Barney Fife had a daughter. . .

Ed Brady — Farmer. Santa. The toughest, sweetest old man in town.

Rainey Cecil — Owns Goldilocks Hair, Nail and Tanning Salon. Bringing big hair to a whole new generation.

Michael Conners — Sexy Chicago Yankee whose Irish pub lures dart-tourney sharks.

Tag Garner — Ex pro-footballer turned sculptor. Good natured when bitten by old ladies.

Maggie Hart — Herbalist. Tag's main squeeze. Daughter of old lady who bit him.

Millicent Hart — See above. Town kleptomaniac. Sorry she bit Tag. Sort of.

Del Jackson — Hunky retired lieutenant colonel. Owns Ida's heart. For now. See Amos.

Bert Lyman — The voice of Mossy Creek. Owner, manager, DJ of WMOS Radio.

Opal Suggs — Retired teacher who adopts needy kids. Talks to her sisters' ghosts who foretell NASCAR winners.

Dwight Truman — Chamber president. Insurance tycoon. Ida's nemesis, along with Ham Bigelow. Weasel.

Swee Purla — Evil interior design maven. Makes even Martha Stewart look wimpy.

Mossy Creek Gazette

106 Main Street • Mossy Creek, GA 30000

From the desk of Katie Bell

Lady Victoria Salter Stanhope
The Clifts
Seaward Road
St. Ives, Cornwall, TR3 7PJ
United Kingdom

Hey, Vick!

Have you ever heard the saying,
"Still waters run deep?"

No? Well, maybe it's an American
"thang." We say it a lot in
Mossy Creek, though most of our
waters aren't <u>still</u>. Right now,
considering it's wintertime and
cold enough to freeze an Eskimo,
our waters — still or not — have
a rim of ice. You know, Vick,
it's strange how we get ice and
cold weather, but not much snow.
Even here in the north Georgia
mountains, we're lucky to have
one big snow day per winter
— meaning enough white on the
ground to grab a make-do sled and
head for the nearest steep hill.

So it's cold and dry here, with
bright blue skies and frost on
the windows. Snuggling weather.
Frisky weather. Bored-indoors-
and-looking-for-excitement
weather.

You know what that means. In
Mossy Creek, it means <u>Trouble</u>.

I swear. One Saturday in mid-
January the temperature went
down, and the calls to the police
went up.

What a day!

Your chilly gossip correspondent,

Katie

A New Year's resolution is meant to be broken.

Ida Gives
as Good as She Gets
Chapter 1

It seemed like just another Saturday in Mossy Creek, but I knew different. Trouble whirled through the cold winter air. My Creekite intuition went on high alert.

I had been punked.

That's how my granddaughter, Little Ida, put it. *Last fall, Nana, you got punked at the Sitting Tree.* Meaning I was *had.* This is what I deserve for buying Little Ida a rap-music version of Mother Goose's fairy tales for her birthday. An eight-year-old who talks like Eminem.

But it's true. Last fall yours truly, the smart and wily Ida Hamilton Walker, got punked. Bamboozled. *Conned.* By my own police chief. Amos Royden threatened to take our relationship public, that is, to court me, to pursue me, to put some moves on me. To make our invisible romance a *real* one.

As mayor of Mossy Creek I can stand my ground on any threat except being openly seduced by my own police chief. So last fall I turned tail and ran, to my shame. But I didn't desert The Sitting Tree. Oh, no. I just went underground with my civil disobedience, on the tree's behalf.

I marshaled the Foo Club and the rest of my loyal troops, and discreetly directed their protests. We managed to stir up plenty of public outrage *and* get the TV news cameras turned on us, a tactic we've perfected several times since we kidnapped the new welcome sign a while back. As a bonus, we antagonized my pompous nephew, Governor Ham Bigelow, who, as it turned out, has a big-money family connection to the scheme to bulldoze the tree. As usual.

Best of all, we got a temporary restraining order against Whoopee Arcades, Inc., the cheesy, underhanded, Bigelow-cronyism-connected amusement park developer who was planning to destroy the Sitting Tree *and* flatten the foothill ridges of Rose Top, the historic mountain where the tree stands in a lower meadow.

Since then I've kept the restraining order alive while feverishly searching for evidence I need to save the tree and its mountain meadow permanently. I know I'll win that battle, but it'll be a tainted victory. I can't forgive myself for my cowardice in the face of Amos's oh-so-not-subtle romantic threat. No way. I've been kicking my own svelte behind for the past four months.

"It must be menopause," I told my cousin and best gal pal, Ingrid Beechum. "Amos gives me *one* indiscreet look and I lose the ability to think straight. How about you and I call a meeting of the garden club, including Eula Mae and every other wise old woman we can think of in Mossy Creek, drink some martinis, then perform one of those 'Embrace Your Inner Crone' rituals? Maybe then I'll accept my middle-agedness and stop wishing for … stop wishing. I'm a grandmother, for godssake!"

Ingrid snorted. "Menopause? You just had your hormones checked. If your estrogen level were any higher you'd qualify as a fertility goddess. Admit it, cousin. Damn the controversy. This is the twenty-first century. Fifty is the new thirty. Older women aren't *old*. They run corporations, they wear thong underwear, they sleep with younger men. *You want to be with Amos.* Until you come to terms with that, your Inner Crone won't be any match for your *Outer Hotti*e."

Ingrid has spewed wisdom like that ever since she squelched her personal demons and became a surrogate grandmother to Jayne Reynold's little boy. Ingrid not only embraces her Inner Crone, she's put thong panties on it.

All right, I admit it: I'm not a crone yet, and I don't want to become one. Ever. I'm proud of my sexy body and proud of being the outrageously sexy mayor of Mossy Creek, the town my family helped create and I'm charged with protecting. If I can keep Mossy Creek safe and secure from the ravages of a world too eager to bulldoze everything sacred, I'll grow old happily. *Some day.* But not right now.

Right now I've got to decide what I'm going to do with the rest of my life. Make hay while the sun shines. Get wild or get mild. *Choose.*

Oh, god, but I don't want to choose. In the past few years, retired Colonel Del Jackson has romanced my socks off — and other articles of clothing — and I've had a great time with him. How can I seriously think about Amos when I've got Del? Del's a brindle-haired hunk of mature man, he's confident, sexy, fun, romantic, and he's *my* age. So why was there always this pestering little voice in my head, this Peggy Lee voice, softly caterwauling, *Is that all there is?*

Peggy Lee? My *mother* listened to Peggy Lee, for godssake. My uptight older sister, Ardaleen, listens to Peggy Lee. But not me. I'm a free spirit, a child of the Sixties, I still have my tie-dyed peasant skirt from college. I'm a Stevie Nicks gal. I own every Fleetwood Mac album and every single song Stevie Nicks recorded after the group broke up. I also own the eight-tracks of those albums, and the cassettes, and the CDs, and when they come out with an electrode that allows me to plug an iPod into my head and pump the music straight to my brain, I'll probably own that, too. I *channel* Stevie Nicks like a psychic channels a spirit. Not Peggy Lee.

Is that all there is? What? All *what* is? What am I wishing for?

Rescue. There's that word, again, the horrible word. *Rescue me. Rescue me. Rescue me.* I've never asked to be rescued in my entire life. Even with Jeb, my husband, my soulmate, the father of my son — I never asked Jeb to rescue me. So why do I keep thinking this way?

Rescue me from myself, Amos.

This is why I've been having nightmares since last fall.

It's the same dream, over and over. I cling helplessly to a high branch of the Sitting Tree, and beneath me stands Amos, looking up at me with his quiet, intensely complex dark eyes.

"Rescue me," I call down, despite the fact that I should feel maternal or something, since he's fifteen years younger than I. Despite the fact that I'm his boss, as mayor of Mossy Creek. Talk about a violation of ethics. Talk about the potential for sexual harassment. Talk about an episode of *Desperate Housewives*. But in my dream I don't care. I have no ethics. And no shame.

"Rescue me," I whisper.

And he nods, and his face relaxes, and he holds up both strong, capable arms. Whenever I'm close to him, he smells like fresh cotton sheets dried in the summer sun. I've never told anyone that, before. Especially not him. But he seems to know my secrets. "Take a chance on me, Ida," he says. "I'm clean. Let go. Jump."

I push myself off the high limb, and I fall happily toward his arms.

And then I wake up. Terrified. No menopausal hot flash could possibly be worse than the flop sweat of my Amos dream. I can't bear to find out whether Amos catches me. I can't bear to find out if he lets me hit the ground, hard. I don't want to dream about wanting Amos. I don't want to remember our torrid conversation at the Sitting Tree last fall. That's sacrilege. I kissed Jeb under that tree, when we were young.

But after he died, I kissed Amos under that tree, too.

I wince every time I think about that fact. Amos was sixteen, but serious and mature for his age, and I was 31, a grieving widow. It was just a kiss. *For comfort,* I told myself. And just once. But still. Twenty years have passed since our kiss, but the infamy of it, and the allure, have never faded. Neither Amos nor I mentioned it again. Never even hinted at it.

Until he punked me at the tree, last fall.

I have to get Amos out of my dreams, my memories, my mind. I have to get him out of the Sitting Tree.

Let me rescue you, Ida.

No, Amos. I've got to rescue myself.

🌿🌿🌿

Dawn had just broken. I got up earlier than usual at Hamilton Farm, after another bad dream about Amos and the Tree. Plus I expected an early phone call from Hope Bailey Settles, my other favorite cousin and co-conspirator, who I'd sent on a mission that was probably a longshot. At the moment she and her husband, Marle, were up in Asheville, North Carolina, a good three hours' drive from Mossy Creek. Hope had spent the past two days ripping old paneling off the attic walls of a historic house that had once belonged to our mutual great aunt, Belinda Hamilton Bailey. With any luck, she'd found the evidence we needed to save the Tree once and for all.

I paced and watched the sunrise from Jeb's favorite window in his study. The day was blue and crisp, a perfect winter morning in January, the kind where the sunlight feels like golden crystals on your skin. A mere trickle of freezing, blue-golden air seeping under a window sash was usually enough to erase my worries and boost my mood like a whiff of pure oxygen. My husband had loved weather like this. *Hibernation time*, he liked to call it, looking at me with a gleam in his eye. We'd dive back into bed. Naked, under warm heirloom quilts, we did everything *but* hibernate. And so I cherished the memories.

But on this day I stood frowning, a steaming cup of gourmet coffee in hand, Stevie Nicks on my CD player, my silk robe bound around me. A human tourniquet of impatience. Rose Top Mountain loomed in the distance, gray-green and majestic. More than a thousand acres of woodland flow from its lower ridges to the edge of the farm's property. I couldn't see the Sitting Tree at its base. But the tree was there, nevertheless. A spectral monument, always in my thoughts.

I clenched my coffee mug, debated adding a slug of bourbon to it, then stiffened my spine and refused. *Keep staring out this window as penance, you punked mayor. Look at the view, and don't flinch from the past, the present, or the future.*

From Jeb's favorite window I could see the entire lovely expanse of the farm's red barns, weathered sheds, and rolling pastures. My herd of caramel-colored Jersey milk cows ambled toward the main dairy barn, called by the lure of sweet grain for breakfast and a friendly pat on the rump, not to mention a pleasant massage from the milking machines. The dairy at Hamilton Farm is run by old Ben Howell, a flatlander from Florida who, along with his wife, Sadie, managed the farm's dairy operation since I was a girl. When I look out my windows, I see my family's history. And my own.

Beyond the cow pasture the rolling land climbs in a broad, gentle swell of brown winter grass covered in glittering frost. For over 150 years my forebears had grown high-protein wheat on that acreage, for hay to feed the cows. I'd kept up the tradition faithfully.

Until now. Now rows of baby grape plants twined their naked winter vines along the wires of sturdy trellises on that land. I've cultivated a good ten acres in vineyard over the past few years. With any luck I'll get the vines' first big harvest by summer. Mom-and-pop wineries are springing up all over north Georgia, and I've contracted with one to distill the debut batch of wine from my grapes. Next year I'll make the wine myself. I've had plans drawn up for a woodsy, Craftsman-style lodge to house the equipment, a wine cellar, and a tasting room. Wolfman Washington, my fellow Foo Clubber and bulldozer operator, just finished clearing and grading a site on a ridge nearby. When the winery building is finished, my guests — and eventually, my customers — will be able to stand on the winery's veranda, sipping a Jeb Walker chardonnay or a Jeb Walker merlot while they look out over the vineyards, toward Rose Top Mountain and the Sitting Tree.

You heard right. Jeb Walker wine. From the Walker Winery at Hamilton Farm. I've already had a logo drawn up. I've already got stationary and business cards. The logo will be an outline of the farm's famous grain silo in rich hunter green with Jeb's initials stamped over the silo in gold. It's classic but friendly. Unforgettable. Like the man who inspired it.

You see, Jeb always wanted to plant a vineyard. Back then, everyone pooh-poohed his daydream, myself included. We chortled at his idea of growing decent wine grapes in Mossy Creek. We thought good wine only came from two places: France and California. Jeb, however, never wavered. "One day," he always said, "I'm going to cover the hill outside my study in grape vines, and I'm going to pick the grapes and stomp them with my own feet and age the juice in oak barrels, and when Ida and I are old we'll sit on the back veranda and drink that vintage wine. We'll have the last laugh."

He never got to plant those grapes. He never got to grow old. I'll never get to have that glass of wine on the veranda with him beside me. But Jeb *will* get the last laugh. I'll make sure of that.

I curled my fist around my morning coffee mug and raised the mug in a salute to Rose Top Mountain and the Sitting Tree. "Nobody's going to build an amusement park over there," I swore aloud. "Nobody's going to ruin the view from Jeb's vineyard." I took a deep swig of coffee.

When my cell phone rang (it plays the opening bars of Stevie Nicks' *Dreams*) I nearly spit French roast on Jeb's mahogany desk. I hurriedly fished around in my robe's pockets until I found the tiny phone. There's something ignoble about trying to field an important call on a phone the size of a matchbox.

"Hope?" I yelled into thin air as I slapped the entire phone to one ear. "What did you find — besides hundred-year-old cockroach skeletons and dirty drawings of women in corsets."

Hope hooted. "It's here! Just like Cousin Farley wrote in that ancient diary you found! Behind the wallboard in the attic, right where he said he put it for safekeeping after Great Aunt Belinda died — stuffed between the pages of the ladies' lingerie section of a 1902 Sears and Roebuck catalog!"

I hooted in return. God bless our great aunt's son — our long-dead mutual cousin, Farley — and his fetish for busty Victorian babes wearing whalebone. "Hurry home," I told Hope. "I'm calling Ingrid. We'll pick you up at Bailey Mill in a few hours."

"Where are we going?"

I chuckled fiendishly. My New Year's resolution — to stay out of trouble — floated past like a small, resigned angel, waving goodbye. "We're driving down to Atlanta to visit the governor. He's got a meeting scheduled with the Whoopee Arcade people this afternoon. Perfect timing." I paused, relishing the image of my pompous nephew roasting on a slow spit of defeat. "Ham's about to get *punked.*"

"The Voice Of The Creek"

Good morning, Mossy Creek! This is Bert Lyman, as always, of WMOS-FM and its sister station, WMOS-TV, local cable access channel 22, bringing you breaking news. Flash! The streets of downtown Mossy Creek are finally safe again. The notorious Miss Irene, age 93, has been captured. No word yet on whether police chief Amos Royden ended her wild spree by running her off the sidewalk, or whether he resorted to shooting the tires off her scooter. More news as we get it. Stay tuned!

Teach a woman to drive, and you give her the world. Teach an old woman to drive a scooter, and you give the world a major scare.

Melvin and Miss Irene Go to Wal-Mart
Chapter 2

There was something about that Saturday that promised trouble. You know, like the feeling you get that makes you want to brush off the centipede crawling up your backbone. For months I had feared it would come to this, starting way back when Melvin called me to tell me that he was "taking Miss Irene to Wal-Mart."

My name is Casey Blackshear. I'm married to Hank, the local veterinarian and Mossy Creek town councilman. Miss Irene is Hank's great aunt, three times widowed, with no children. In all fairness, I have to say that all three of her husbands adored her. Unfortunately, being a wife was the only thing she excelled at.

Husband number three died twenty years ago. Now she's ninety-three and a diva, as much as a diva can be, who, except for a church-organized tour to Niagara Falls, hasn't been out of Bigelow County since she turned seventy-five. Until two years ago, she and her three cousins, all widows, lived in the same trailer court down in Bigelow — in separate trailers, of course.

They got up each morning promptly at 7:15, made their beds, brushed their teeth, combed their tightly-curled perms and dressed, always with ear bobs (clip-ons of course) and lipstick. Each ate a bowl of cereal — fiber for their systems — and drank one-half cup of prune juice and one cup of decaffeinated coffee. Then they washed the dishes and waited for someone to come by or call.

Most days someone did. Of course the cousins went to prayer meeting on Wednesday night, shopped at the Bigelow Ingles on Friday, went out to eat on Saturday night, and went to Sunday School and church on Sunday, with the youngest cousin driving. Then Aunt Irene fell and broke her good hip; she'd already done a job on the other one. That's when the Bigelow cousins pronounced with greatly exaggerated regret that they could no longer care for Irene since they were in their eighties and needed looking after themselves. Against her wishes, and Hank's, we brought her to the assisted living section of Magnolia Manor, here in Mossy Creek.

I should now explain about Melvin. He was Hank's best boyhood friend, becoming even closer after he was wounded in Desert Storm and sent home. Melvin's parents had died by then, and he had no other family. Hank offered him a job, and Melvin took it. Then Melvin built himself a one-room apartment at the end of the clinic, where he lives now.

Since then he's been our self-appointed keeper, handyman, kennel man, and veterinary assistant when Hank has to make house calls. And every Saturday he looks in on Ed Brady, a local senior citizen. Ed is a crusty old-timer who is just as set in his ways as Aunt Irene. Doesn't seem to bother Melvin, who just ignores their preferences and makes them do what they need to do, when nobody else can.

Since I'm in a wheelchair, Melvin thinks he has to make sure that my daughter, Li, and I are always safe. He doesn't need to, but we humor him by agreeing. When Aunt Irene came to Mossy Creek, Melvin just extended his bodyguarding services to her, whether she wanted them or not.

Melvin shaves his head. The color of warm cocoa,

he looks like a dark-chocolate Mr. Clean. He's a handsome man, a good man. Everybody loves Melvin, except Aunt Irene. At first, she didn't consider it proper to ride around Mossy Creek with a black man driving her car. No amount of discussion changed her mind. Her racism embarrassed us, but we were stuck.

Didn't bother Melvin. He went out and rented *Driving Miss Daisy*, and we had movie night. After the movie, he brought out his new chauffeur's cap and announced that he'd drive and Irene could sit in the back. Nobody else in Mossy Creek had a chauffeur.

That appealed to her, but there was another problem. Aunt Irene didn't want anybody driving her car except herself or me. The obvious problem here was that, as drivers, neither of us could use our legs — she of the broken hips and me of the auto accident that left me in a wheelchair. Hank and I tried to get her to sell the car, but she refused. She fully intended to drive the car herself — after her hip healed. We realized that dream was important and stopped nagging her.

The state of Georgia didn't help our "Ground Miss Irene" cause. When it came time to renew her driver's license, the license bureau gave her a new one —good for another five years — without so much as a question, despite her tottering along on a walker.

She can no longer read street signs, but the bureau never even tested her eyes. To make matters worse, she forgets how to get where she is going in Bigelow and she's never learned the streets in Mossy Creek. At least she's confined to Magnolia Manor unless someone takes her out — which is more than you could say about Ed before he had his cataract surgery. You remember? After Chief Royden took his license, Ed drove his tractor into town and directly into Mossy Creek — the actual creek — thanks to an encounter with Ham Bigelow's limo.

Still, Aunt Irene managed to move about enough to keep her own battery charged; her Pontiac wasn't so lucky. Finally, Hank told her that the car needed to be driven to keep its battery charged and its parts working. He didn't have time to drive it, and I couldn't. Reluctantly, she agreed to let Melvin drive the Pontiac at least once a month.

Dutifully, he drove it over to Magnolia Manor every week. She'd walk out to the car and sit in the back seat while Melvin cranked the engine. But she continued to refuse his offer to take her for a ride.

Until one weekday.

I was at the clinic. Melvin called on his cell phone to tell me that he wouldn't be back for a while. He and Miss Irene were going to Wal-Mart.

Now you understand, there is no Wal-Mart in Mossy Creek. They had to go down to Bigelow. I didn't ask what they were shopping for. I just told him to drive carefully, glad that I didn't have to accompany them. Taking Aunt Irene anywhere means we park in a handicap area, Hank goes into the establishment and finds a store wheelchair, and he pushes her around while I drive my motorized scooter.

On that day, I expected Aunt Irene and Melvin to be back in a couple of hours. That estimate gave them thirty minutes to Bigelow and thirty minutes back, and an hour to do whatever they were doing. Two hours turned into three, and I began to worry. Finally Melvin drove into the clinic parking area at three o'clock. He parked and locked the car and came into the house, beaming from ear to ear.

"You're not gonna believe it, Casey, but Miss Irene drove one of those electric scooters all over Wal-Mart."

I was stunned. We'd tried to get her into one of the electric chairs for months. She'd refused. She always said firmly that she was too old to learn how to drive one of those *things*.

"How'd you manage that?' I asked.

"Well, they were out of regular wheelchairs and I just told her she was going to learn how. If she could drive a car, she could drive a scooter. I told her she could even get her own scooter and drive it on the sidewalks from Magnolia Manor to church. The idea of being able to go to church by herself did the trick."

"Melvin, I'm amazed."

"Me, too. We turned the scooter on, and I walked beside her and cleared the way until she got the hang of it." He smiled. "She didn't run over but one lady. That lady saw us coming and just stood there. Miss Irene panicked and pinned her to the cashier's counter before I could pry her fingers off the accelerator."

"Oh, Melvin, was the woman hurt?"

"Heck, no. Besides, wouldn't have mattered. We were in the pharmacy."

"So what did Irene buy?"

"Nothing. The other ladies at the home have started going to Wal-Mart every week, but Miss Irene doesn't want to ride on that little bus with them. She just wasn't gonna let those other ladies have anything on her. So we not only went to Wal-Mart, we went them one better."

"I'm afraid to ask. What did you do?"

"We went to lunch at the Bigelow Cafeteria. That's what took so long. I got the cafeteria wheelchair for her, and rolled her up and down the line first to see what her choices were, then we had to go back and fill up her plate. Do you know how many different things they offer there? I counted thirty dishes, not including the salad bar, the pizza bar and the dessert bar. She had to have one little spoonful of everything. Apple season in Mossy Creek doesn't create a traffic jam like we did in the Bigelow Cafeteria. Good thing it wasn't on the weekend."

I was stunned. For six months, Hank's great-aunt had

refused to allow Melvin to drive her around. Now they were having lunch together. I couldn't wait to tell Hank. He rolled on the floor laughing. That was before we realized that Melvin had created a monster.

❦ ❦ ❦

If an electric scooter worked at Wal-Mart, it would work in Mossy Creek. Aunt Irene and Melvin put their heads together and ordered a scooter advertised in the AARP magazine. It would go anywhere, and it did.

Last summer, Aunt Irene became the terror of Mossy Creek, beeping her horn and zipping along the sidewalks, sending both residents and tourists fleeing into the street. She was a pinball gone amuck. Mossy Creek Drugs and Sundries sent her flowers in appreciation of the business her collisions sent to them.

Melvin and the maintenance man at Magnolia Manor, Bunkin Brown, concocted an umbrella stand on the back of the seat, which shielded Aunt Irene from the rain and the sun. So on a cool morning in autumn, Aunt Irene was out and about, enjoying her hobby: hot-rodding.

And Amos busted her.

"Miss Irene," our police chief said politely, "Can you slow that thing down enough that I can walk along with you?"

"Well, I can, but I was heading for the Hamilton Inn to have lunch. If I hurry I can get there before Millicent Hart Lavender and her group of old harpies."

"Miss Irene," Amos said, "we have to talk."

"Well, make it fast," she said, blowing her horn as she swerved to miss Win Allen, who jumped out of the way so quickly he dropped the five-gallon container of stew he was about to load in his Bubba Rice Catering van. Dwight Truman, on his newest racing bike, hit the stew head-on.

Dwight and his bike landed in the arms of some big azaleas. Win's stew seeped from the broken plastic container, making a steaming, gumbo-ish puddle on the street.

Miss Irene never even slowed down.

Amos jogged along beside her. "Tell me the truth. During World War Two, you were trained to drive a tank."

"Don't be sassy to your elders! It's about time you did something about these rude pedestrians. They can *see* my handicapped tag hanging from my handlebars."

"Miss Irene," Amos explained patiently, still jogging, "it's not the pedestrians. It's your driving that's causing concern."

"I'm a very good driver, Amos. I haven't hit anyone since my trial run at Wal-Mart. And *that* woman had plenty of time to get out of the way."

"You haven't hit anyone because everybody in Mossy Creek knows to get out of your way. You drive too fast and you expect your horn and your handicapped sticker to clear a path for you."

"I certainly do. I've done a little research. The handicapped vehicles have the right away."

"Only when you're parking. And that's what I'm going to have to do with your scooter. Park it. *Permanently.* Unless you slow down and show your fellow citizens some courtesy, I'm going to have to impound your vehicle."

Miss Irene came to a stop. "On what grounds?"

"Speeding and reckless driving."

"Young man, this isn't an automobile. Now, get out of my way."

Amos blocked her. "Sorry, Miss Irene, I can't do that."

She stared firmly at him. He stared firmly back. It was a stare-off.

A crowd gathered. Half the onlookers sided with Amos and the other half egged Miss Irene on.

"Stand up for your rights, Granny," one yelled.

Another yelled, "Chief, call Hank and tell him to get over here and take his senior delinquent in hand."

"Aw, come on, cut her some slack. She's crippled," a man with a cane yelled.

"Somebody call Bert Lyman over at WMOS and tell him to get over here with his video camera."

Aunt Irene's eyes lit up when she heard *that*. The only thing that Aunt Irene liked better than dressing up was to be the center of attention. The two things were mutually compatible. And she wasn't above using her age as a tool for getting her way. She was having the most fun she'd had in years.

Lifting her chin, she tilted her head and adjusted her sun hat. "Please do call Bert. I think Mossy Creek's mistreatment of the elderly should be shown everywhere. I bet it even gets on CNN. Now, down in Bigelow, this would never happen. Only Mossy Creek would persecute a ninety-three-year-old woman."

Amos realized he'd opened a can of worms. Aunt Irene wasn't going down without a fight. Melvin arrived on the scene. Melvin came to the rescue.

"Miss Irene, Casey needs you at the clinic right away."

"Needs me? What for?"

"Hank's on a call and one of the patients he's boarding is going into labor. She needs your help."

It was obvious that Aunt Irene was torn between being needed by her great nephew's wife and being persecuted. Obligation and family need took precedence. She pointed her finger at Amos and gave him one last parting shot. "Amos Royden, whether or not I want to be, I'm a tax-paying citizen of Mossy Creek, (well, she paid sales tax) and I have rights. We'll talk about this after I've handled Casey's emergency."

With that, she beeped her horn, backed up and with Melvin running along beside her clearing traffic, drove quickly back to Magnolia Manor. There, Aunt Irene traded her scooter for her Pontiac and, with Melvin wearing his chauffeur's cap, she ignored the cool autumn air and let down her window, waving as if she were Miss America on parade as they drove out of town.

When they reached the clinic, I sheepishly admitted to getting her there under false pretenses. There was no labor and delivery problem. But there was trouble of a different kind. Dwight Truman had just called Hank on his cell phone. As chairman of the town council, Dwight was calling an emergency council meeting for that very same night, to declare Aunt Irene a menace.

Dwight wanted her banned from the sidewalks of Mossy Creek.

❦❦❦

A few nights later, Creekites packed the courtroom where town council meetings are held. Bert Lyman was present, his WMOS-TV camera in hand. Ingrid Beechum, Jane Reynolds, Hope Bailey Settles, and most of the other shop owners were there, and all the residents of Magnolia Manor. Irene's friends held up signs. *Irene is Innocent. Seniors Will Overcome. Go, Irene!*

Dwight Truman called the meeting to order. "Good evening, fellow Creekites. I'm filling in for Mayor Walker, who will be here any minute. She called to say she's conferring with a lawyer about protecting the Sitting Tree, and the meeting's running a little late." He rapped the gavel. "You all know that we're here tonight because we seem to have a little problem: Miss Irene is terrorizing the citizens on her scooter."

"And the tourists," somebody called out.

Dwight put a serious expression on his face. "With our apologies to Dr. Blackshear, we have to decide what we need to do about his great aunt."

"I'm sure we'll do what's fair," Hank said stiffly. He doesn't like Dwight. Very few people in Mossy Creek like Dwight. Look up "pompous" in the dictionary, and you'll see Dwight's picture.

Dwight nodded. "The citizens love Miss Irene, and we have made every effort to accommodate her new means of transportation. However, we can't have our town's commerce threatened by her. I say that not only as head of the town council, but also as head of the chamber of commerce. Commerce is clearly *my* responsibility. And she *does* threaten it. Chief Royden, what do you have to say about the situation?"

Amos stood. "I've handled a lot of dilemmas in my career as a law officer, but a ninety-three-year-old menace on a scooter is a first. I've had Teresa Walker research the legal aspect of this case, and she tells me that we have no regulations to cover this."

"Thank goodness," a female voice said. "Unlike our council chair, other lawmakers have better things to do than regulate handicapped citizens."

We all turned to look as Ida strode up the center isle. She was wearing snug jeans, cowboy boots, and a quilted windbreaker over a white turtleneck. Her red hair spilled from a casual twist. I snuck a peek at Amos's expression. He watched Ida with the quiet, intense focus of a man who knew what — and who — was important to him. Everyone in town saw how he looked at Ida whenever Ida wasn't looking back.

Dwight turned red and looked annoyed — his usual look around Ida. She took the gavel from him and sat down behind the "Mayor Ida H. Walker" sign on the council table.

She settled her firm, green eyes on Amos. "Chief," she said, making it sound like a caress, whether she realized that or not, "Chief, Miss Irene wasn't exceeding any speed limit, was she?"

Amos smiled slightly. He never let Ida get the upper hand, if he could help it. "It's hard to say. What is the speed limit on the sidewalk, these days?"

People laughed. Ida thumped the gavel, giving Amos a slit-eyed smile that promised repercussions. She was always touchy around him now. The controversy over the Sitting Tree wasn't helping. "Very funny, Chief. The city ordinance clearly says any handicapped person can park their vehicle in wheelchair-marked spaces."

Dwight piped up. "It doesn't say she can drive like a demon on the sidewalk! Because of her, I bent the front wheel of my new bike!"

Someone called out, "You're always bent, Dwight."

Ida rapped the gavel.

In the back of the courtroom, old Ed Brady cupped a hand around his mouth. "Good manners and a Christian attitude demand that we show consideration for those less physically fortunate than the rest of us. Let Miss Irene run free!"

Applause. Mr. Brady had a crowd of supporters who celebrated his rebellions against authority. Especially when it came to driving vehicles, like Miss Irene's scooter and his farm tractor, in hair-raising ways.

Melvin walked into the courtroom. "Here comes the freedom fighter now!" he announced loudly. He stood at attention. In came Aunt Irene, puttering along on her scooter. She was dressed in a World War II helmet and a flight jacket. "Don't pussyfoot around and lose your Constitutional rights," she said to the audience. "I can tell you from experience, the streets are a war zone. It's every man for himself."

People applauded again. Dwight slapped a hand on the council table. "Not when one man, er, woman puts others in danger."

Ida rapped her gavel. "Chill out, Dwight. You're *dissing* a veteran."

Miss Irene beamed. With her pale, Max Factor face powder and her Revlon Red lipstick, she looked like a gray mouse with pink cheeks and squinched-up lips. But my toddler, little Li Ha Quh Blackshear, took one look at Irene's strange get-up and began to cry with fear.

Miss Irene stopped her scooter. Tears welled up in her eyes. "See what you've done," she said to the council, accusingly. "You've scared my great-great niece. She thinks you're persecuting me. Have you no shame?" If she'd been auditioning for the part of a dying swan, she'd have won, wings down.

She was ninety-three and being persecuted. Melvin had definitely created a monster when he got her a scooter.

The courtroom went silent. I hugged Li and shushed her. She quieted, but kept staring at Irene as if Irene were stranger than usual.

Amos cleared his throat. "Where'd you get the war gear, Miss Irene?"

"From Ed Brady. In that he's had some experience with the law suspending driver's licenses, he's been advising me. Ain't this a kick in the pants? Me, and my *tank*, at war with Mossy Creek. And I don't even have a gun."

"Miss Irene, until we can figure this out, you're free to go, but I'm arresting your scooter."

"You can't do that." She looked at Hank, sitting on the dais behind the council table. "Speak up, Hank. You're supposed to be looking after me, aren't you?"

Hank grinned. "Sorry Aunt Irene, but you're on your own."

Aunt Irene drove her scooter as close to Amos's toes as she could manage. "I've not broken any law, Chief. You said so yourself."

"Well, you have, now. You're blocking the aisle with your vehicle. I'm within the law to impound your scooter as a ... hazard to the public right-of-way."

Aunt Irene looked around helplessly. Then she caught sight of Dwight Truman's racing bike, parked in one corner. "Well, are you impounding Dwight's vehicle, too? It's blocking that corner."

Dwight came to his feet. "That's outrageous!"

"Arrest Dwight's bike!" someone yelled.

People began to chant. *Dwight's bike. Dwight's bike. Dwight's bike.*

Ida silenced them with her gavel. She cut her eyes at Amos. "Chief? I think Miss Irene's got a point."

Amos nodded, barely holding back a smile. "I believe she does. Melvin, if you'll accompany Miss Irene back to Magnolia Manor and then bring the scooter over to the jail, I'll take care of impounding Dwight's bike."

Dwight exploded. "This is absurd! Chief Royden, you can't just stick my expensive racing bike in the jail parking lot. Someone will steal it."

"Oh, I'm not putting in the parking lot. I'm going to lock it and the scooter in a cell. Visiting hours are on Sunday afternoon, one to three."

Dwight sputtered.

The audience applauded.

Hank and Ida hid smiles behind their hands.

Irene raised a fist. Victory, even a symbolic one, was sweet.

Ida rapped her gavel. "I declare this issue resolved. Good night."

Irene's admirers leapt up and surrounded her, patting her shoulders and offering congratulations. With Li seated in a car seat attached to the side of my own scooter, I backed up. That was when I discovered that Melvin had put an automatic back-up horn on my vehicle. *Beep, beep, beep* it went, as if I were driving a fork lift through a warehouse. Already spooked by Aunt Irene, the Creekites gathered in the courtroom scattered, giving me a wide berth.

"Beep, beep, beep," Li said, imitating the horn. I waved to Hank, who waved back. Li beeped us outdoors to my handicapped van. Ed followed us.

"Miss Casey, I'm sorry. I didn't intend to get the town in an uproar. Melvin and I just thought Irene needed some help making her point. She ought to be able to navigate around town on her own, even if she is a mite reckless."

"Well, I think you were certainly right. She's having a ball. So, what do we do now, Ed?"

"Been thinking about that. Don't suppose we could talk the mayor into reactivatin' the Foo Club and get some civil disobedience going, do you? Maybe Wolfman Washington could bulldoze a hole in the jail. Spring Miss Irene's law-breaking scooter."

I laughed. Ida and her Foo Club escapades had become legendary. "I think we've had enough civil disobedience already," I told Ed. "Melvin and you started this. Now you need to put on your thinking cap and get Irene out of it."

He tipped his head to me. "We'll figure something out."

❦❦❦

Amos released his wheeled captives with a stern warning to Aunt Irene and Dwight about the proper use of their vehicles. Neither person was receptive to the chief's suggestion that they take a taxi.

Everything calmed down through the rest of the year. Aunt Irene lay in wait during the holidays. She let the new year begin peacefully. She, Ed and Melvin debated ways to make Mossy Creek scooter-friendly, but didn't appear to be up to any mischief. But then this cold, clear morning in January arrived, the day I should have seen coming for months.

Aunt Irene and her army of cohorts took to the streets in a protest march.

❦❦❦

Mt. Gilead Methodist Church was having their winter fundraiser on the square. Yes, it takes tough, faithful people to schedule an outdoor event in mid-January, but that was part of the appeal. Kind of showing off to the other churches in town. *See? No ice storm, no snow, not even a drizzle of cold, winter rain to mar our event. A perfect winter day. God obviously likes us best.*

They set up nice tents with propane heaters to keep everyone comfortable. The creative church women sell the crafts they've made all year long. They also sell pickles, canned tomatoes and anything else that can be put up in jars. For two days before the event, they assemble and cook their famous homemade chicken stew. They bake dozens of cakes and pies and cookies. Since the new minister, Mark Phillips came, the parsonage has been completely refurbished from money raised through such events.

As usual, people from all over our end of Bigelow County came to town to buy stew and other goodies. I held Li on my lap as I drove my scooter among the tents, hugging her close to me, loving her laughter and wondering how anyone could be as lucky as Hank and I. Hank managed to get away from the clinic for an hour that morning to accompany us to the event. Li picked out a rag doll we bought it, and then she preceded to throw it to the ground with regularity.

She giggled. She threw the doll. Hank fetched it. She had him trained.

About eleven o'clock there was a humming sound, faint at first, then louder. Gradually the murmur caught the attention of the crowd, and they turned toward it. That was when I recognized the lyrics — *We Shall Overcome*. Around the square came a slow-moving line of scooters — there were at least a hundred — headed straight for the church fundraiser. Aunt Irene was leading the charge.

"Casey," my husband said, "what do you know about this?"

"Not a thing, I swear."

I drove my scooter over to Sandy Crane. Mossy Creek's short, curly-blonde police officer was bent so far over a big trash can that her top half disappeared inside. Her gun belt clanked on the basket's metal rim.

"Gotcha, you little mooch," she said, and straightened. She held Ingrid Beechum's Chihuahua, Bob. He had a french fry in his mouth.

"Sandy," I called. "Look what's coming."

You know, lots of towns say they have a town square, but Mossy Creek's town square was a *true* square, with sidewalks and parking spaces built all around it. The difference, unlike most small towns, was that our courthouse wasn't in the center of the square. Instead we have a park with a Confederate statue, a gazebo, picnic tables, big shade trees, little sidewalks and lots of brown winter grass. That day, tents and booths selling the church's goods and chicken stew dotted the area.

You could stand in the square and, turning, see the panorama of downtown Mossy Creek, including Aunt Irene's "Charge of the Scooters," which headed towards us from the north, where Magnolia Manor was located. Sandy and I stared. "Oh, lord," she said slowly. "And here comes Amos."

A police car arrived from the south.

"Did you know about this scheme of Irene's?" I asked. Sandy, like our gossip columnist, Katie Bell, knows almost everything before it happens.

Sandy shook her head. "Not this. Oh, lord. This isn't gonna make the Methodists or the chief happy. On top of which, I gotta go tell him the rumors I've heard about Ida's plan to —"

She clamped her lips shut. I stared at her hard. "Ida's plan to do what?"

"Never mind. It's police business." Sandy hurried away, handing Bob off to someone else.

I drove quickly toward the intersection of Aunt Irene and Amos.

He stepped out of his patrol car, blocking her advance. They met in the middle of the street, eye-to-eye, again.

"Good morning, Miss Irene," Amos said. "Does this mean we're being invaded?"

"Absolutely."

"Do you realize you don't have a parade permit, and you're impeding the flow of traffic around the square?"

"Absolutely. Do you realize how many of your senior citizens are coming to this fundraiser for the first time in years? Senior citizens who expect to spend a great deal of money here and everywhere else in Mossy Creek, now that they can get around the square as easily as anybody with two good legs?"

Amos looked at the hundred faces behind her in the scooter line, all nodding at him beneath yarn caps and mufflers. He sighed. I felt sorry for Amos sometimes. He'd come home from a successful stint as a big-city cop, but still had to prove he was as good a law officer as his daddy, Mossy Creek's legendary police chief, Battle Royden. So Amos dutifully judged beauty contests, looked for lost cats, solved disputes between neighbors, and put up with being the most-watched bachelor to ever secretly court our mayor.

And now he had to face down Aunt Irene.

Her group of protesters started singing a hymn titled *Walking With Jesus*, only they changed the words to *Driving With Jesus.* This time, other Creekites joined in, and even some tourists. Near the front of the line, ancient Eula Mae Whit began beeping her scooter's horn. "I'm a hundred-and-one," she called, looking like a wizened brown fairy in a kinte-cloth coat. "Do I look like I got time to waste on this argument?"

Suddenly, two of the scooters pulled out and glided smoothly to stop on either side of Aunt Irene. Melvin drove one; Ed drove the other. Ed's late wife, Ellie, had been a resident at Magnolia Manor, and it had nearly broken his heart when she died. After that, Ed had almost given up playing Santa Claus for Mossy Creek's Christmas parade. The last few years had been hard on Ed. Now it was obvious he had a new mission in life. He and Aunt Irene had become friends.

He grinned. I looked at Hank. He looked at me and nodded. It had been a long time since anybody had seen Ed smile.

"Amos," Ed said, "I believe that Melvin and I have come up with a solution to our traffic and sidewalk problems."

"I'd be glad to hear it, Ed, but don't you think it could be better addressed at a town council meeting?"

"Why? We got pretty much everybody from the council right here."

Amos ran a hand over his hair. "The thing is, Ed —"

"Come on, Amos," Melvin put in. "Don't you want to at least hear the plan?"

"All right. I'm game. Tell me."

"Wasn't really our idea," Ed said, "it was Amelia's." This produced murmurs in the crowd, since Amelia was the wife of Pastor Phillips. Everyone turned to stare at her. She waved and smiled from a church booth. Ed grinned. "Smart woman, she is. She looks like my Ellie, when Ellie was young."

"I'm listening, Ed," Amos reminded him.

"Look around this square. Our founding families were pretty smart people. They made the streets extra-wide. There's enough room to move the parking lanes out four feet or so. That will give us space to make a bicycle and scooter lane between the parking spots and the sidewalk. Think of the publicity. We even got Dwight Truman on board with the idea. He says Mossy Creek will be the only town he knows that can welcome both the handicapped and the biking clubs."

"We'll put together a volunteer group to paint the new parking lines," Melvin interjected. "It won't cost the taxpayers anything. And think of the new business it will bring in. Buses full of retirees with their wheelchairs and scooters."

You didn't have to be a psychic to see that Amos was thinking this might work. "Sounds good to me, but you'll have to run this past the mayor. I don't know where she is today." Amos spotted Ingrid across the street, leaving her bakery in what appeared to be a hurry. "Ingrid," he called. "Where's Ida? I thought she'd be here by now."

"I don't know a *thing*," Ingrid said, looking guilty of *something*. She tucked Bob tail-first into her over-sized purse, then headed down a back alley, clearly rushing to her car. Sandy pivoted to watch Ingrid with the intensity of a curly-blonde hawk. Something was up, something involving Ingrid and Ida and who-knew-who-else.

Amos frowned, then turned his attention back to the scooter brigade. "Without the mayor on hand —"

"I'm right here," Ida said.

Well, she wasn't right there, exactly, but she was on

the screen of Bert Lyman's laptop computer. He held it up for everyone to see. "She text-messaged me," Bert explained. "I told her to hold her cell phone up and look into its camera. Then I put her on-line. Wireless technology is wonderful."

Amos frowned at Ida's suspicious lack of bodily presence. "Mayor? Where are you? Why don't you hop in a car and just drive on up to the square? We'll wait."

"I've got cookies in the oven."

"You don't bake."

"I've taken it up. The Food Channel seduced me."

"Oh?" Amos studied her shrewdly. "Do you bake *outdoors*, dressed in a business suit, standing beside your Corvette? Because it looks like that's where you are."

"Are we here to discuss my baking habits? Or Irene's mission?"

"Hurry it up, Mayor, Chief," Bert interjected. "I'm on battery power."

Ida smiled sweetly. "Thank you, Bert. I hereby convene this impromptu meeting of the Mossy Creek town council. I like Ed and Melvin's suggestion about the scooter lane. I wasn't aware of how many of our citizens owned their own scooters."

"Mayor, they really aren't ours — yet," Ed admitted. "When the manufacturers heard about what we were planning, they loaned them to us. Ain't it wonderful? We get to keep them, too, if Mossy Creek puts in the scooter lane and we agree to be in a Medicare commercial."

Ida gave a thumbs-up. "Good work. Is Casey Blackshear there?"

"Right here, Mayor," I said.

"What do you think of a scooter lane, Casey?"

As the only person on a scooter who wasn't in the protest, I said, "Let's ask Aunt Irene."

Ed took Aunt Irene's hand. "You tell them, Rene."

"You know," Irene said, "Everybody always says that Mossy Creek is 'the town that ain't goin' nowhere and don't want to.' That's the town motto, even. I think what that means is that you all welcome the world to Mossy Creek, in person and in spirit. Including the ones of us who can't walk anymore."

A number of people began wiping their eyes and sniffling. She had them crying.

Ida winced. "Okay. That's enough of a discussion for me. Have we got a majority of the town council on hand?"

"Yes, Mayor," Hank answered.

"Then let's vote."

Hank said loudly, "I move to approve the new scooter lane."

"I second that," said councilman Egg Egbert, Ida's second cousin, from about tenth back in the line of scooters.

"All those in favor, say, 'Aye.'"

Other council members chimed in, and a resounding "Aye," rang out.

Cheers and applause filled the air.

Ida smiled. "Glad that's settled," she said, way too cheerfully. "Bye, now. I have to go check my cookies."

"*Ida.* Mayor," Amos said grimly. "I want to talk to you —"

"Catch you later, Chief."

The screen went dark.

So did Amos's expression.

I had watched that little exchange with great interest. Li wiggled in my lap. "*Beep, beep, beep,*" she said, as if warning everybody we were backing up.

I had a feeling Ida was going to need a warning beeper, too. *Catch you later, Chief?* Not if he caught her first.

"Three cheers for Irene," Ed called.

The cheers went up.

Irene smiled.

To think it all came about because Melvin took her to Wal-Mart.

Mossy Creek Gazette

VOLUME V, NO. ONE　　　**MOSSY CREEK, GEORGIA**

The Bell Ringer

Come Early, Ready To Rumble

Biggest Estate Sale Of The New Year
This Saturday

by Katie Bell

Ready, set, shop! You all know how I feel about yard sales. I love yard sales the way a quarterback loves football! Ah, the smell of the turf as I race across a lawn to catch a velveteen painting of a fruit bowl! The roar of the crowd as I knock down three teenagers and an old man on my way to score a vintage Barbie missing only half of her hair!

Well, folks, put on your helmets and grab your shoulder pads, because Russell King is hosting not just an ordinary old yard sale, but an estate sale of his late Uncle Ernest's treasures. As we all know, an estate sale is the same as a yard sale, only with fabulous *antique junk*.

I'll be there with my game-face on and my reporting instincts turned to "High gossip." Because you *know* what turns a good yard sale into a *great* yard sale, right?

The post-game fights.

Christmas comes only once a year,
unless you leave your decorations up.

Blinded by the Lights

Chapter 3

I like few things better than a leisurely Saturday morning with the great expanse of the weekend stretching before me, especially when there were bargains to be found on the cold but sunny horizon. I was happy. Never let it be said that yours truly, Patty Campbell, can be bested at a bargain table.

Old Mr. Ernest King's nephew and heir, Russell, had decided to conduct an estate sale today, which was unusual for this time of year, but I'm not one to quibble when there are "visionary pieces" to be found. That's what my husband Mac and his best friend, Amos Royden, call my flea-market and garage-sale finds. Once I've sanded, painted, and sanded some more, these finds transform into treasures. I've even sold a few to Mossy Creek's own interior designer and my good friend, Josie Rutherford.

But the notice Russell put in the *Mossy Creek Gazette* brought me more joy than my visionary pieces. The ad said, *Bargains galore. Everything Must Go*. I knew "everything" included Mr. King's Christmas light display that had seemed to grow in abundance every year, as if it were a living thing. It wasn't so much his love of the holiday season that had bothered some Creekites, including me, it was his habit of never taking those lights down. I relished the thought of driving along West Mossy Creek Road without having to view the icicle lights dangling from his gutters, twelve months out of the year, tacky as white shoes after Labor Day.

Forgetting for a moment that my coffee was missing a necessary ingredient for full enjoyment, I sipped my cup-o-joe without sugar, one of my New Year's resolutions, and tried not to wince as I waited for the aftertaste to hit me. Splenda wasn't bad; I would survive.

Mac, who's a lawyer specializing in family law, set down the newspaper and eyed me as if he were a wealthy Bigelowan instead of a Creekite, wanting to change his will to spite his relatives. "What's got you in such a good mood?"

"I plan to spend part of the morning trolling for vision-ary pieces at Mr. King's estate sale."

"Maybe your resolution should have been to give up searching for visionary pieces rather than to give up sugar," Mac said with a twinkle in his deep blue eyes.

I couldn't help but smile at his teasing. But removing sugar from my diet was my resolution, and I was sticking to it. The closer I approached forty, the more weight I seemed to gain over the holidays. Being a tiny woman, I can't hide those extra lumps and bumps that every buttery-sweet cookie packs on my behind. So in a moment of either su-preme brilliance or utter stupidity, I gave up refined sugar until I could zip up my favorite pair of jeans without lying on the bed.

You may wonder what prompted my decision. It was quite simple, really. I saw my hind end when I exited the shower on New Year's Eve and thought I saw my mother in the mirror. So ... no pancakes with sorghum syrup on Saturday mornings, no sugar in my coffee, no honey ham, no chocolate. You get the picture.

I called out to my son, Clay, "Honey, we're going to leave in about fifteen minutes. Get your shoes laced, your jacket zipped, and I'd better see gloves on your hands and a hat on your precious head."

"Aw, Mom, do I have to? The sun's shining."

"Mom" is a simple word, but I don't ever take it for granted. I blinked away the tears that filled my eyes at the way he'd said "Mom" in that whiny, I'm-irritated-but-I-love-you tone. And at the way he'd knit into the family. It was like he'd always been ours. God had truly blessed us when he made the way smooth for Mac and me to adopt Clay. "It's cold, honey. You need to keep the top of your head and your ears covered."

He groaned as if we'd been having this argument for years. I nearly teared up again.

Mac rolled his eyes that way men do when they think mothers are being overprotective. Or maybe it was Katie Bell's *Bell Ringer* column in the paper. He had it folded over so he could read it. Oh, Mac pretended he never read Katie's column because he didn't like gossip, but he read it from opening gambit to the byline at the end.

Recently, Katie had outdone herself. She'd come up with the brilliant if devious idea of recording all the resolutions spouted at the Hamilton Inn during the New Year's Eve party. Shortly after publishing the town's resolutions for one and all to see, she started outing people when their resolutions failed. I had to give her kudos for cleverness. The last time she'd done a piece like this was when she sent out that survey asking Creekites for their deepest, darkest memories to share leading up to the Mossy Creek Reunion.

More than a few townspeople are unhappy about having their lack of fortitude commented upon in print. Take Eula Mae Whit, for example. Filled with the New Year spirit, she proclaimed to one and all that she planned to stop dipping her favorite peach snuff. Katie caught her with a pinch between her cheek and gum and a plastic spit cup in her apron pocket last Sunday.

Katie recently enlisted an assistant — Sandy. And Sandy's so annoyed about Creekites failing in their resolutions only two weeks into the new year, she's begun to drive everyone crazy making sure they *don't fail*.

"So what sort of visionary pieces are you looking for today?" Mac asked, as I brought my mug of coffee over to the sink to dump.

"I never know until I see one. Then the ideas come to me."

He nodded. "Sort of like a sculptor finding the form in the marble."

"Exactly. I knew I married you for some reason. You understand me."

"More than you suspect. For example, I understand that looking for visionary pieces makes you happy, but I also know, even if you won't admit it, you're in a good mood because you'll never again have to see Ernest King's icicle lights hanging off his roof in the middle of July."

A twinge of guilt pricked my good mood. I was glad one of the town's eyesores would be gone, not that Ernest himself was gone. "Is it petty of me?"

"Yes," Mac teased. "I still don't understand why it bothered you and Josie so much, anyway. And don't launch into an explanation of *feng shui*. It makes about as much sense to me as 'shabby chick.'"

I let that one pass. 'Shabby chick' was what Mac called my shabby chic slipcover-loving, go-ahead-and-put-your-feet-up-on-the-coffee-table decorating style.

"And where does playing *Beatles* music on the bagpipe fit in with making sense?" I asked and was rewarded with a slow, Scotsman's grin.

I'd made short work of dropping Clay off at the house of his best friend, John Wesley McCready. The boys were pretty much inseparable these days, a bond formed because they'd both lost someone they loved. I hoped they'd stay friends like Mac and Amos had. Having a friend over a lifetime was a precious gift.

When I arrived at the estate sale, I wasn't surprised to see Orville Gene Simple there in his ever-present *John Deere* cap and his favorite overalls. He liked a good bargain, too. Orville was definitely a visionary challenge if I ever saw one. He was a good man, a fair farmer, but he had no sense of fashion, nor did he understand curb appeal. When I drove past his place this morning, I purposely looked away from the hubcap-lined driveway and the commode he uses for a lawn chair. Sue Ora had tried unsuccessfully to convince him to get rid of the toilet, but Orville was a man who'd lived by himself too long.

I headed toward the icicle lights piled up on a card table about twenty feet from me. I was going to make certain they didn't fall into the wrong hands. But then I saw a jumble of linens and quilts thrown on a blue plastic tarp. I passed the icicle lights, my eye on the corner of a wedding ring quilt at the bottom of the pile. Katie Bell was making a beeline for the linens and my quilt. But I beat her to it, short legs and all. She snorted at me like a frustrated football tackle. "I'll out-run you on the *next* play," she warned.

As I examined the fine stitching on the old quilt, so heavy I knew it had real cotton batting, I heard Orville tell Russell that he wanted *all* of the icicle lights. I tossed the quilt over my shoulder, determined to double Orville's offer, when I saw a vintage 1940s chenille bedspread under some worn flannel sheets. I had to have it for the guest room.

"Deal!" I heard Mr. King's nephew say, and I turned back toward the card table with the icicle lights, my heart pounding like I was in Argie's aerobics class.

"You got the fasteners to go with 'em?" Orville asked.

"No, sir," Russell said. "But you're welcome to climb up and get them off the gutters yourself."

No way was I going to allow Orville to bring those icicle lights home. He'd probably hang them over his commode. "Hey!" I shouted, then waved and smiled.

Orville looked over at me and frowned. "Morning, Mrs. Campbell."

"I was wondering if you would do me a favor?"

"Depends on what the favor is."

"How about selling me those icicle lights?" I didn't bat my eyelashes, but I thought about it.

"Nope."

"Come on, Orville. Clay's always wanted some, and I waited too long to pick any up during the after-Christmas sales. All the stores are out." I gave him my tried-and-true, sad-puppy-dog eyes, the expression I learned from Butler, our black lab.

Orville narrowed his gaze and sized me up, which didn't take long. "Drive Clay by the house, then."

"I'll double what you paid," I offered.

"No, thank you." He glanced at the gutters, then checked his wristwatch. "I don't have time to climb up and get them fasteners. I gotta go down to Bigelow and spend the whole afternoon loading some lumber I bought. So I'll just go by Derbert Koomer's after I leave here, and buy some new ones."

Besides being stubborn, Orville was odd. Most people would have taken the money I offered, and if they didn't, they would just wait until the next fall, during the after-Thanksgiving Day sales, to buy Christmas light fasteners. Thanksgiving was ten months away. Why would he need the fasteners now?

About an hour later, as I was driving home, pleased

as could be with the old pie safe, two quilts, and chenille bedspread I'd bought for me, and the stack of Beatles albums I'd bought for Mac, I found out why Orville needed the Christmas light fasteners right away. I made the mistake of slowing down as I approached the Simple farm. It's like a wreck on the interstate, you can't stop yourself from taking a peek.

I noted the new mailbox he'd fashioned and painted to look like a beaver. Orville was still proud of winning the battle with the "denizen of the deep" who'd tried to dam up his pond. The mailbox was folk art at its best, which surprised me. Maybe there was hope for Orville yet.

But then my eyes followed the rusty hubcaps lining the driveway, drawn as always to that damned commode he'd set in the front yard. The commode resided under an ancient elm tree that shaded a good portion of the yard, south of the porch. A big, faded, red-plastic bow, made from what looked like red garbage bags, sagged from a leafless branch of the elm. Just below the bow, a dried-out evergreen wreath hung by a series of unbound wire hangers. The dried-out wreath and faded bow were centered directly above the white porcelain commode. The display looked like a throne for a redneck Santa.

Unfortunately, Orville never understood why most people wouldn't consider using an old commode as a yard chair. He didn't much care if the neighbors saw him sitting on it reading the paper, or that they might think he was doing his business in the front yard. He worried even less if a stranger driving along the West Mossy Creek Road saw him sitting on the pot.

I slammed on the brakes with a screech when I witnessed something worse — Orville atop a ladder attaching those damned icicle lights to his porch roof.

I pulled off on the shoulder and dug in my purse to find my new flip-phone. I never remembered to turn it on and, no, I hadn't set up my virtual mailbox. I sometimes worried I'd get dependent on it and get a whopper of a bill for going over my monthly minutes. But this was an emergency. I'd get Josie to rally the troops. There was no way Orville Gene Simple was displaying Christmas lights twenty-four-seven.

🐛🐛🐛

Josie called Jasmine Beleau — our local beauty, fashion and image consultant — and Sandy, who carries a badge and a gun. After they opted in on "Project Curb Appeal," I picked up Clay from the McCready's, brought my finds into the house, and fixed lunch for the family. It was almost time for me to leave. Mac was watching an old football game on TV. He referred to these old games on some sports cable channel as classics, and who was I to argue? Liking old things or things that looked old bound us together.

Clay was wrestling with Dog, our Australian Shepherd. Maddie and Butler, our labs, were snoring near the fire. Mac was winning the competition with the dogs for the loudest snore. Now if I turned off the football game blaring on the TV, I knew he'd claim otherwise.

I pressed the *off* button on the TV console.

Mac opened one eye. "Hey, I was watching that."

"Really?" I asked, waiting for the line that always followed.

"I was just resting my eyes." He sat a little straighter in the oversized, club chair I'd slipcovered in a striped ticking. He grabbed the remote in his lap and pressed the *on* button. Some team in maroon and white was on the forty yard line.

"I thought you only snored when you were sleeping," I said.

"I wasn't asleep. I was listening to the game."

I blocked his view of the TV screen as best I could. "So what's the score? Who's playing?"

"Okay. I give up. You win. I was just having a little cat nap." He yawned as Dog woofed low at the word *cat*. "Where are you going?"

"Oh, I'm just meeting up with Josie, Jasmine, and Sandy for a consultation."

"I like our 'shabby chick' house just fine."

"*Shabby chic*," I said. "A shabby chick is a disheveled female. And the consultation isn't for us."

Dog stopped tickling Clay with his nose. His ears raised to full attention.

"So who's it for?" Mac asked.

"I'm sorry. I can't tell you. I've been sworn to secrecy."

"You're up to something, Patty."

I grabbed my purse and wrapped my scarf around my neck. "Don't be silly."

Mac removed himself from his comfortable spot in the chair and walked over to the front picture window. He peered through one of the wooden slats. "And why do you have my ladder hanging out the back of the Expedition, and my Adirondack chair?"

Thankful that he didn't realize I had the space heater as well, I picked my key ring off of the key rack by the door. "Not everyone is six-foot-four inches tall. Some of us have to get up on a ladder to measure for curtains."

I got as far as opening the front door before he placed his towering frame between me and the front porch. I knew I shouldn't look him in the eye, but I couldn't help risking a quick peek.

Mac was frowning. "Why do I get the feeling you're leaving out some important details?"

A good offensive move was needed, so I shrugged, then

kissed him like I had when we were first dating. Men can be distracted that way. Jasmine gave me that little piece of advice. It worked like a charm.

"Maybe you can be late for the consultation," he said with a familiar gleam in his eye.

❧❧❧

I'd picked up two of my accomplices, Josie and Jasmine, in record time. We stopped at Mossy Creek Hardware and Gardening and bought red paint. Josie said Orville needed a red door to improve his *feng shui,* and his dog Duke needed some distraction. She'd brought a sack of *Gour-mutt* dog treats she'd picked up from Beechum's Bakery. Ingrid's Chihuahua, Bob, loved the liver-and-herb biscotti. Josie figured Duke would like those, and she had Ingrid toss in a couple of bison biscuits, too. My labs, Maddie and Butler, prefer Ingrid's carob pupcakes. Dog's favorite is the banana nut biscotti. I doubted Duke was that discerning since he rarely roused himself to bark at anyone's intrusion, and when he did it was on a delayed basis. He was too lazy to be persnickety about which treats he ate.

It took us about twenty-five minutes to decide that we couldn't all agree on the right shade of red. So we bought three different quarts. Actually, I did the buying since the whole "While You Were Out" makeover of Orville Gene's exterior was my idea. Plus, I thought buying three different shades of red would help keep Amos off my trail, just in case Orville decided to file a report.

Tom Anglin winked at me when I handed him my debit card. "Kind of cold for painting today, Patty. Working on another visionary piece?"

"Yes," I said with a smile. "I bought an old pie safe at Ernest King's estate sale. And we can't decide which shade of red would be best for the crackle treatment."

"Right," he said, with another wink. "You make sure you paint it in a warm-enough space. Otherwise it won't adhere right."

I had my electric space heater in the back of the SUV, so I wasn't worried about the paint adhering. I was a little worried about the winking. I was a happily married woman. Why was Tom winking at me?

We headed down West Mossy Creek Road, certain that by the time Orville arrived back from Bigelow, we'd be long gone.

Sandy, who'd enjoyed her part in fixing up Michael Conners' bachelor pad last year, was already pulling up the rusty hubcaps lining Orville's drive by the time we arrived. She had a couple of bales of white wire edging in the back of her truck. We didn't have time to use the plastic stuff you had to pound in, and we'd decided the wire stuff had that quaint, old-fashioned feel anyway.

"Please tell me you bought the wire edging in Bigelow," I said.

"Why should we give those Bigelowans our hard-earned money?" Sandy asked. "Tom'll keep our secret. I explained everything to him."

"Great," I muttered under my breath. We probably should have thought to bribe Tom. At least the winking hadn't meant he was hitting on me. But Tom was the least of our problems.

Josie's face turned pale as she stared at Orville's front door.

"What's wrong?" I asked.

"The door. I can't paint it if it's locked."

"No problem," Jasmine said, then dug in her purse for a bobby pin. She picked the lock on the front door without any explanation of where she'd acquired that particular skill, and none of us girls asked any questions.

I wondered where Duke was. If he never showed, I'd

bring my babies, I mean dogs, the treats.

Once the door was open, Josie took the opportunity to grab a bucket and scrub brush and wash down the door in preparation for the red paint.

While Josie started sanding the door, Jasmine and I worked as a team pulling all those icicle lights down. I wanted to clean the gutters while I was up there, but we only had so much time. You know it's bad when the leaves in the gutters turn to soil and pine saplings grow in them. There was no question about it, we'd have to come back. The daylily bed beside the porch needed cleaning out, too. The brown, flattened fronds of last summer's greenery hung over the bed's rock border like the legs of dead spiders.

Jasmine and I had our system down. She held the ladder for me. I'd remove the lights, coil up the strands, bind them with plastic wire twists and hand them to Jasmine, who'd place them into the large plastic wheeled tub she'd brought. I plucked the light fasteners and deposited them in my builder's apron until I had enough to bind with rubber bands.

We stopped our disassembly line once to judge the three test patches of paint Josie dabbed on the door. I drank some water, while everyone else had hot chocolate that Sandy had picked up from Mama's All You Can Eat Café. Sandy made a point of telling me she knew I'd given up sugar, so she'd made certain to ask Rosie Montgomery for bottled water, so as not to tempt me. She'd even outright refused the chocolate meringue pie Rosie offered.

By the time we'd taken down the last strand of lights, had the tub packed in the back of the Expedition, removed the dried-up wreath and the faded plastic bow, and even swept the leaves off the porch, Josie's second coat of Barnyard Red was dry. Sandy was about done securing Orville's new driveway edging. I stood back, trying not to think about hot chocolate or chocolate meringue pie, and surveyed our progress.

The red door cheered up the old white farmhouse immensely. Josie was busy inside, drawing up plans for a complete renovation. All we had left to do was get rid of that commode in the yard. I knew it was heavy, but figured Jasmine and I could lift it. I didn't want to interrupt Josie. Maybe my New Year's resolution should have been to accept my small stature.

We put Mac's Adirondack chair under the elm without much trouble, though Jasmine and I must have looked like Mutt and Jeff carrying the thing. I placed a cute red gingham pillow made of water-repellant fabric against the fanned back of the chair. Josie was still sketching away inside. Sandy was answering a call over the radio.

As Jasmine and I proceeded to take either side of the heavy porcelain toilet, Jasmine asked, "Are you sure you can lift this?"

"Absolutely," I said.

I knew what my tall, sturdy friend was really saying. *You're too little to pick this up. You're not strong enough.* I might be what some people would call tiny, if you didn't count the ten pounds of sugar cookies plumping out my posterior. But my determination to do things for myself despite my lack of stature is what you might call Mac-sized. I should have realized Jasmine was just worried about me and what might happen. But I had to prove myself like *The Little Engine That Could*, my favorite children's story of all time.

We hoisted the commode. About halfway to the SUV, my arms felt like rubber bands stretched to their limits. I tightened my grip. My knuckles whitened as I huffed and puffed.

"Let's set the commode down for a minute and rest," Jasmine suggested.

Little did she know those were fighting words to tiny

women the world over who carry off more than they can haul. "I'm fine," I grunted.

"See if you can lift it higher on your side," she said, probably thinking she was being helpful. "Or maybe you could balance some of the weight on your shoulder."

I attempted the adjustment, and the commode started wobbling, sort of like a canoe that's about to tip over.

That's when Sandy shouted, "Holy cow! We're done for!"

Orville's battered old pick-up was speeding up the driveway where we were standing. That's when the commode slipped from my grasp. Jasmine, bless her heart, couldn't hold on to it either, and it smashed to the cold, hard ground, breaking into three pieces. Too many for Orville to have any hope of gluing it all back together. Thank goodness. I kept hoping I'd feel a little remorse, but I didn't.

❧❧❧

Mac pressed his lips together tightly as he glared at me. Clay stood next to Mac, mimicking his expression, but looking far less menacing. I was in trouble, big trouble.

Amos, notepad in hand, leaned back against his Jeep. His expression was almost gleeful, like he'd caught his sister sneaking out at night and was ratting on her to his parents. "Let's start with *breaking and entering*."

"Only because Josie couldn't paint the door with it closed, Chief," Sandy said.

He raised a dark eyebrow at her. "And we have *destruction of property*."

"It was a toilet that he kept in the front yard, for goodness sake," I said in my best big-sister voice.

He ignored my comment and continued his litany of

offenses. "We have *attempted theft* of twenty strands of icicle lights and fifty rusty hubcaps."

"Fifty-three," Orville said. "And don't forget conspiracy involving an officer of the law."

That's when Duke, Orville's old hound dog, decided to run out from the woods to growl and bark at us for intruding.

"A little too little and a little too late," Orville said. He bent down and grabbed a stick. "Shut up, Duke. Go fetch." He threw the stick, and the dog lumbered after it, tail wagging.

He came back, without the stick, and lifted his leg to give the Adirondack chair a good dousing.

"Stop that, you damned mutt! That's my good..." Orville stopped and scratched his head, apparently rethinking his position. "Go ahead, Duke. Get the chair good and wet, and then you women can haul it off to where you found it. And you're gonna buy me a new commode, too."

Amos frowned at Sandy. "Orville has a point about you being an officer of the law. I doubt I'll like what I'm going to hear, but what do you have to say for yourself?"

"It wasn't stealing. I swear. We were only storing the lights for safekeeping. We planned to bring them back at the start of the holiday season and even help Orville put them up."

"And take them down once the season ends," I added.

"For perpetuity," Jasmine said and smiled at Orville, who looked startled at the beautiful woman's attention.

Mac wagged a finger at me. "I think it'd be best if you declined to make any further comments." Mac's lawyer tendencies had kicked in, his need to protect his client overtaking his husbandly anger.

"But I have proof of our good intentions," Sandy said. "I've got the certificate we printed up for Orville."

Her blonde curls bobbed as she ran back to her pick-up truck.

"This is why women are nothing but trouble," Orville said, folding his arms over his chest, then sniffing like he smelled something bad. "I don't care what that piece of dadblame paper says. I didn't ask for no help with my Christmas lights, and I don't see how hanging them all the year 'round hurts anybody."

Amos and Mac didn't refute him.

I wanted to elbow my silent husband, but I couldn't reach him.

"Do you keep Halloween decorations up all year?" I asked.

"I don't have Halloween decorations, Mrs. Campbell."

"How about Valentine's Day? If you had them, would you keep big pink and red hearts hanging from your elm tree? Or turkeys and pilgrims? Or Fourth of July flag banners?"

"Well no, except maybe the good ol' red, white and blue."

I groaned. "Orville, my point is that Christmas lights are for Christmas. You don't turn them on except during the holidays. Why keep them up there? Quite frankly, it denotes laziness on your part."

"*Laziness*? Do you know it took me two hours to string up them lights this morning?"

"And it took us no time at all to take them down. So what are you complaining for?"

Orville turned to Amos again. "See, this is what happens when you start thinking maybe having a woman around might be nice. Then they start messing in your business, and you realize you're better off alone. Fate stepped in today to remind me why I don't need a woman around."

Amos wore a conflicted expression, like he wanted to

agree with Orville, then thought the better of it.

"So where were you when you had this revelation?" I asked Orville.

Mac sent me one of his patented "mind your own business" looks.

Orville scratched his head again as he debated whether he'd tell us. "One time I made me an appointment with the Hair Club for Men people down in Atlanta. I thought maybe if I got all fancified I could get me a woman to court. About halfway there, I changed my mind." He glanced over at the urine-soaked chair. "You took the most comfortable seat I have and gave me that contraption with the girlie pillow on it. What kind of crime would you call that, Chief Royden?"

"Have you sat in the Adirondack?" Jasmine asked, her voice all honey-smooth.

"No," Orville said, eyeing the chair.

"Then how can you say you don't like it?" she asked.

"On pure principle."

"Well, Mac liked that chair," I said. "I don't see why it wouldn't be comfortable for you."

Amos grinned. "You want me to add that to the list of crimes, Mac? Your wife giving away your oversized Adirondack?"

Mac's frown deepened. "No comment."

"Yeah, no comment," mimicked Clay.

Jasmine sidled up close to Orville. "May I?" she asked and removed his cap before he had a chance to say *yes* or *no*. She revealed the thin comb-over, swirled from back to front, then swept to the side in a curve nearly as intricate as the one Donald Trump created on a daily basis. "So what made you change your mind about the hair?" she asked.

Orville shifted from one foot to the other. "I, uh, remembered how painful briars were when I got some stuck in what you might call one of my sensitive spots, and those things are smaller than a hair plug. So I figured maybe I'd just get me some of that Rogaine. Can't be any stinkier than linament."

"Why not simply clip it short, like Sean Connery or Bruce Willis? Sexy men embrace their baldness."

She gave him a once over, rotated her finger, and he actually spun in a circle for her as she sized him up. "I don't think I'd have any problem finding a woman for you to court. But you will need some new clothes. I'm in the beauty consultation business. Meet me Monday at Hamilton's Department Store. We'll pick out a new wardrobe, then swing by Rainey's for a trim and a facial."

Mac snorted at the idea of Orville getting a facial.

Sandy returned from her pick-up truck at that moment. "And maybe you can join our aerobics class to get in shape. There's a few single ladies in the class." She handed Amos the gold-embossed, good-for-a-lifetime, Christmas Decorating Gift Certificate we'd created for Orville. She recited, "We hereby promise to decorate Mr. Orville Gene Simple's house for Christmas every year, and after Christmas is over, we hereby promise to un-decorate his house. See, Chief, we were telling the truth about storing the lights for him."

Amos perused the certificate. "Uh huh."

"And you really should make some changes inside the house, Mr. Simple," Josie said. "The kitchen and baths at the very least need updating. The furniture, too. I took the liberty of making some sketches while I was waiting for the paint to dry." She handed Orville her interior design card. "I could turn this house into a showcase."

"Women like nice houses," Mac said, then shrugged when Amos frowned at him.

"What do you say, Orville?" I asked. "Will you let us help you? You know we mean well. And we're really sorry about the commode."

"No, you aren't."

"Okay, so I'm not sorry. I hated that commode more than Sue Ora did."

Orville glanced at Jasmine, who winked at him, at Josie, who smiled hopefully, at Sandy, who shrugged, and then he turned his gaze to mine. "Oh, all right, Mrs. Campbell."

Mac's expression was hard to decipher. He looked pleased that I might be off the hook, but worried about Orville. "Since the ladies are willing to help you become one of Mossy Creek's most eligible bachelors as reparation for the pain and suffering they caused in today's activities, will you drop all the charges pending against my wife and her partners in crime?"

Orville sighed. "I guess so."

Amos shook his head as Josie whipped out her appointment book and started paging through for a good date. "You don't know what you're getting yourself into, Orville," Amos told him. "You'll be discussing paint chips and learning white is *bisque*."

Mac clapped Orville on the back. "Congratulations, my friend. You're now one of Patty's visionary pieces."

Clay offered Orville his hand to shake. "I think I'm a visionary piece, too, and I like it just fine."

Orville couldn't resist. Slowly, he smiled.

Mossy Creek Gazette

VOLUME V, NO. TWO   MOSSY CREEK, GEORGIA

The Bell Ringer

Local Hero Catches Mysterious Library Prowler

by Katie Bell

Miss Marple, Sherlock Holmes, and Hercule Poirot can rest easy now — their books aren't going to take any more midnight strolls around the Mossy Creek Library. I'm happy to report that the case of the book-loving ghost has been solved. Hannah Longstreet, head librarian, says the culprit was caught, but no charges are being filed.

"The capture went down as easy as a slug of cold gin on a hot night," Hannah told me. "Yeah. It was sweet. Sweet like a soft bed in a cheap hotel next to a back-alley diner where the sign flashes EATS in neon the color of a doll's lips right before she pulls a loaded piece from her purse and ... excuse me, I seem to be channeling Mickey Spillane."

Hannah gives full credit for the caper closure to library intern, Linda Polk, and her daddy, Jimmy. The detective duo set up a sting operation Saturday night and nabbed the ghost red-handed.

"You shoulda seen my daddy," Linda said. "He tackled that ghost like Hulk Hogan doing a smack-down on the Rock. I'm calling the World Wrestling Federation."

Indeed! Check out the accompanying photo, courtesy of Hannah's digital camera.

Even pay-per-view can't show you better wrestling action than this. I think we should give Jimmy Polk a stage name to use in his new sport.

How about, "The Ghostbuster?"

*Books can "talk," sure, but can they take a walk
when you're not looking?*

The Ballad of
the Bookworm

Chapter 4

"Listen to me, Linda Polk, we are *not* calling the police and reporting we have a ghost moving books. For goodness sakes, Amos would most likely tell us we were a couple of doughnuts short of a dozen. Besides which, this is a busy Saturday, and I hear he and Sandy and Mutt are getting all sorts of strange calls. I hear that Amos just came back from some fiasco over at Orville Gene Simpson's place, and you know anything involving Orville couldn't have been *normal*. Well, this call would be even stranger! Beyond that, the county library supervisor might find out and fire me for not keeping the library shelves under strict Dewey Decimal System control." Hannah Longstreet, the head librarian of Mossy Creek Library, adjusted her black-rimmed glasses, the better to stare me down. She wasn't going to listen.

"What else can we do? It's not like we can call the ghost busters or something." I sighed.

I'd only been working part-time at the library since before Thanksgiving, and I liked it better than clerking at my Aunt Effie's fabric store, but so far every time Hannah, I mean Mrs. Longstreet, opened the library and found books rearranged we had the same conversation. Heck, I didn't mind if we had a word-starved ghost in our midst. Yes, it made a little more work for the rest of us, but on the whole,

I thought it was kinda cool. My friends at school would freak if I could tell them I saw a ghost. But Hannah, her being in charge and all, she'd had her back up about it since she'd accused one or all of us high school part-timers (there were only three — Junie Biddly, Willa Sawyer and me) from the Friends of the Library of playing tricks on her. An epidemic of punking had broken out at the Bigelow high school and moved due north to Mossy Creek. So Hannah had started setting traps to catch us, then realized when she'd been the last one out and the first one in the next morning that we couldn't have shelved the Civil War books next to the Nazi occupation of Europe, or the hunting and survival books next to our collection of local cookbooks. None of us had a key.

We couldn't really be upset about her suspicions. After all, what normal ghost would want to learn how to cook?

And now the ghost had taken to poetry.

You know, I love my job, reading to kids, helping them pick out books, keeping them from landing blows over the latest *Harry Potter*. But sometimes, in the dead of winter, especially after all the excitement of Christmas, our younger readers seemed a little *possessed* themselves.

These were mountain kids — kids used to being outside and, as my granny used to say, *runnin' wild*. So us volunteers had to keep busy staying one step ahead of bored seven-year-olds with library cards. This gave me a whole new respect for my elementary school teacher, Mrs. Hammer. She'd spelling-bee'd us into learning, offering a small prize for the winner.

Since I was planning on becoming a teacher myself, I had to have a few tricks of my own.

And the poetry contest was born. Anything to keep them mostly in their chairs and relatively quiet. First, we read poetry and nursery rhymes out loud, *Dr. Seuss* being voted the favorite for the second year running. *The Night*

Before Christmas coming a close second. Next, we sang nursery rhymes like *Itsy-Bitsy Spider, Baa, Baa, Black Sheep*, and I had to explain that no, nursery rhymes are not just for babies.

You get the picture.

So yesterday afternoon, after reading and singing, I assigned the group to write their own poems using the example of *Hey Diddle Diddle.* I promised that when they were done, we'd read them out loud and post the best ones by vote on the bulletin board near the front entrance of the library for everybody to read. And the winner would get the cherry flavored *Tootsie Pop* I carried in my pocket.

Besides complaints of "Nothin' goes with diddle," the assignment went well. Mossy Creek kids learn how to compete on their mommas' knees since none of us knew when we'd be called upon to best those snooty Bigalowans. At least it occupied eight kids for nearly forty minutes. At the end we had four readable examples due to an overuse of *piddle.* One of the diddle dissenters wrote:

Hey, diddie, diddie,
You look like a biddy,
Your hair looks just like a broom.

I didn't take this personally since I knew my hair looked just fine. That lesson in beauty I'd gotten last year from Miss Jasmine Beleau, Mossy Creek's sophisticated image consultant, had settled over me in permanent fashion. I never went out of the house now without primping just a bit. I could almost hear Miss Jasmine's voice, "You never know who might wander into the local library."

Then there was:

Hey diddle, diddle,
a cat can't play the fiddle
and my dog Spenser barks at the moon.

Also:

Hey diddle, diddle
I don't care if you're little
Put your dish away with the spoon.

This from one of the girls who did a lot of babysitting for her younger brother.

And, my own personal favorite:
Hey, who are you callin' diddle?
My name is Joe.

Boys just don't get poetry.

There you have it, the whole enchilada of our Mossy Creek poetry talent in the ten-and-under group. That is until Hannah opened the library this chilly Saturday morning and while posting the new book list for the week, found an extra poem tacked up with the rest. This poem hadn't been written by the children. She showed the carefully written verses to me as soon as I came in.

Ballade of the Bookworm

Far in the Past I peer, and see
A Child upon the Nursery floor,
A Child with books upon his knee,
Who asks, like Oliver, for more!
The number of his years is IV,
And yet in Letters hath he skill,
How deep he dives in Fairy-lore!
The books I loved, I love them still!
                    —Andrew Lang

I held the paper by one corner in case it did something weird like disappear or flutter on its own. I might think it was cool for the library to have a ghost, but I didn't necessarily want to shake hands with him, if you know what I mean. "So our ghost's name is Andrew Lang?"

"I don't think so," Hannah replied. "Andrew Lang died in Scotland around the turn of the century. I don't see why he'd be haunting our library."

I gingerly placed the paper on the counter. "We have a book on handwriting, don't we?" I wasn't going to suggest calling the police again so they could dust the paper for fingerprints like they did on *CSI*. Especially with my own big ol' thumb print on one side. "I could see if the book says anything that would help us figure it out," I offered. But even I knew there was a slim chance the author knew anything about the handwriting of a ghost.

"We did have a handwriting analysis book, but I think Sandy Crane borrowed it." She wrote Sandy's name on a piece of paper and underlined it twice. "I think I'll call her."

"Excellent," I said under my breath. Calling Sandy in most cases was even better than calling Amos. I settled near the counter to listen in.

"Sandy, this is Hannah over at the library. Do you still have that handwriting analysis book you checked out last year?"

There was a long space of silence on Hannah's part. I imagine the air time was being filled up by Sandy making an excuse for not bringing the book back. Everyone in town knew Mrs. Longstreet guarded the books and her library territory with the jealous eye of a pit bull in charge of the dumpster behind *Mama's All You Can Eat Café*.

Then Hannah said, "Well, we need it because —" She caught herself and glanced at me. I pretended to be totally busy checking in the books that had been left in the overnight box. "Never you mind what we need it for. The overdue fine must be at least five dollars."

More silence.

"I see. Well, no. No need to have the chief call. I suppose I can make an exception for books used in a criminal investigation but you need to bring it by — oh. Yes, I know you have other calls — important calls, but we —"

I had to do my best to hide my amazement. Someone

was actually getting away with a known overdue book.

"I also wanted to ask you about a problem we're having."

This time I did stop, book in hand, to look at her.

"Yes, I believe we have a prankster in the library. No. Not really vandalism. It's . . . someone is moving books, and I want to find out who it is."

Mrs. Longstreet yanked off her glasses and rubbed one eye. I'd seen her do that before. It usually meant she was gathering words for a storm. In this case I was willing to bet my volunteer salary that she'd love to just hang up the phone.

"Security camera?" The eye-rubbing stopped and the glasses were resettled. "I'm not spending good library funds on *cameras*. Why, the Grim sisters would roll over in their graves, especially Sadie." Everyone knew Miss Sadie and Miss Sarah Grim had donated money for the library with the stipulation that only Hannah would decide how to spend it. "The money the Grim's left was only for books and book-related technology. If I use my tech budget to buy security cameras, I won't be able to buy new bar code scanners this year —"

Sandy must have cut her off at that point, because Mrs. Longstreet met my open-mouthed attention and scowled. I looked down quickly and concentrated on the book in my hands. The title was: *Scottish Poetry*.

"Holy —" I dropped the book.

"Linda!" Mrs. Longstreet admonished. Then to Sandy, "I have to go now. I'll think about what you suggested. Goodbye."

Then she was picking up the book I'd dropped. "I've told all you volunteers to be careful with our books. One good drop to the floor can break the spine —"

My first impulse is always to confess. In fact, back before I'd met Miss Jasmine I'd even confessed to some things

71

I hadn't done, just to make everybody happy — everybody meaning my daddy. In this case, pure startlement overcame my usual claim of guilt. "I'm sorry Mrs. Longstreet, but read the title."

She looked down, and I heard a small intake of breath. She fanned the book open to the index. "A sampling of Scottish Poetry." One finger skimmed down the page. "Andrew Lang, 1844 - 1912. *Ballade of the Bookworm*." Turning the book over, she examined it as if it might give us a clue.

Nothing.

"I'm going to get to the bottom of this," she declared. "If I have to watch the shelves twenty-four hours a day."

Before I could offer to help, she assigned me a job. "Linda, I want you to forget what I taught you about always helping people find books. Let Junie do that. You and I are going to watch the shelves."

She tucked the Scottish poetry book under her arm like someone might snatch it away from her. "It should be safe for you to watch the 200's to the 500's, mostly philosophy, religion and the sciences, and I'll watch the 600's to 900's. Whoever this is, they seem to be partial to the arts and history. If you see something strange come and get me."

"Maybe it's the Grim sisters?" I whispered. "They sound like they'd make good local ghosts to me."

Mrs. Longstreet looked like she was actually giving my question some thought. Then she shook her head. "No. Sadie and Sarah loved this library. They'd never do anything 'out of order' to it. Now go find a good place to set up a watch." She patted the poetry book like our little secret. "We'll catch this prankster red-handed."

We watched all day and as far as I could see, nothing happened except Junie got mad at me for 'shirkin.' In other words, making her do more work while I supposedly lounged around. I couldn't tell her what I was really doing, so she'd just have to get over it. When it was time to close up and go home I helped shut down the computers at the front desk. Mrs. Longstreet was busy making some kind of list.

"Do you want me to stay awhile longer? I could call my mom —"

"No, that won't be necessary, dear. I'm going to run out and pick up a few things from home. I'll drop Rachel off at the Blackshears'. She loves to play with Li. Then I'll come back. I've decided to spend the night here."

"Spend the night in the library?"

She stopped writing and arranged her glasses to look at me. "Yes. I told you I intend to get to the bottom of this. After watching the shelves this afternoon, I realized this ghost or vandal — whoever — usually does his dirty work after the library is closed. So, I'll lock up like I always do, but instead of going home, I'll wait at my desk and see once and for all what goes on when the building is empty and quiet."

For some reason Mrs. Longstreet's plan to stay alone in the darkened library worried me. Enough so that I spoke before thinking. "I could come back and stay with you."

"Absolutely not. What would your parents say when you asked their permission to stay an entire Saturday night in a county building? I think the word 'No' would only be the beginning." She smiled slightly. "Thank you, Linda, for the offer. But I'm sure I'll be fine here."

I wasn't so sure. Every ghostly tale I'd ever read from the Headless Horseman to the scary books of Peter Straub and Stephen King flashed through my mind. I knew in my bones that if we had a real ghost in the Mossy Creek library then Mrs. Longstreet shouldn't be hunting it down alone. So I did what any confused teenager would do. I went home to tell my mother.

Mossy Creek Gazette

106 Main Street • Mossy Creek, GA 30000

From the desk of Katie Bell

To: Chip Brown, Spruce Street

Chip —

Thank you for writing to me at the Gazette. You know, the newspaper's office is just a short walk from your house. You could have left your letter on my desk, instead of mailing it. However, I appreciate your formal manners. You have style. And you bought a postage stamp. I'm honored.

In answer to your first question: No, you're not too young to write an article for the paper. I wrote my first gossip column when I was your age. Only eleven!

In answer to your second question: I'm not sure the subject you suggested is such a good idea. "How To Get Girls, Like My Cousin Rory Does," might upset some of the Gazette's readers. Especially the ones who are parents or grandparents of teenage girls. And I'm not sure

Rory will appreciate the publicity, either.

Why don't you stop by the Gazette office sometime soon, and we'll discuss ways to "spin" your angle. I'll teach you how to get your point across without making readers mad. Or, at least, without getting caught.

Your friend,

Ms. Bell

*A bad combination — the coolest kid in town,
on the coolest day of the year.*

The Day Rory Lost His Mind
Chapter 5

I'm Chip Brown, and I think I'm a pretty cool kid. But when it comes to being *really* cool, there's no one in the world cooler than my cousin Rory. You can ask any kid in Mossy Creek, except maybe the MacGruder boys. The only reason they won't admit he's cool is because Rory stuck them both head-first in a snow drift last winter for picking on my little brother and his friends. The girls will definitely say he's cool, but for silly reasons, like his blue eyes and blonde hair. When my mama said she'd like to take a pair of scissors to his "shaggy mop," Ashley Winthrop nearly had a conniption fit, and she'd just met him.

The girls talk about his muscles, too. He sure enough has some muscles, now. He's only three years older than me, but shoot, you'd think he was sixteen or maybe even seventeen. He's a big ol' boy — almost as tall as my daddy — and strong as all get-out for just being fourteen. And man, can he fight. Some of the biggest, baddest boys from Bigelow County come looking for trouble when he's around, just to see if they can whup him. Rory usually has 'em hollering uncle in no time flat. He's just naturally talented that way. He's also the star wrestler at his school in Chattanooga, Tennessee. He's always sending us pictures of his trophies and articles from the newspaper about his victories.

Daddy says it's a crying shame that Rory's own father

didn't live to see him wrestle. He died in a car wreck when Rory was four. It wasn't your ordinary everyday car wreck, either. I heard mama telling her friend, Miss Francine, that he was running from the law. "Billy Tom is the skeleton in the Brown family closet," Mama said.

Scared me to death. I had nightmares about Rory's daddy being a skeleton in our closet, until Mama told me she only meant Uncle Billy Tom did something we weren't proud of. I heard Daddy say, "If that ain't the pot calling the kettle black, Tammy Jo. Folks 'round here still talk about you throwing that knife at an officer of the law."

Mama hushed up about Uncle Billy Tom. She's real sensitive about the fuss she caused when we first moved to Mossy Creek, thinking the neighbors held a grudge against her for being a Bigelow by blood and that the Mossy Creek police were going to sic their dogs on us. Daddy would have calmed her down, but at the time, his jaw was wired shut from his fall off the roof. I never was so glad to hear my daddy's voice than when those wires came off. Miss Francine told Mama not to give another thought to that knife incident— anyone with half a brain knows she gets a little crazy about dogs since that time a Rottweiler attacked her just before the county beauty pageant and scarred her face and all.

As sensitive as Mama is about her run-in with the Mossy Creek police, Daddy's even worse about Uncle Billy Tom's breaking the law. The only time I ever heard him talk about it was when my little brother Toby walked off with a *Pokemon* card hid up under his shirt at the Up the Creek Flea Market. Daddy was madder than fire.

"I wasn't stealing it, Daddy!" Toby had cried. "I was only borrowing it. I was gonna bring it back next time."

"If you take something that doesn't belong to you and you don't have permission from the owner, that's stealing, and I will not stand for it. I watched my brother take to thievin', and I watched him die trying to run. I'd rather cut my heart out than go through that again. If you *ever* steal another dad-gone thing, you'd best pack your bags and hit the road, son. You won't be welcome in my home."

Later I told Rory about what Daddy said. Rory didn't say much. I guess it can't be fun, knowing your daddy was a thief. Then again, it's a whole lot better than thinking he's a skeleton in your closet.

🌻🌻🌻

For as long as I remember, Rory came from Chattanooga to spend vacations with me and my family. Mostly because his mama, Aunt Lou, is a career woman, as my mama puts it, and has to travel all over tarnation selling lumber to Latin American countries so as to keep food on her table, though why she'd keep food on her table when she's never home is beyond me. Most of the time, Rory lives at a private school that costs a pretty penny. To hear him tell it, he'd rather she keep that penny and let him come live with us. She says he'll be glad for all that fancy schooling when it comes time for him to go to college. Rory don't give a flyin' fig about that, though.

"I don't need college," he says. "I want to work on motorcycles with Uncle Bunk." That's what he calls my daddy. Everyone else calls him Bunkin, except me and Toby, of course.

Rory happens to share Daddy's never-ending fascination with motorcycles. Daddy is the maintenance foreman at the retirement home, Magnolia Manor, but cycles are his full-time hobby. Heck, Rory spends more of his vacation working with Daddy in his garage than hanging out with me. Once the two of them get to talking about Harleys and taking apart engines, there's no stopping them.

That's why I was surprised that Daddy wasn't happy

when Rory got suspended from his school for two weeks in January for throwing a stink bomb into the teachers lounge. Sounded like something Rory would do. I told you he was cool as all get-out, didn't I? But when Daddy and I drove up to Chattanooga to pick him up, Daddy laid into him about how much trouble you'll get into nowadays for having bombs of any kind, anywhere.

"It wasn't my bomb, Uncle Bunk," Rory told him, "and I wasn't the one who threw it."

Daddy didn't look a bit glad to hear that. In fact, he glared at Rory as if he'd just tossed a grenade at a passing school bus. "The principal said you owned up to it."

"Only to keep my buddy, Joe, from being expelled. Shawn McElroy, the sorry jerk who happens to be our quarterback, blamed the stink bomb on Joe. Joe didn't do it, but the principal wouldn't believe him. So I said I did it. I knew they wouldn't expel me. Coach needs me to win the wrestling championship. Joe doesn't wrestle or play football or anything important. They'd have kicked him out, for sure. I *had* to help him."

Daddy studied Rory like he wasn't sure he was telling the truth. I remembered Mama saying that Daddy couldn't look at Rory without seeing his own brother. Maybe that's why Daddy doubted him — because Uncle Billy Tom always lied to get out of trouble. He was a charming son of a gun, that Billy Tom, Mama told Miss Francine, but he'd climb a tree to tell a lie, if it would get him what he wanted.

"You sure you weren't after a two-week vacation from school?" Daddy asked.

Rory's eyebrows bunched together in the middle and his face turned red, like he was ready to fight, which he'd never do with my daddy. "I'm not lying about what happened. All the kids know Shawn McElroy has a mess of them stink bombs in his locker, and he ain't above throwing 'em in the teachers lounge. But a two-week vacation from that school is fine by me. A permanent vacation would be better. I hate living there."

"Why? Is someone giving you problems?"

Rory hesitated, and I knew he wanted to say yes. I could see the word pushing to get out of his mouth. But then he fell back against the seat, looking annoyed with himself. "No, sir," he mumbled. "Not really."

"Are the kids unfriendly?"

"No, sir."

"Is the coach unfair?"

"Not to me."

"Is the school work too hard?"

"Boring, but not hard."

"Then why don't you like it there?"

"Well, heck, Uncle Bunk...would you like living at school?"

Daddy and Rory frowned at each other for awhile, then Daddy shook his head and lectured all the way back to Mossy Creek about how Rory better not throw away his opportunity to get educated, and how the best motorcycle designers are mechanical engineers with college degrees, blah, blah, blah.

By the time we got home, Rory's good mood at being off for two weeks was ruined. We'd been emailing each other about my new video game system since Christmas, and he'd been wanting to try it out, but now he barely looked interested.

"Aw, c'mon, Rory. Don't feel too bad. At least Daddy only talked. Heck, if I'd been kicked out of school, he'd have me 'clocking it' for days."

He scrunched his brows together again. "What do you mean?"

"You remember what happens when Toby or me have to 'clock it', don't you? That means we work our butts off, round the clock. Oh, they let us eat and sleep a little, but then every waking minute, we have to do chores. And when Mama and Daddy run out of chores, we have to stand in the corner and just stare at the gall-dern wall." I shook my head at the memory. "There's nothing worse than clocking it."

"Yeah, I do remember," Rory said in a slow, pondering way. "You had to do that after you dropped the chain saw in the creek. And Toby had to clock it when he trampled all over Mrs. Lavender's flower garden."

"That's what happens to Toby and me when we mess up too bad."

Rory squinted at me, as if I'd said something extremely important. "Then why not me?"

I barely heard his question, he asked it in such a low, hushed voice.

"Daddy never punishes anyone but his own kids," I explained, surprised he hadn't known that. "Doesn't matter how bad the neighbor kids are— they never have to clock it. He just sends them home."

I'll never forget the look on Rory's face then. He turned pale and still, almost like he was about to throw up. He didn't, though. He just stood there.

Looking back, I believe that was when the trouble really started.

🐛🐛🐛

"Good game, Chip." Rory dropped the video game controller and pushed his chair back to stretch his muscles, as if he'd been playing for hours instead of minutes. "But I'm ready for a break."

"A break? We only beat one puny level. Heck, we haven't even got to the good part yet. You know, where you turn the aliens into gobs of green goo then splatter 'em with your turbo-laser."

"Let's take a walk into town. Maybe to Poppy's Ice Cream Parlor on the square."

"We've got ice cream in the freezer downstairs. Three kinds. Cookie dough, Moose Tracks, and— "

"Ashley Winthrop still works at Poppy's, don't she?"

I don't believe he even heard what kind of ice cream we had. He was too busy looking in my dresser mirror and combing his hair. Guess I should've known what he had on his mind. Girls — the only thing Rory likes better than motorcycles, wrestling or pulling pranks. Last summer he even passed up a poster of Chipper Jones at bat for one of Paris Hilton in a bikini. Can you believe it?!

"I guess Ashley still works there," I mumbled, trying to think of something that might interest him more. "Hey, you want to see the deck we built by the creek in the backyard? It's cool, man. Almost like a fort. And we can make a bonfire in the fire ring Daddy built."

"Ashley still going with that Charles Huckleby?"

I shrugged. I didn't pay much attention to that kind of thing, especially considering they were both older than me. "I s'pose so. I see 'em together now and then."

"Does he spend a lot of time at the ice cream parlor while she's working?"

"How would I know? And so what if he does?"

Rory laughed at that and ruffled my hair. I punched him in the chest, and he swung me into a headlock and rubbed his knuckles against my skull. Before we could get into a decent tussle, though, he pushed me away. "You go on downstairs and tell your mama we're heading into town. I'll meet you out front."

That seemed kind of odd, seeing as how he could have come downstairs with me then and there, but I figured he had to go to the bathroom. Little did I know he had an ulterior motive for sending me away ... and for going into town.

I also thought it a little strange when he met me on the front porch wearing his backpack. "Just in case I buy DVDs or posters, or something cool from Derbert Koomer's I Probably Got It store," he explained when I asked about the backpack. After we walked a good little ways, he added, "I also brought along something for excitement."

"What is it?" I asked, mystified.

He slanted me a look that promised fun. "You'll see."

My spirits perked up considerably. Rory had something up his sleeve ... or in his backpack, to be more precise. I couldn't imagine what it might be.

When we strolled into Poppy's, Ashley Winthrop stood behind the counter scooping up ice cream for a couple of ladies, and Charles Huckleby, the kid Rory had mentioned, was sure enough sitting at the counter, sipping a cola. Ashley's big green eyes lit up when she spotted us. "Well, as I live and breathe ... Rory Brown! I didn't know you were visiting."

Three other teenage girls at a nearby table jumped up to greet Rory and fuss over him. Almost made me wish my hair was blonde instead of red-brown and that I had muscles instead of "skin and bones," as some people put it. Not that I really liked girls all that much, but still ... no one wants to be left out of the action.

I reckon Charles Huckleby was feeling near the same, judging from how he swiveled around on the stool and gave Rory the evil eye. Rory just sauntered up beside him and leaned against the counter, smiling at the fluttering, giggling girls. "We might go bowling down in Bigelow tonight, Rory," a short blonde named Chantal said. "You want to come along?"

"Chip and I were thinking of starting a bonfire in our backyard," he answered. "I'm sure we wouldn't mind company." He glanced at Ashley when he said it, and she grinned at him. The others all talked at one time, mostly about bringing a thermos of cocoa and bags of marshmallows to roast.

Ashley finished with the customers she'd been helping, tossed her head in a way that made her long dark hair shimmer and slide, then sallied over to us. "What flavor can I interest you in, Rory?"

He slid the backpack off his shoulder, set it on the counter and leaned in toward her. "What kind you got?"

It was a simple question, but I noticed Charles Huckleby getting all tense and huffy on Rory's other side. Charles was even bigger than Rory and at least two years older, but he never caused the stir Rory did with the girls. Last summer Charles threatened to whup Rory's butt if he ever talked to Ashley again. Personally, I was hoping Charles had forgotten about that threat, but something told me neither he nor Rory had.

"Let's see now ..." Ashley drawled with a flirty little smile, "I have Chocolate Mousse Surprise, Strawberry Banana Fantasy, Peaches-n-Cream Paradise —"

"Why don't you just read the sign?" Charles cut in, glaring at Rory,. "Or can't you read yet?"

I stiffened and glanced sideways at Rory. Guys couldn't talk to him like that without expecting trouble in return.

Surprisingly, Rory didn't scowl at him or shove him or even tell him to take a flyin' leap. In fact, he smiled at him. "Why, hello, Charles. I didn't notice you sitting there." He actually put an arm around his shoulder. "How you been, buddy?"

"I ain't your buddy, and I told you last summer that if you —"

Charles's words broke off, and he looked down at his lap. His eyes grew wide and with a mighty holler, he pushed himself clean off the stool. Next thing I knew, girls were screaming, Charles was flailing around on the floor and Rory was diving to grab something from under the counter.

It took me a while, but I finally spotted the cause of the commotion. A snake. A big ol' black rat snake. Just like the one that belonged to my brother Toby.

"I think it's a rattler!" someone yelled, which started more girls to shrieking.

"No, it ain't," Ashley said, dropping to her knees behind the counter. "Aww, he looks scared slap to death, bless his little heart. Charles, you brute! You nearly rolled over him ..."

Amidst all the shrieking, cooing, shouting, and cussing, I heard Rory say, "Now how the heck did Oscar get loose? I thought I had him packed up good and cozy."

🐛🐛🐛

You should have seen the looks on Mama and Daddy's faces when we arrived home in a police car. Officer Mutt Bottoms explained that no charges were being brought against us, but only because they couldn't prove we meant to let that rat snake loose in the ice cream parlor, and that witnesses swore Charles Huckleby threw the first punch.

"But you're lucky," Officer Bottoms said, "that these two aren't in jail for inciting a riot and fighting. Adele Clearwater almost had a heart attack at the sight of that snake, and Charles Huckleby nearly knocked a tourist through the plate glass window."

I felt sick thinking about what could have happened, and I know Rory felt pretty bad, too. Throwing a few punches at Charles had to please him some, but I knew he hadn't meant to give old Miss Clearwater a heart attack or get a tourist knocked through a window.

The minute the officer left our house, I launched into a profuse apology. I knew Rory and I were in big trouble. Just the mention of the police was enough to put Daddy on edge, let alone seeing us hauled home in a patrol car. We did have one point in our favor, though—our crime had nothing to do with stealing. Which meant I could surely handle any punishment Daddy might dish out, even if I had to clock it for a day or two. But what worried me more than my punishment was what might happen to Rory.

Because Daddy never punished kids that weren't his own. He always just sent them away. And heck, Rory and I hadn't even beat level two on my new video game yet. This was no time to cut his two-week vacation short.

"The whole thing was my fault," I said, stabbing my thumb into my chest for emphasis. "I thought it would be funny, seeing those girls run from Oscar. I never meant to cause any real trouble."

"It wasn't his fault." Rory nudged me aside and faced Daddy squarely. "I was the one who took Oscar from his cage, and I was the one who let him loose."

"No, it was me," I insisted, elbowing my way in front of Rory, hoping he'd get the message and lay off. He never had been one to tell lies, but I hoped he'd have the sense to go along with mine. "Rory didn't know anything about Oscar until I let him loose at the ice-cream parlor."

"Chip Brown, you're lying through your teeth," Rory charged, angrier than he'd ever been with me. "You know dang well that I —"

"Both of you are to blame," my mother snapped, "and I've never been so disappointed in all my born days. Just think how Toby would feel if Oscar had been squished flat..."

"We're both sorry as we can be, Mama. But really, Rory had nothing to with —"

"That's enough." My father's deep, quelling voice cut through the noise like a hot knife through butter, and we all fell silent. Daddy's a man of few words, and he rarely gets mad, but when he does, we all pay attention. "Chip, you go to your room."

I knew better than to argue. I headed for the stairs.

Before I'd taken more than a few steps, though, Rory burst out, "What about me? Aren't you going to punish *me*, Uncle Bunk? I'm the one who did it!"

My father blinked a half-dozen times, as if he wasn't quite getting a clear view. "I'm not sure what's going on here, Rory, but you and I need to have a talk."

"A talk? That's it ... *a talk*?" He was scornful and furious and almost near tears — and I ain't never seen Rory cry. "Why won't you punish me? Why?"

Daddy just stared, looking too surprised for words. I stood and stared, too. Taking his rightful blame for letting the snake loose was one thing, but begging Daddy for punishment! Had Rory lost his mind?

"Don't you take that tone with your uncle, young man," my mother finally said, breaking the silence.

Rory didn't spare a glance for her, but glowered at my father as if he hated him. "The only reason Chip's taking the blame is because he knows you'll send me away."

Again, Daddy found no words, so Mama came up with some. "Send you away? Don't be silly, Rory. Letting a pet snake loose ain't all that bad."

I considered that to be good news, but it seems Rory didn't. His mouth stretched thin, his fists clenched at his sides, and with one last glare at Mama and Daddy, he took off through the front door.

Sometimes there's no understanding a guy as cool as my cousin Rory.

🐾🐾🐾

Everyone's got something they treasure, something they consider more important than anything else — and I'm not talking about love, friendship, family or anything mushy like that. I mean real, honest-to-goodness things. Mine is my video game system. If the house burned down, that's the first thing I'd grab. Toby would grab Oscar, I'm sure, but since pets might count under the "mushy" category (like a brother or a parent), I'd say his most important item is his dirt bike. Mama's is her Little Miss Bigelow beauty-queen tiara she won when she was a girl, before Tyrone Laslow's Rottweiler put the scar on her face. And Daddy's prize possession, without a doubt, is his FXSTDSE Screamin' Eagle Softail Deuce Harley Davidson.

You can hardly blame him for thinking it's so special. Heck, it's got a fuel-injected Twin Cam 95 cubic inch power train, a custom leather seat and pillion with chrome inserts, three-spoke custom wheels, dual front disc brakes and a custom "Candy Cobalt and Starlight Black" paint job with a color-matched frame. Trust me, it's sweet. He and Rory spent weeks last summer polishing it, gazing at it and listening to its engine roar. Rory, more than anyone, knew how sacred Daddy's Screamin' Eagle was.

That's why a short while later, just before dark, when I heard the first rumble of a powerful engine coming from the barn Daddy used as a garage/workshop, I figured Daddy must have decided to take his motorcycle out to try and find Rory while there was still enough daylight to see by. I'd been pacing across my room, waiting for Rory to come back to the house so I could find out why he'd run off. But then I heard a surprised exclamation from Mama in the kitchen followed by a muffled curse from Daddy, and I realized Daddy couldn't be the one who cranked up the Screamin' Eagle. Since Toby was off spending the day at a friend's house (and he probably wouldn't know how to start up the Screamin' Eagle, anyway), that left only Rory. And Rory knew everything there was to know about that motorcycle, including where Daddy kept the extra key in the garage.

But surely Rory wouldn't take Daddy's motorcycle without permission. Why I couldn't think of a single thing he could do to get into more trouble, short of doing bodily harm to somebody. He might as well pack his bags and never come back — a fact that Rory knew as well as I did. So, no, it couldn't have been Rory starting up that Screamin' Eagle.

The roar grew louder. Clearly the motorcycle was out of the garage, heading down the drive. I heard Mama and Daddy running for the front door. I tore off out of my room and flew down the stairs, not wantin' to miss whatever action was taking place. I reached the front porch just in time to see that Screamin' Eagle fly past the house, toward the road. And sure enough, Rory was driving!

Man, oh man, I always knew he was cool, but you shoulda seen him on that Harley, all hunched over the fat chrome handlebars, not even wearing a helmet, his shaggy blond hair streaming out behind him.

Daddy ran to his pick-up truck and flung open the driver door, while Mama headed for the passenger seat. Daddy already had that old gray truck in gear when I vaulted into the back. No way was I gonna miss whatever Rory did next. I hung on to the side of the truck bed with a deathgrip while I poked my head out to the side, trying to watch Rory while Daddy sped after him.

Rory barely slowed down when he turned out onto the road, and I held my breath, watching the motorcycle fishtail before it finally straightened up. He'd turned away from the town square, thank goodness, or he'd have had to stomp on the brakes to keep from running red lights or plowing over pedestrians in the crosswalks, I'm sure. As it was, he was headed for the main highway that led out of Mossy Creek.

"Rory!" Daddy yelled through the open driver's window of the pick-up. "Rory, pull over!"

Mama was hanging out the passenger window and yelling something, too. Rory gave no sign of hearing, though. Just kept that Screamin' Eagle flying.

Daddy sped up and gained on him. Just as we were closing in, Rory hung a left onto an old dirt road that led to Whitaker's Pond. Daddy turned behind him, and Rory led us on a merry chase all the way 'round the pond. Daddy was just a-cussing, which is something he rarely does, and Mama took to praying. Me, I just tried my best not to be pitched over the side of the truck bed, what with all them ruts and bumps we were hitting and all. And let me tell you, it ain't easy holding on to cold truck metal with your bare hands in January, or braving the winter wind without so much as a jacket. I liked to have froze my butt off. My fingers, at the very least.

But I was too worked up to pay much mind to the cold. Rory rounded that pond, then headed back the way he'd come on the dirt road, with us in hot (actually, cold) pursuit. When he reached the main road, he stopped at the stop sign, which let us close the distance, but before Daddy could do more than holler out the window, Rory took off again, turning toward town. I hoped like heck he wouldn't pass by our house and wind up on the town square. Mutt or Sandy would surely spot him then and haul him off to jail. He was three weeks shy of 15, when a body could get a learner's permit, and even then I believe he'd have been in big trouble for driving that Harley all by himself.

He hung a smooth right into our driveway — he was really getting the hang of steering that thing from the looks of it — and I let go of the breath I'd been holding. Shoot, he looked like a pro, the way he slowed down nice and easy and brought that baby to a halt just inside Daddy's garage. A guy can't help but admire a kid who can handle a Harley.

Daddy didn't look anywhere near admiring him,

though. Lord a' mercy, was he mad! I saw steam spouting from his ears, I swear, as he climbed out of the pick-up, slammed the door behind him and stalked into that barn-garage-workshop. Even Mama hung back some, taking her time getting out of the truck. I saw no use in moseying too close, neither. I stopped next to Mama just outside the garage, where we had a good view of the action.

Daddy clenched his fists at his sides as he approached Rory, who had cut off the Harley, swung his leg clear of it and turned squarely for a confrontation. He didn't look like he'd taken a bit of pleasure from that ride. And he didn't look the least bit cocky for having handled the Screamin' Eagle so well. Though I ain't personally seen it, I suspect he had the look of a condemned man getting ready to die.

His body stiffened and his face grew even paler as Daddy stalked close. It must've been like looking into the face of hell's own fury.

Oddly enough though, Daddy walked right past him, clean over to the far wall. And when he reached the wall, he pivoted and strode the other way. With every step, he shoved his fist into the palm of his other hand, harder and harder each time. His face was redder than I've ever seen it, and his mouth slanted this way and that. And his eyes ...

Good gosh a'mighty ... his eyes were shining with tears. They weren't dripping down his face or anything girlie, but they sure 'nough hovered in his eyes. And his throat worked like he'd swallowed a chicken bone.

He passed by Rory again without paying him a glance, then stopped at a stack of baled hay ... and plowed his fist into that hay with a growl I'd never heard from a human. He hit the hay again and again, and when he whirled around, his chest was a'heaving. He looked a little crazy, and we all took a step back — even Rory.

"You could have been killed."

He didn't say it loud, but rough and gravelly, like his

throat was too tight to let such a roar come through.

Surprise loosened Rory's jaw. He clearly hadn't given his personal safety a thought — and sure hadn't expected my father to.

"Damn it all to hell, Rory," he thundered then, loud enough to shake the barn, "you could be lying out there on that road —" He pointed in that direction, but his words broke off, and his throat muscles clenched again.

And I knew what he was thinking. He was remembering his brother. Rory's daddy. How he found him on the road, after some high-speed chase had killed him.

Rory didn't say a word. Just stood there staring at Daddy.

"Why, Rory?" Daddy asked, his voice pure hoarse now. "Just answer me that."

Rory didn't answer. In fact, he pressed his lips together until they nearly disappeared. The silence was heavier than any I'd ever known.

"You took my Screamin' Eagle without permission, and risked your life, your limbs, your everything, for nothing but a silly joyride. You scared us all sick. And you haven't even tried to apologize." Daddy frowned at him, as if he couldn't for the life of him figure Rory out. Heck, I couldn't either. "So what do you think I ought to do with you now?"

Rory lifted his chin in a show of strength, but I could see he was hurtin' something terrible. "I reckon you're gonna send me away."

Dread clutched at me. Of course he'd send him away ... and not just for the time being. Stealing the Screamin' Eagle is one of those unforgivable offenses.

"Is that what you want?" Daddy asked him.

A muscle moved in Rory's jaw, like he was chewing on something tough. "No, sir. But why do you bother asking me questions? You never believe me when I answer."

The air itself grew still and close in that garage.

Daddy narrowed his eyes. "What are you talking about?"

"You always think I lie. But I don't. And you probably think I steal, too. But I don't. And if you think I was stealing your Screamin' Eagle, you're wrong."

"Then just what were you doing, boy?"

Rory let out a big rush of breath, and dropped his head, then lifted it again and looked at the ceiling, the wall, then Daddy ... and his eyes were as shiny as Daddy's had been. In a whispered little croak, he uttered, "I don't know."

"Do you want to go to your mama? If you do, I'll get you a flight and drive you to the airport right now. Do you want to go back to school? I'll get on the phone to the principal and have him search that quarterback's locker. You'll be back in school by Monday."

Rory eyes widened, and I guess mine did, too. I hadn't thought Daddy believed Rory about the quarterback throwing the stink bomb.

"Whatever you want, Rory, I'll help you get."

Rory swallowed hard then, and his eyes grew even shinier. "I don't want to live at school, or in the apartment my Mama rented in Puerto Rico, or ... or ... " he choked up some.

"...Or in a place where I'm just ... company. I want to live at home."

Daddy looked as lost and confused as I felt. Where exactly was Rory's home?

Rory turned away suddenly and jammed his hands into his jacket pockets and looked like he wished he was anywhere but here. "Never mind about any of that," he mumbled, nudging a stone on the ground with the toe of his sneaker. "I'm not your son, and I guess don't deserve to be. Everyone knows you just send company away when they do something wrong, so —" he shrugged, "— call my mama, or the school, or —"

"Wait just one cotton-pickin' minute," Daddy cut in.

Rory glanced at him.

"We haven't settled the matter of you taking my Screamin' Eagle without my permission."

Rory blinked, Then he frowned and flushed a little. "Oh. Well, I ... I apologize ..."

"It'll take a whole lot more than an apology." Daddy seemed to be gathering steam, like a locomotive, and his voice grew loud and stern. "What you did was wrong. When you take something that isn't yours without permission of the owner, that's stealing."

"But I —"

"And I will not tolerate it in my family. My brother took to thievin', and he died tryin' to run, and I'd rather cut my heart out that to go through that with anyone else I love."

Rory gaped at him with the strangest expression.

"I believe you're gonna have to clock it, Rory."

Clock it. Daddy was making Rory clock it. Rory looked like he might be in shock at the news.

"And I don't mean for just one day," Daddy went on in his sternest tone. "You'll be clocking it for a full week."

"A full week!" I cried, aghast at the very thought. "Aww, c'mon, Daddy —"

Mama pinched my arm, cutting my protest short.

Daddy kept his attention on Rory. "And then, for the week after that, you'll go straight to your room every day after school."

Rory pondered that, and so did I. How could Daddy know what Rory did after school, seeing as how his school was way up yonder in Tennessee ...

"Mossy Creek might not have a school as fancy as the one you're used to," said Daddy, "but the one we've got will have to do. You can go to college just as well from Mossy Creek as you can from Chattanooga. I have no doubt your mama will agree. It's time we bring you home."

It took a good minute before I fully realized what he'd said.

Rory understood straight off. His eyes went to brimming, and his mouth wobbled some, but happiness beamed from that boy in rays so strong, it warmed me like the summer sun. "Yes, sir," he said to Daddy. "Yes, sir."

"Report to your aunt for duty. Your clocking starts now, son."

🐞🐞🐞

I heard tell that folks take to harsh punishment in different ways. Some try to think of happier times while going through the worst of it, some rant and rage at every turn, and others wallow in self pity. Toby and me are more of the wallowing kind. We've learned over the long, hard years the secret to surviving a clocking sentence. If you look and act pitiful enough, Mama might go a touch easier on you while assigning the chores. The same can't be said for Daddy. There's a definite knack to keeping your pitiful looks for Mama's eyes only.

Rory didn't seem to grasp the wisdom of this strategy, or maybe he didn't quite understand my advice during the few stolen minutes I found to whisper to him. Since communication with other family members is strongly discouraged during a body's clocking term, I wasn't able to give the benefit of all my hard-won wisdom.

Boy, was he screwing up. Whereas Toby and me would take our time with every chore, knowing that when you were done, you'd only get another, Rory zipped through every task, as if he was racing against the clock. Not only that, but he took extra pains to do a good job — a really good dang job — at even the most menial of tasks, like cleaning the kitty litter box, doing the supper dishes, and sorting out Daddy's tool chest. I started to worry he was setting too high a standard for Toby and me to follow.

The most amazing part was, Rory didn't look at all put out by anything Mama or Daddy told him to do. He actually took to whistling while he worked — and every now and again, he'd flash a smile at one of us. Very ill-advised, if you ask me. If he kept this up, they'd surely have him scrubbing the toilets before too long.

Daddy and Mama, meanwhile, closed themselves up in the den to phone Aunt Lou, Rory's mama. In no time at all, Daddy came strolling out, looking well-pleased with himself. Next thing I know, Mama's chatting on the phone with Miss Francine, telling her the news about Rory staying in Mossy Creek.

Not fifteen minutes later, the coach from Bigelow High School, Buck Looney, called to talk to Rory. Kids in Mossy Creek still have to bus down to Bigelow for school, since we're still waiting on the governor to make good on his promise of rebuilding Mossy Creek High. Daddy told Coach Looney that Rory was "otherwise occupied" at the time. No phone use allowed while clocking it. I heard Coach's voice through the receiver, even though I was clear across the kitchen. He wanted to know if Rory was intending to wrestle. Daddy speculated that he very well might. And while he said it, Daddy got this gleam in his eyes, like he did every year at the start of football at the University of Georgia. Something told me he could barely wait to see Rory in action on the wrestling mat. I could barely wait, myself. Coach sounded so excited at the prospect of signing Rory up, I'll bet he let out a great big "Yee-Hah" after he hung up.

It was almost too much to take in all at once. I'd have Rory here year-round. How cool was that?

Hamilton's Department Store

312 Main Street
Mossy Creek, GA 30533
Est. 1901
Marble floors. Old-fashioned service. Modern selections.
Visit our on-line catalog at www.hamiltons.com

From: Robert Walker, executive manager
        Hamilton's Department Store

Rosh:

You were right about the new glow-in-the-dark knit jogging caps with the iPod pockets. We can't keep them in stock. Every kid in town wants one. Every kid, and my 50-ish mother, too. She's been working outdoors a lot this winter, getting ready to build a winery at her farm. She likes the "Raging Pink" color. She puts her iPod in it and listens to Stevie Nicks. I stopped by the other evening right after dark. She was driving a tractor in from the field. I spotted her glowing pink cap a good quarter-mile away. If you knew my mother, you'd under stand why I like to have that much warning.

But the reason I'm faxing you is to ask a favor. Can you hook me up with one of your custom uniform designers? Just between you and me, I'm putting together a community-league soccer team up here. Adult men, thirty-and-over.

Don't laugh. Yeah, so maybe we'll need a few uniforms in sizes like "Xtra-Large Beer Gut" and "Double-Wide Comfort Fit," but just wait until you see us kick a ball. By the way, do you have any connections among the sports linament and Ace bandage wholesalers?

Rob

You can run, but you can't hide.

Amos Comes to a Decision
Chapter 6

I checked my watch. I was hungry enough to eat a horse, but I doubted I'd be left alone long enough to chew my lunch. I'd have to settle for a cup of hot coffee. Before I headed into the Naked Bean, I glanced around the square for troublemakers. When I didn't see any, I shot a glance skyward. Just to be sure the sky wasn't falling. After this morning's mayhem, I wouldn't have been surprised to see two suns, a meteor coming at me or an unexpected eclipse.

Instead I found the perfectly ordinary, clear, cold blue of January, which meant the only thing left to blame was the metaphysical universe. To be fair, my horoscope had tried to warn me about Mercury in retrograde. Next time I'd listen.

The day started out with my retrieving the paper and catching a criminal in the act. My next door neighbor was across the street stealing Ms. Zola Hartley's newspaper. "Joshua! Do not tell me you are doing what I think you're doing."

Joshua was a twenty-something living on a budget with two roommates. They all worked at the candle factory out on Trailhead Road and until this moment I'd considered them good neighbors — a little loud with the music but since I liked their play list, I wasn't complaining. He had the decency to look sheepish. I think he would have scuffed the toe of his shoe, too, except he was barefoot and dancing back and forth to escape the cold.

"Hey, man." He pitched his voice in a whisper that carried across the street. "They cut the cable off. I need my news."

"Here's a newsflash. That's not your paper."

He crossed the street, bringing the paper with him and quick stepping. That asphalt had to be torture. He halted in the grass at the edge of my yard. "Come on, Amos. Zola wouldn't mind sharing. She sleeps late. I can have this baby read, folded and back in her driveway before her coffee pot kicks on. She'll never know."

"This isn't the first time you've *shared* her paper is it?"

He knew better than to lie. "No."

"You'll be telling her how generous she's been later today."

"Right. I guess so."

"Good."

The day went downhill from there. Mutt, Sandy and I were busier than I could ever remember. Battle would have enjoyed today's call sheet. Especially the most recent part that pitted me against the Gray Panthers. I'd have to remember to tell him next time I visited the cemetery. My visits weren't obligatory lately. Funny how a year or two of walking my father's beat had brought us closer than over thirty-five years of being his son. I understood him a little better and I'd convinced myself that he'd begun to appreciate me as well. We had a truce of sorts finally and a fair-to-even chance of maintaining it.

Of course, one of us being dead had improved our chances tremendously.

The Bean's shop bell jingled and a herd of freshly ground scents washed over me in their rush to escape through the door. I couldn't tell Peruvian Dark from aged, canopy-grown Brazilian, but that didn't matter. Jayne hadn't ever put a bad cup of coffee in my hands. A few months ago she'd switched my regular with something. It was pretty good. Now I didn't even bother to order. Just took my chances with what she gave me, from whatever pot struck her fancy. As long as it wasn't decaf.

Battle thought decaf was a waste of good cup. I agreed. If you're going to drink unleaded you might as well drop by Maggie Hart's herb shop and guzzle tree bark tea sweetened with clover honey. *Gak*. I knew Battle wouldn't have tried the tea either. I wondered if he would have switched his coffee allegiance to the Naked Bean or kept getting his refills over at Mama's café?

The answer followed right on the heels of the question. Mama's. Yep. *Mama's*.

Taste actually had nothing to do with it. Money did. Battle never surrendered a nickel without a fight. Rather than cough up an extra buck, he'd have drunk coffee so bitter you couldn't have distinguished it from a three-time divorcée whose husbands cheated. Nope. Battle would have still been getting free refills down at Mama's. Somehow that made gourmet coffee and its price slide down real easy.

Okay, so the truce isn't perfect. But we're working on it.

The Bean was empty for once. The Methodists and their baked goodies were luring the lunch crowd away. Jayne looked up from something on the counter. I did the hey-I'm-here-for-my-coffee wave. She nodded and came to meet me, carrying and wiping some piece of stainless equipment that was essential to the espresso machine. At least I think it was essential because she constantly fussed and fidgeted with it. As she walked she smiled that wide, welcoming smile of hers, the ponytail swishing just a bit. I decided that Battle might have switched his trade after all. And she was definitely easy on the eyes. Battle liked easy-on-the-eyes. Plus Jayne had a way of making people like her.

Until they got sucker-punched by her. Like now. "How can I help you, Vlad?"

Vlad? *Vlad the Impaler?*

That Jayne packed a wallop when you least expected it. Reminded me of another strong, blunt woman I knew. A corner of my mouth kicked up. You couldn't fault her reference. She was spot on. Vlad and I both shared the love of our villages. His neighbors showed their love with pitchforks and torches. Mine used electric scooters. Let me tell you, electric scooters coming at you are every bit as unsettling as pitchforks and torches. Especially the way Miss Irene drives.

"Jaynie, darlin', do not start with me. I've had a wicked bad morning. I've got a ticket book, a short temper and I know for a fact you've got trash cans blocking the alley out back."

She snorted and reattached the espresso part. Jayne didn't stand on ceremony with me. "Amos, you give me a ticket for blocking the alley and I can guarantee you a new protest march by two p.m."

It was my turn to laugh. "Only by two? I thought you were better connected than that. I'm a bit disappointed. I'd have thought you could pull it together sooner."

She grinned over her shoulder and grabbed a to-go cup for my coffee. "Well, I could. But without Ingrid here to help I'd have to forgo the torches."

"Yeah, what's a march without torches? Although it's probably best if we don't put another deadly weapon in Miss Irene's hands. By the way, where did Ingrid go in such a hurry, packing Bob along for the ride? She usually asks me to keep an eye on her place."

"Just gone for the day." *Snap.* The lid settled into place.

"She and Ida are sorting out some city business. I think it was an old paperwork thing." She traded me coffee for money. "Just as well they aren't here stirring up more trouble for you. Looks like you got enough restless natives."

Before I could agree, a yellow plastic duck came sailing out of the little office in the back. I'd never been around a baby long enough to watch them grow from little lumps to little people. The process was interesting in a watching-a-train-wreck sort of way. The little sucker had quite an arm.

Jayne pushed my change at me but made no move to retrieve the duck, which teetered forlornly on its broad nose, butt in the air. "Irritating isn't it?" she asked. "That compulsion to run pick up the stupid duck? I'm convinced he's working on his first science fair project."

I snapped out of duck-focus. "Come again?"

She finally ambled toward the duck. "I'm convinced that kid has a little notebook and when I'm not looking he's writing down things like, 'Today the subject reliably retrieved the duck eight hundred forty-six times. Speed of return noticeably slower than with the binky. Must try the red block tomorrow.'"

"Which you'll retrieve reliably."

"Absolutely."

I headed for the door, warming my hands on the cup and asked a question that surprised me. "You like this? Being tortured in the name of science? Giving up sleep?"

Duck in hand, her whole body radiated the answer and she cast a glance toward the play yard hidden just inside the office door. "Yep."

Baby Matthew tuned up for a scream. He'd apparently reached the end of his tolerance for the play yard. I sought the relative peace and quiet of the station. I liked my train wrecks without soundtracks.

❦ ❦ ❦

Caller ID for the station was a bit of technology that Sandy'd just had to have. Said it made her more efficient since we couldn't afford a proper emergency response system. Probably did make her more efficient. But she wasn't here and I had to pick up the phone *knowing* who was on the other end.

I think I'd have been faster and more efficient about picking up the line if I hadn't known it was Dwight Truman. I don't think he could actually hear me swear under my breath as I picked it up.

"Mossy Creek Police. Chief Royden here."

"Amos?" He sounded cranky, but then it's hard to tell with Dwight. In the dictionary, the word *crank* has his caricature beside it. All nose and ears. Think of a human Dumbo but with less charm.

"Yes, Dwight. It's Amos. Unless you've hired another one, I'm the only Chief Royden we have at the moment."

"Good grief, Amos! Why are we paying a dispatcher if you're going to answer the darned phone? That's a waste of money. I never thought we needed another city employee anyway. It's just a drain on the budget. And if the girl can't even be trusted to properly answer the phone —"

"Whoa. No one works seven days a week around here except me. The girl has a name, you know? It's 'Sandy.' She spends most of her time out on calls now. She's earning her pay as a full officer."

Best not to tell him about the dispute at Orville Gene's place. He wouldn't understand that Sandy considered trespassing and committing vandalism part of her job description.

"More money wasted," Dwight complained. "You know the insurance went up when you made her an officer."

He didn't actually accuse me of costing him business,

but he was a mite touchy over the ruling that forced the city to get three bids for every contract. Dwight had lost the insurance deal recently. Right after we added Sandy.

Tweedle ruffled in his cage. The parakeet had a sixth sense about Sandy and he didn't like anyone who didn't appreciate her. I had to agree. I was about out of patience with Dwight today. "Look, Councilman, I'm a little busy, and I'm not the one you should be having this discussion with."

"Oh, like talking to Ida would make any difference if you're involved. You barely say two words at the town meetings and she interrupts to agree and rushes to the next item. If she weren't so busy agreeing with you, I'd say you'd done something to rub her the wrong way."

Rub her the wrong way? Ha! That would assume I'd gotten close enough to Ida to touch her. All I saw of Ida lately was her shapely backside as she ran the other way. I'd never thought of her as cowardly but she was about to make a believer of me. A smarter man might have given up hope, but I figured if she wanted me out of the picture she'd have set me straight rather than avoid me.

"Dwight, I'm burning daylight here. What did you want?"

"Hooligans are using the football field. It has to be stopped."

"We don't have a football field."

The gasp was a piece of performance art. I thought he'd hyperventilate before he stopped. "We most *certainly* have a football field. Just because the Governor hasn't made good on his promise to allocate funding for the new high school doesn't mean that the land shouldn't be protected and preserved for our boys."

By *our boys*, I'm assuming he meant the football boys and not our troops overseas. By *land* I assumed he meant the big patch of ground inside the almost nonexistent track oval. To call it a football field was a great leap of faith.

"Are you saying that someone is using the ... football field for illegal activity?"

"They're practicing soccer."

"In England that *is* football."

Another gasp. "Amos, your flippant attitude isn't helping. That land is a treasure and they'll ruin the grass. Besides they don't have a permit from the parks department."

I bit my tongue and didn't volunteer that there were more weeds than winter-shriveled grass left. Whoever was practicing on the field would just save us the cost of a weed killer. "It's winter, Dwight. Winter. Are you sure they are regularly using the field?"

"Every Saturday at one o'clock. Last week they left the field in a muddy mess."

"Are you sure it's every week? Maybe it was just a one-time deal. Did they ask you for a permit, Dwight?"

"Not yet. But I've seen them out there when I'm doing my bike laps."

I tossed my pen on the desk and closed the folder on the report I'd been drafting. "I take it their chances of getting a permit are nonexistent?"

"Well, I'm not the only vote on the parks commission."

"Yes or no, Dwight?"

"No. I don't believe they'll be able to obtain a permit. Go and throw them off."

I sincerely doubted that Dwight had seen rabid sports parents or he wouldn't be sending me out to do his dirty work. I didn't like it, but my hands were tied. No permit. No practice.

"All right. I'll head out there. Get there before they start practice."

"Thank you." He hung up.

I stared at the now-dead phone in my hand. "You're welcome, Dwight. Anytime. Happy to be of service."

Then I hung the phone up with unnecessary force. Three or four times in rapid succession.

Tweedle approved.

❦❦❦

Rob Walker and his daughter, Little Ida, were the only ones on the old football field when I got there. Rob was fifteen or twenty feet in front of Little Ida, demonstrating some footwork with the soccer ball. He didn't look half-bad for an over-thirty department-store manager. The baseball cap looked oddly out of place though. I called out and waved. Little Ida turned, waved back and ran toward me executing a perfect cartwheel along the way. I clapped. The one thing I knew about the pint-sized version of people was that if you paid attention to them, they'd return the favor. Besides I was just about to ruin her day. Might as well soften the blow.

"Hey, Chief! You gonna play, too?" She grabbed my hand and swung it back and forth as we walked back to her dad.

"I think I'm a little too big for your league."

"Bubba Rice is going to play. He's as big as you. Daddy promises we can crush Bigelow."

Win Allen and his alter ego, Bubba, were indeed as big as me. I slowed, let go of Little Ida's hand. Details I'd ignored suddenly formed a crisp picture in my mind. Little Ida wasn't dressed for soccer. She had play clothes on. Regular tennis shoes. Her hair wasn't pulled back. Rob had on sweats and cleats and was expertly herding the ball with his feet as he sprinted over. When he stopped the ball, flipped it up with his foot and bounced it on his knee before snatching it from the air ... well ... I knew that

Dwight's definition of hooligans and mine were very, very different.

Car doors slammed behind me. No doubt the rest of the hooligans were arriving. I twisted to get a quick look. Strapping big hooligans, one and all.

While we waited for them to stroll over, I stated the obvious to Rob. "You're putting together an adult soccer team."

"Yep." He didn't volunteer anything else, just waited.

"You didn't ask me."

"Nope."

I nodded slowly — absorbing his answer, checking the faces beginning to lineup behind him. They were almost all younger than me. I'll admit that stung. I didn't think I was a vain man, but I was more than unhappy at the thought of being officially past my prime. Judging from the vague apprehension on the faces and hastily averted gazes there had at least been some discussion about inviting me to join the team. Win Allen, who had managed to crack the age barrier and uphold our generation's honor, shrugged as if to say, he'd tried to sway them. He made eye contact with me and very deliberately cut his eyes toward Rob, the only player not the least bit embarrassed.

Curiouser and curiouser.

Rob'd been the deciding factor. Maybe the only dissenting vote. I'd bet money on it. Sometime between last fall and this moment, Rob Walker had taken a dislike to me. A subtle one. I sure hadn't noticed. Until now. Only one transgression of mine would cause the quiet challenge in the stare Rob directed at me. That transgression was personal and had nothing to do with foot speed. As awkward as the next few minutes might turn out to be, I was more than a little relieved to realize my foot speed was no longer the problem. Hell, I was downright cheery as I crossed my arms and returned his stare.

"Sorry, folks, but we've had a complaint."

That startled them all. "About us?" three or four of them chorused in unison. Even Rob's expression lost some of its confidence. "About what?"

"You don't have a permit to assemble on city property."

Again, the guys responded in disgusted unison. "Dwight."

Rob tossed his ball at Dan McNeil. "You start practice while I straighten this out."

Funny. To my ears, the word *this* sounded an awful lot like *Amos*. Apparently he was going to straighten me out. If I'd been Battle I might have taken offense. But I wasn't Battle. I was, however, his son and blood will tell. "Yeah. Y'all hit the field. Rob and I will get a few things straight."

I think I must have been wearing my "scary smile." The one Sandy says gets people's attention. The team took the field so fast I began to believe they could handily crush Bigelow. Dan called for passing drills, and Rob told Little Ida to scavenge runaway balls for them. I watched her take off and then turned back to Rob.

"Which first? Personal or soccer? And let's walk. Ground's too cold to stand still long." I didn't give him any choice about following.

"I wasn't aware we had any personal business."

That made me smile for real. "She's your mother. I think that qualifies as personal. How'd you guess? I'm sure Ida hasn't said a word."

"Not one. You used to tick her off on a regular basis. We'd hear about it at Sunday dinner. And then one day, we didn't. I wondered why. I watched her. I watched you. I don't like it. Leave her alone, Amos."

"Or what? You'll kick me off the softball team? What are you? Twelve?"

He opened his mouth and shut it. Twice. Suddenly he

relaxed his shoulders and called a truce. "It was all I could do to keep you off the soccer team and I only managed that because no one had ever seen you play soccer."

"That's disappointing. They should have trusted me to figure it out."

"Yeah." His mouth tightened a little. "I know. You put your mind to something and you figure it out. Always have. I don't know how but you figured out Mother. You got her running scared."

"As long as she runs in any direction but Del Jackson's, I can live with that."

"Current problems aside, he's a good man."

"Del's an idiot. He and that clingy wife of his are a train wreck waiting to happen. I'm angling to pick up the pieces."

"Angle for a different fish."

"I got this one on the line."

He snatched the ball cap off his head and whacked his thigh good, struggling not to say something. Failing. "Dammit, Amos. You're not that much older than me."

"Yeah, your mother's hung up on that, too. Must be genetic."

"You're serious?"

"As a heart attack. She's a grown woman, Rob. I am more than a few years older than you. Not that it matters because I couldn't care less if you approve. I'm not asking for your blessing. I'm just asking you to get out of the way if Ida looks in my direction. Ida will cross just about anybody to get what she wants. Except you."

He jammed the hat on his head and paced in a circle. "Is she putting up with Del's nonsense because she's afraid of what I'd say if she dated you?"

I shrugged and stuck my hands in my pockets. "Ida does what Ida wants. But I wouldn't be having this conversation if I didn't think your opinion about the men she dates mattered to Ida."

A noise similar to a strangling cat came out of his mouth. "Arrgh. Dating you. This could go wrong in so many ways."

"Absolutely. Want me to list them?" I raised my eyebrows and held up a thumb, ready to go.

"No. I won't be able to sleep tonight as it is."

"Out of curiosity ... you have a talk like this with Del?"

Shaking his head, he turned back toward his players. "Nah."

"Why not?"

"He's a good man but he's not in the same league as my father. His potential to break her heart is limited."

Rob was ten feet away before I realized my feet weren't moving. I was still trying to process the bomb he'd dropped. Whatever problems remained between Ida and me, Rob wouldn't be one of them. He'd paid me what was probably the highest compliment in his arsenal and then warned me not to break his mother's heart. I had no intention of hurting Ida so I was okay with the unspoken warning.

Unfortunately I still had Dwight and the damned permit to deal with. "Hold up, Rob. We need to talk about the permit."

Arms spread wide, Rob whirled back to me. "Come on, Amos! The permit nonsense is a bunch of bull. You know that. You aren't seriously telling me that we can't practice here. Give us a break. I've already ordered team uniforms. And I've lined up a corporate sponsor."

"Let me guess. Hamilton's Department Store."

"Being the store's executive manager and a major stockholder has its perks."

I looked around. There wasn't much of anything that could be hurt. Someone could break a leg but the risk wasn't any greater than over at the baseball diamond. I didn't roust every bunch of kids taking the field over there. Besides, Dwight's problem wasn't the permit or the damage to the football field.

No, thanks to my own little reaction to being excluded from the soccer club, I had a very good idea why Dwight's panties were in a bunch. And I was human enough to enjoy dropping a little bomb of my own.

"Rob, you can practice here if you add at least one more man to the roster."

"You mean you."

"Nope."

"Then I don't need anyone else."

"Yeah, you do. I bet Dwight's pretty fast now that he's been doing all the bike training."

"*Dwight*? You want me to ask Dwight? *That's* why he complained? Because his feelings were hurt? You gotta be kidding. Asking him is going to make the permit problem go away?"

I shrugged and dug some sun glasses out of my pocket. "Forget the permit. I'd do it because he'd make one nightmare of a goalie. Nothing's gotten past that man in years. But it's your call."

Smiling, I settled my sunglasses and headed to my Jeep. Rob was sputtering behind me, but I kept walking. The phone was already ringing. I'd had the station phone forwarded to my cell. I didn't have Caller ID but I knew who was calling without looking.

Mercury in retrograde.

🐾🐾🐾

At least this crisis came with more coffee. Jayne had been vague on the phone. She had something to tell me and a problem she wanted handled. Wouldn't tell me the *something* until after I'd handled the *problem*. Just when I

111

thought she had good sense she joined the ranks of the cryptic. I hated cryptic. Didn't have much use for shades of gray either.

I saw the problem as soon as I circled around the square. Jayne had a squatter. Right there in front of her store, big as life, was a first-class lemonade stand, only this one sold hot chocolate. Seventy-five cents. Not only was he in front Jayne's shop, he was competing with the Methodists and the hot chocolate stand at their festival, in the park just across the street.

Poster board was neatly lettered and taped to hang down from the edge of a card table. Several thermos bottles sat to one side of the tabletop along with cups and napkins. I couldn't tell what, but he had a paperweight holding down the napkins.

I parked the Jeep and watched the kid — the Greevy boy — tidy his business. When I got out he perked up, ready to make eye contact and a sale. Good technique. I had a psychic vision that this one would be class president or die trying. All the Greevys had red hair and glasses. This one had big feet, the kind of feet that would make a basketball coach happy someday. He was mid-chest on me already.

"Afternoon, Chief. It's a cold one. A little hot chocolate would probably taste good, huh?"

"Pour me up one." I fished in my wallet and pulled out a buck. "What are you planning to do with your profit? A good cause?"

He hesitated for a second as he made change. "No cause. Well, maybe a lost cause."

"How so?"

"You know anything about women?"

"Nothing useful."

I frowned at Jayne through the window. Her face instantly disappeared. "But I'm willing to learn. What's your problem?"

"Scarlet Masterson."

I took the cup. "Don't believe I know her."

"Wish I didn't. I didn't even like girls 'til her. Now I'm out here in the cold selling hot chocolate so next month I can get her a better Valentine's present than the other guys in the class. Plus Chip Brown's cousin, Rory, is in town. He gets *all* the girls. If I knew Scarlet liked him—or any other guy—better than me, I could just not embarrass myself. But I don't know, so I'm out here. You know if a girl likes you, she just ought to tell you. There ought to be rules or something."

"Rules would be good." We nodded silently, in complete agreement with each other. Then I paid him for his hot chocolate and asked him not to set up shop in front of any food establishments in the future. He said that was a rule he could live with. I left him to pack up and found Jayne.

"Problem solved. Now, cough up the intel."

"You won't like it."

"I'll like it less if you make me wait."

She actually wrung her hands. "Sandy just reported in from a reconnaissance mission out at Hope Settles' apple farm. She confirmed what we both suspected. Hope and Marle just got home from North Carolina. Ingrid picked Hope up at the farm, then they met up with Ida. The three of them are headed to Atlanta to confront the governor. The 'old paperwork' is the deed to the Sitting Tree property. They found the deed. There's going to be serious trouble at the governor's mansion."

I was dialing before she stopped talking. I had the key in the ignition before the county dispatcher put my call through to the governor's security detail. I was already on the road when they agreed not to do anything until I got there.

Before this day was done, Ida and I were going to agree on a few rules.

113

Mossy Creek Gazette

106 Main Street • Mossy Creek, GA 30000

From the desk of Katie Bell

Lady Victoria Salter Stanhope
The Clifts
Seaward Road
St. Ives, Cornwall, TR3 7PJ
United Kingdom

Hello, again, Vick!

I've got lots more to tell you
about our rambunctious winter
day, but I just want to mention
that there's no ill will between
me and Patty Campbell over that
little estate sale incident. I
mean, okay, she beat me to the
quilt, fair and square. That's
what I get for not working out on
the treadmill since Thanksgiving.
I was a little off my game. But
I'm back in the gym now, and next
time Patty grabs for an heirloom
quilt, I promise you, she'll find
herself holding nothing but a
few threads and a tuft of cotton
batting.

I'm very busy in town right now,
following up tips and leads

on the local New Year's resolution breakers. You know, it's strange how people don't appreciate a friendly reminder that they failed at their good intentions.

More winter gossip coming atcha,

From your quilt-less friend,

Katie

Never get between a woman and her bad habits.

Resolutionary War
Chapter 7

My name is Pearl Quinlan and I'm a carbo-holic. A fat-aholic, too.

As testament to my addiction, I'd just spent the last five minutes determining how I could sneak a pack of Little Debbie Swiss Cake Rolls out of my sister Spiva's stash at home without her noticing.

"They were on sale at the Sam's Club in Bigelow," was Spiva's excuse for purchasing a jumbo crate of my all-time favorite snack cake. If caught, lying and blaming my pet ferret, Twinkie, would be my best line of defense. I wondered if Spiva knew ferrets didn't like sweets.

I glanced up at the clock on the wall behind my register at Mossy Creek Books and Whatnots, then checked my wristwatch. Fourteen minutes to closing. I shut down at two o'clock on Saturday afternoons in the winter. I'd best stop thinking about cream filling and start adding my register.

My store had done a pretty brisk business today, despite the cold, since a lot of people visited the town square for the Mt. Gilead Methodist Church January fundraiser. I realize most churches don't conduct fundraisers in the heart of winter. They prefer the spring. Creekites, however, like to be different. After all, we are the town with a motto that says we "ain't going nowhere, and don't want to."

Well, before I'd been coveting my sisters' snack cakes, I'd been trying to put out of mind all the delicious baked goods being offered just across the street from me. Ever since Doc Champion had me on strict orders to lower my cholesterol, visions of fried pies and brownies danced in my head. Not surprising, I know, especially for the woman who usually wins the Bigelow County apple butter contest and has the size eighteen Levi's to prove that she eats it, too. For the past three weeks though, I'd been making an honest attempt at following Doc's advice. All short-nosed Quinlans end up with high cholesterol, and I was going to be the one who won the battle the hard way — through diet and exercise. So far, I'd lost ten pounds and an inch around my considerable middle.

Spiva, who is both my older sister and my roommate, is also a brown-haired, short-nosed Quinlan who packs weight on her middle. She was diagnosed with high cholesterol long before me. And with the way we chow down, it's no wonder the town thinks of us as the dynamic duo of artery-clogging, gastronomic delights. We did name our charitable organization the Chubby Cherubs with good reason — we are chubby, and we like to do good works.

Although Spiva takes her medication faithfully, what she does three times a week on a dilapidated treadmill Patty Campbell found for her at a garage sale can't truly be called *exercise*. She doesn't even break a sweat. And she continues to eat whatever she wants, which, quite frankly, irritates the heck out of me. The only joy in all of this deprivation is that I seem to be irritating the heck out of her, too.

Doc Campbell told me at the first of November that I might be able to forgo the cholesterol-lowering medications if I cut back the fat and carbs and started exercising. I liked the idea of accomplishing my goal without the drugs and committed to it. Then I ignored the doctor's advice because I couldn't start a diet and exercise program with Thanksgiving and Christmas looming on the horizon.

Two days after a snowy, house-bound, full-eats Christmas, I realized that I didn't have much time left to effect a change in my March blood work. By New Year's Eve, amid the splendor of the town's annual gala at the Hamilton Inn and after consuming a plate full of stuffed mushrooms, mini-quiches, shrimp cocktail, and those scrumptious little pigs-in-blankets, the combination of fat-laden foods and the sweet *Asti Spumante* went to my head. I announced my resolution to one and all. This chubby cherub had seen the light. I would lower my cholesterol by my March appointment with Doc Champion.

Of course Katie Bell took note, which has, I hate to admit, kept me on the straight and narrow and off the butter and bacon. I did not want to gain notoriety as one of the resolution failures mentioned in the *Bell Ringer* column.

All too soon I discovered I didn't need Katie's help. In the two weeks since New Year's, my minor announcement at the New Year's party had caused my cholesterol problem to become the town's crusade. People constantly ask me how much weight I've lost after church, in line at the *Piggly Wiggly*, and even in the bathroom stall at the cinema-plex in Bigelow. If I miss a day of walking because of rain or cold, folks comment about not seeing me out and about. I have to explain I use my sister's slow-as-sorghum-syrup treadmill during inclement weather. I don't tell them that I have to stay on the thing darned near an hour and a half before my face glistens.

I foolishly believed Katie Bell would be my biggest problem, since she's always watching me in the hope I'll mess up, but I have two worse problems — Sandy Crane and Spiva. Sandy, bless her big heart, has been getting my lazy butt out of bed for my morning walk before the roosters crow. She even changed my order at Mama's All You Can Eat Café the other day when I backslid and the words "country-fried steak with mashed potatoes and sawmill gravy" came out of my mouth. Sandy looked over at waitress, Ellen Stancil, and said, "Pearl's such a kidder. What she meant to say was that she'll have the diet plate without the cottage cheese."

I could have predicted Sandy would make a nuisance of herself trying to help me, but I never expected my own sister to turn into a supreme saboteur. Spiva's three years older, and she thinks that means she's three times wiser when it comes to battling cholesterol. Only you can't call what she's doing a *battle* because she still eats everything she shouldn't.

Popping a pill is not fighting the good fight by my way of thinking, even though she'll be sure to tell you it is. What's truly upsetting about this sabotage is that Spiva is the same sister who once protected me from bullies at school. She even listened to my whining about sales profits with equal sympathy as she listened to my whining about the dearth of datable, middle-aged men in Mossy Creek— especially ones who like mature, literate, chubby women. I just didn't get it. My sister was my best friend. Why did she want me to fail?

Rather than add up my register so I could leave on time, I glanced at the clock again, then pondered how best to deal with those beckoning Swiss Cake Rolls. Maybe I could ask Sandy to exercise her police powers, perform a search and seizure, or just come into the house and hide them from me. Nope, that wouldn't work. I'd tear up the place looking for them. Best to exercise my shaky willpower. Maybe it would get firm, too.

The bell attached to the front door chimed. Relieved that I finally had someone to divert my carb obsession, I looked up from where I stood at the register to find Spiva bearing toward me like a member of the Benevolent Society looking for a donation. She was carrying a styrofoam plate full of brownies and homemade peanut-butter cookies with crosshatches scored across the top. And I thought the Little Debbie cakes were a diabolical temptation.

Cherub my big toe! I could almost see little red horns sprouting from her ultra-short hairdo. She set the treats on the counter right in front of me, where I used to display chocolate truffles.

"Want one?" she asked, her mountain twang lost in breathlessness from her jaunt across the square.

Although my mouth watered at the thought of biting into one of those moist, chewy brownies, I summoned my willpower. "No, thanks."

"One little ol' brownie isn't going to hurt you," she said, lifting one pencil drawn eyebrow. Spiva had an unfortunate tendency to over-pluck and therefore relied on her meager artistic skills to fill in.

Yes, eating one brownie would hurt me. Mostly because I had no willpower to stop at one.

The door bell chimed again, and I looked up, hoping against hope that I'd have a real customer to distract me. No such luck. It was Katie Bell, notepad and pen in hand, here to watch me succumb to my sister's temptation and record it for posterity.

Great. Just what I needed. "Can I help you? Don't you have another estate sale to go to? Missed any good quilts lately?" Patty Campbell's end-run around Katie was already sashaying down the gossip trail.

Katie, who was a good ten years younger and about thirty pounds lighter than me, brushed her highlighted hair out of her face in order to make eye contact. She wore one of those trendy hairstyles where the long sideswept pieces kept falling in front of her eyes and made me think of Cousin It from *The Addams Family* television show. Those eyes narrowed to evil slits. Her upper lip curled.

"I'm looking for a cookbook," Katie said. "All those baked goods at the church fundraiser have inspired me.

I want one that includes downhome Southern fare, too. Crowder peas with salt pork. Fried chicken. Biscuits. That sort of thing."

My stomach growled in appreciation. Katie smiled at the noise and scribbled something on her notepad.

Dinner. I would have my sensible dinner of broiled, skinless chicken breast, steamed carrots, broccoli, and cauliflower soon. Woo-hoo!

Glad to have an excuse to remove myself from the chocolate and peanut-butter aroma wafting toward me from Spiva's plate, I came around the counter and pointed Katie to the cooking section just as Sandy whisked into the store, nearly as out of breath as Spiva had been.

"Drop the brownie!" she yelled, pinning me with her signature curly blonde Barney Fife stare.

Thank goodness she didn't have her gun drawn. I might have peed in my pants.

I raised my hands to show there was no chocolate residue. "I'm clean, officer."

"You didn't eat one before I got here, did you?" she asked, eyeing the tower of treats like they were made of hashish.

"No. They're Spiva's." I said and transitioned into my patented I-love-my-customers salesperson voice. "I don't suppose you're here to buy a book."

"Well, of course, I'm here to buy something," Sandy said. "It's just that I've had a busy day. Plus I've been working on a special investigation, and uh, let's just say me and Jayne Reynolds have finished that investigation and given the chief our findings. And those findings kinda upset him, so he's taken off down to Atlanta. So it's just me and Bubba Mutt on duty right now." She called her brother and fellow officer "Bubba Mutt." To me, that always sounded like a character from *Star Wars*.

Sandy surveyed the store, her gaze meeting Katie's

briefly as she noted the cookbook in her hands— *The Soul Food Queen's Big Ass Cookbook*. "I'm interested in a book about nutrition."

"Knock yourself out," I said, wishing she would literally, and pointed her to the row where Katie stood. "Bottom shelf."

Besides the impromptu visits, like now, and morning walks, Sandy had taken to phoning me at night, too—when the temptation was greatest, to provide me with what she called "positive reinforcement." Shortly after I'd made my pronouncement at the New Year's party, Sandy had also spent several days staking me out. She then presented me with a map of my bad eating patterns, such as my stop in the Naked Bean every morning for a scone and a caramel macchiato, my high-fat lunches at Bubba Rice's and Mama's, my Sunday Beechum's Bakery doughnut habit. It's not that I didn't appreciate the help. It's just that ... I didn't want it.

I decided to leave my food angel and devils to their own devices. "Since you're here, Spiva, you can watch the register for me. I've got some boxes to unload."

I was actually looking forward to ripping the cardboard and getting a piece of sugarless gum out of my desk in the storeroom. Gum would help me stave off the temptation lurking so innocently on the front counter. One could always hope.

Spiva rolled her eyes but agreed to do as I bid. I did hear her moaning in ecstasy over the fudge brownies as I slammed the storeroom door behind me.

All too soon I was done with the computer inventory and checked off the special order DVD I'd gotten in for Argie Rodriguez. Broadway Dance Moves — the hot new exercise craze. A picture formed in my head of big, burly, kilt-wearing Mac Campbell, a khaki-clad Amos Royden, who bore an uncanny resemblance to a dark-haired George Clooney, and former Atlanta Falcon Tag Garner, leaping in synch and snapping their fingers to the *When You're a Jet* gang dance number from *West Side Story*. Not that any of those three beefcakes would be caught dead in a dance class. Still, Argie's class at Wisteria Cottage had to be more fun than power walking through town in the cold with taskmaster Sandy.

Smiling, I returned to the register and the angel and devils battling for my high cholesterol soul. I quickly dialed Argie's number at the dance studio. She wasn't answering so I left the message that her DVDs were in and that I was interested in her new class.

Sandy grinned and nudged Katie. Spiva rolled her eyes and sighed deeply like I'd signed *her* up for class.

"What's your problem?" I asked.

"I don't have a problem, other than you pretending to be someone you're not." Those imaginary horns grew about another half-inch.

"Excuse me?" I said.

Spiva removed a palm-sized peanut butter cookie from the plate on the counter, bit off a substantial crescent, and jabbed what was left of the cookie at me. "You've changed since you started with this whole ridiculous diet and exercise kick."

"Okay, first of all it isn't a kick. It's a lifestyle change, and that's a good thing. I don't want to have high cholesterol."

"Then take the Lipitor, like me."

"I don't want to take medicine if I don't have to."

Spiva shrugged. "Well, it's working for me."

"Is it?" I challenged.

She took another nibble of her cookie, then set it down on the counter. "Have you for one minute thought about how what you're doing affects people other than you? For example, how is this kick going to affect Chubby Cherubs? Those old people at Magnolia Manor count on us."

"And you think my diet and exercise regime is ridiculous!" I took the plate of goodies off the counter and dumped them in the trash.

Spiva reached out, like she was going to dive in after her cookies and brownies, then stopped.

"I'm still helping out at Magnolia Manor," I said. "And I've got a long way to go before I get from chubby to svelte. I doubt that's even possible. But hey, why not call our organization Cheerful Cherubs?"

Spiva flushed red from her neck all the way up past her penciled eyebrows. "That's just plain stupid."

"And so is that excuse you call a treadmill," I said.

"Doc Champion says exercising three times a week for thirty minutes is fine."

"Hah! What you do isn't even a snail's pace. Your machine has only has two speeds —slow and slower."

"You just have to succeed at everything, don't you, Pearl? Miss Perfect. Well, maybe I think you're showing off."

I heard a button click and saw Katie try to sneak out of the store with evidence of the Quinlan sisters' argument on her handy dandy recorder. Great. Now we'd both be quoted in the *Bell Ringer*.

Spiva moved her much larger body in a surprisingly agile glide to block Katie. "Hand over that tape."

"So now I'm the enemy? And you're all buddy-buddy with Pearl?" Katie asked, pushing her hair out of her eyes. "Pearl?"

"Sometimes blood ties are more important than cholesterol levels and treadmills," I said.

"You tell her, Pearl," Sandy chimed in.

That's when Spiva took hold of the hand held tape recorder. Katie wouldn't let go, and they careened into my display of *Cliffs Notes*. Yellow and black pamphlets scattered across the room, landing on the counter, several rows of bookshelves and the carpeted floor.

"Stop it, both of you!" Sandy yelled. "In the name of the law!" She was in uniform and duty-bound to stop a brawl. Spiva shoved her with one hand. Spiva is big. Sandy is ... not so big. Sandy bounced off a display of romance novels. Love hurts.

Spiva used her weight to her full advantage and at long last ripped the recorder from Katie's fingers. Spiva sprawled backwards and sat down hard on the floor. So did Katie. Spiva pressed the delete button. "No one gossips about my little sister. Except me."

"Thanks a lot, Spiva," Katie spat out. "It might interest you to know that I had other material for my New Year's resolutions column on that recorder."

Sandy chuckled. "And I bet not a bit of it was nice. Why not come up with something better, like sisters who can fight but still love each other deep down?"

"That won't sell papers."

"Don't be so sure," I said and went over and offered a hand to help Spiva get up. "You know I'm on this diet and exercise jaunt because I want to live a long time without having to move into Magnolia Manor. I'd like you to live a long time with me too, Spiva."

"I don't think I can do it," Spiva said. "I never met a food I didn't like, except maybe brussel sprouts."

"If I can do it, you can do it."

Spiva eyed the trashcan holding the baked goods I'd tossed. "I don't know."

"Come on, all you've gotta do is try. And I'll be there trying right alongside you. *We* can do it."

"Okay. I'll give it a go," Spiva said, then offered a hand to Katie, who was attempting to upright herself from a pile of paperbacks. Spiva handed her back the recorder. "You might want to start writing about Creekites *succeeding* with their resolutions rather than focusing on the ones breaking them, Katie. You could start with Pearl, here. Do you know she's already lost ten pounds?"

There was the sister I'd grown up with, the one who championed me and made me feel like I could be anything I wanted.

"Ten pounds?" Katie looked impressed.

Spiva looked down at her comfortable shoes. "I'm sorry I was jealous of your success, Pearl. I don't know what came over me."

"Me neither, but that's okay. And I bet you a whole wheat, no-fat banana muffin that Dan McNeil could turbo-charge your treadmill. I'll help you cart it to his shop."

Spiva wiggled her eyebrows and shook an imaginary cigar in an imitation of Groucho Marx. "That's not all he could turbo-charge."

"I ought to arrest everybody in sight," Sandy announced. She glared at Spiva. "You assaulted me. A police officer."

"Aw, you're not hurt. You bounce just fine."

Sandy confiscated Katie's recorder and pushed the delete button again. Katie apparently had started taping their latest exchange.

"What did you go and do that for?" Katie whined.

Sandy placed her hands on her hips. "This is a private reconciliation between sisters."

"Not when it's in a public bookstore," Katie said, pushing open the door and causing the bell to chime. "Listen to that. Every time a bell rings, a gossip columnist gets her wings. Gimme my tape recorder back."

Sandy followed her outside, still holding the recorder. "Don't make me confiscate your property."

Katie shook a finger at her. "Don't make me trot out my First Amendment rights."

"You can trot 'em, jog 'em, or make 'em dance to rap

music for all I care. You're not getting this recorder back until you promise to keep quiet."

"That's police brutality!"

"Not unless I *stomp* the tape recorder. Hey, there's an idea."

"Don't you dare!"

My door closed on their argument, bringing a swoosh of cold air into the shop. Spiva and I grinned at each other.

"The way they fight, you'd think the two of them were sisters," I said.

We hugged.

Mossy Creek Gazette

VOLUME V, No. THREE   MOSSY CREEK, GEORGIA

The Bell Ringer

by Katie Bell

Dear Faithful Readers:

I'm postponing my New Year's resolutions exposé while I hammer out some problems in my investigative methodology. Some of your fellow Creekites are being, shall we say, *less than forthcoming* about admitting they've already broken their year-end promises.

I'm not asking for praise or pity, but do you realize how often your intrepid gossip reporter risks public scorn and even physical violence to bring you the latest juicy news? And that's just toward my tape recorder!

Sometimes you get carried away. Literally.

Ida Gets More Than She Bargained For

Chapter 8

By mid-afternoon my posse and I arrived in Atlanta, ready to raise hell for the good of Mossy Creek and the Sitting Tree.

The Georgia governor's mansion is a big, brick, white-columned faux-plantation house surrounded by manicured lawns, beds of azaleas, and tall iron fences. It's located smack in the middle of an exclusive Atlanta neighborhood called Buckhead, where all the driveways are protected by gates and all the mansions come with maids, gardeners, and lifetime tickets to the Atlanta Ballet. Even on a cold Saturday afternoon in the barest depths of wintertime, Buckhead feels luscious.

Ingrid, Hope and I feigned polite patience as we waited in a foyer. We were mature businesswomen in handsome suit-dresses. Who would have guessed what we plotted? We gazed demurely at a huge oil painting of a southern fox hunt. It was done in arch, 19th century style, but featured beagles instead of fox hounds and antebellum gents on prancing Tennessee Walking horses.

"Ardaleen commissioned this bloated thing as a gift to the governor's mansion," I told Hope and Ingrid. "My sister wanted the artist to include a few happy slave children running along with the beagles. Ham's staff had to explain why that might tick off every black voter in the state."

Hope chuckled. "Ida, that's a weird painting any way you look at it. Those horses have the biggest butts I've ever seen. They need to join Jenny Craig."

Ingrid nodded. "And the beagles are pop-eyed. Do they have thyroid conditions? Not that I dislike a pop-eyed dog." She peered inside a voluminous leather purse hanging from one shoulder. "Isn't that right, my little cupcake?" A low, nervous yip came from the bowels of the purse.

I looked around quickly. "Sssh. Keep Bob quiet." A uniformed state trooper glanced our way from the end of the long hall.

Ingrid huffed. "Bob doesn't like being stuffed in a pocketbook. Chihuahuas have a natural sense of dignity, you know."

"Could have fooled me."

Hope elbowed us. "Here comes Gloria."

Ham's administrative assistant rounded a corner and tipped-tapped toward us, her lacquered faux-leopard high heels — bought at some Atlanta boutique with taxpayer money, no doubt — clicking like a cat's toenails on the hallway's glossy wood floor. In the finest tradition of Bigelow nepotism, Gloria was the wife of Ham's second cousin. Thanks to Ham, so many Bigelows lived off the state payroll they could almost form their own credit union. Gloria, a typical Bigelow, was a humorless little tyrant. She pursed her lips in a permanent strawberry.

"If all her holes are that tight," Ingrid side-mouthed, "I don't know how she passes gas."

Hope choked on a laugh.

I focused on Gloria's arms. To be precise, what she was carrying in her arms. Bingo. My instincts had been perfect. I knew Gloria couldn't resist showing off for Ingrid, a fellow Chihuahua fan. In Gloria's arms lounged the fattest blonde Chihuahua in the world, a foot tall and a foot wide. As she walked, he lapped the air with bored disdain. His pedigreed name? Regal Von Doggin. As in AKC Champion Regal Von Doggin. And no, he didn't have a folksy nickname for home use. In fact, Gloria got miffed whenever anyone addressed him by less than his full moniker.

"Hi, Gloria," I said pleasantly. "I see you brought Porky The Obese Wonder Mutt with you, today."

She leopard-tapped to a hard stop in front of us. Her strawberry lips shrank to a raspberry. "What are you doing here, Ida? You're an hour early for your appointment."

"A little bird told me the reverend's meeting with Ham right now. I have something to show *both* of them."

"You're well aware that Reverend James refuses to meet with you in person."

"The so-called reverend can refuse all he wants, but I intend to see him."

"After all you've done to discredit him? No way. This is what you get for calling a man of God — and a cousin-in-law of the Governor's — a con artist! How dare you insinuate Reverend James received his ministerial degree in a home study course! He could have sued you for slander, but he has too much dignity for that."

"I didn't *insinuate* anything. I came right out and *said* it: He's a crook and a fraud. He's trying to pass Whoopee Arcades off as a tax-exempt business project owned by his so-called church. If he weren't a Bigelow cousin he'd probably be doing a Martha Stewart in some white-collar prison by now."

Gloria's left eye twitched. She glared at me pop-eyed, like her dog, who growled. Gloria hugged him and took a step back from my evil influence. "Why do I waste my breath attempting a civil servant's conversation with you? You're lucky Ham agreed to see you at *all*. Sit down and wait. You can't get your own way around here, Mayor Walker."

She pivoted toward Ingrid. One hand rose in a preening posture over Regal Von Doggin's head. "Hello, Ingrid. Have you given any more thought to trading Bob for a Chihuahua with *good* bloodlines? How *is* Bob these days? Have any more hawks mistaken him for a rat and tried to carry him off? Has he been beaten up by any more kitty cats? Is he still neurotic and incontinent?"

Ingrid cut her eyes at me. I nodded. Now.

Ingrid held out her huge purse and grinned at Gloria. "See for yourself."

Bob popped his scrawny, wild-eyed head out.

Bob saw Regal.

Regal saw Bob.

Bob hates Regal.

Regal is terrified of Bob.

See Bob launch himself at Regal.

See Regal freak out.

Gloria shrieked and chased the dogs. Regal scrambled like a hamster on ice skates, trying to get a toenail-hold on the slick hallway floor. Bob bit him in the butt and Regal made a sliding left turn through an open office door. Bob followed with all the fervor of a pop-eyed tornado, dribbling pee and nipping at Regal's Von Nuggets. Hope and Ingrid headed off to rescue Bob from the stampeding Gloria, who shrilled as she galloped after the dogs, "Don't you dare hurt Regal Von Doggin's testicles! He's a stud!"

Ingrid pulled a wad of tissues from her purse and flung them here and there as she ran, making a half-hearted effort to hit Bob's puddles. Regal shot back into the main hallway, yelping, with Bob still nipping his tail.

"Save my champion!" Gloria called.

Hope dodged right and left, proving that she could body-block the smaller, faster Gloria even while confined to a snug skirt and high heels. The state patrol officer loped past me with his mouth open in astonishment and both hands splayed as if he were desperately attempting to herd Chihuahuas and women at the same time. Gloria sprinted past Hope and Ingrid, grabbing a miniature U.S. flag from a flower arrangement on a hall table. She flailed at Bob.

Ingrid yelled, "It's unpatriotic to whack Bob with the Stars and Stripes!"

"I'll show your little runt some *real* stars and stripes," Gloria yelled back.

Bob bit Regal in the behind, again. Regal yelped and farted. Loudly. Or maybe it was Gloria. Hard to tell.

The state patrol officer slipped on one of Bob's puddles and did a pratfall worthy of The Three Stooges. As he went down he grabbed for thin air and caught one corner of the frame on my sister's redneck fox-hunting painting. Beagles, Tennessee Walkers, and antebellum southern gents swung wildly, then popped off their hanger.

Gloria squealed and did a belly flop with both arms over her head as the large, tacky painting landed on top of her and the state trooper. Bob bit Regal in his Von Doggin again and they vanished up another side hallway at a dead run, leaving sprinkles of Bob's pee in their wake.

Ingrid and Hope were now laughing so hard they nearly rolled on the floor. I gave them a thumbs up. They managed to salute.

My diversionary tactic had worked. This punking stuff was highly effective, not to mention, fun.

I headed for the governor's office.

🐾🐾🐾

Some sacred places are made by God, and some are made by man, but some take root without any help from either, defiantly waving a hand toward heaven until God and man notice them like annoyed teachers acknowledging a precocious first grader. That's how the Sitting Tree achieved its fame — by its sheer determination to survive and be noticed. And that's also how its fate came to be tied to the yellowed, fragile letter I carried into Ham's office.

My great-great grandfather, Samuel Alton Hamilton, cleared the meadow where the tree took root one hundred years ago. Rose Top Mountain was Hamilton land, then. Samuel and his men chopped down an entire grove of old-growth maples — a sacrilege, but that's how things were done at the time, to make way for pastureland. A single young maple sprang up from the carnage, growing on the windswept foothill despite the cold and heat, alone in the home where all its kin had once kept company. A lone sentinel. Even the wild cattle and deer couldn't nibble it to death.

Samuel gave the land to his oldest daughter, Becky, and her husband Lucias Royden (yes, ironically, an ancestor of Amos's) as a wedding gift. Becky and Lucias built a small farmhouse and barns near the young maple tree, that only living memory of the beautiful maple forest. Their only child, Amelie, loved the tree, watered it, talked to it, and persuaded her father to build a picket fence around it when the family's growing herd of cows decided the tree's supple trunk made a great rubbing post.

When Amelie died of influenza at only twelve years old, Becky and Lucias, heartbroken, sold the farm to the neighboring Baileys. The sale contained one odd clause, specified in a letter that accompanied the deed: if the Baileys should ever decide to sell the land, they had to notify the Hamilton family and give them a chance to bid.

That was in 1872. The farm's abandoned house and barns were eventually struck by lightning and burned. The stone foundations gradually sank into the earth. Wild grasses and blackberry briars overtook the pasture fences and well house, pulling them down. The land went back to itself. The maple, by then a grand, mature tree, was all that survived. It guarded the empty meadow, all alone. The legend of Amelie and the Sitting Tree became a symbol of love and loyalty to Creekites, and soon the secluded spot turned into a favorite of the local romantics. Not just teenagers looking for a safe make-out spot, but sentimental lovers.

The Bailey-Hamilton deed, along with a handwritten letter outlining the special right of us Hamiltons to buy the land back, was filed at the Bigelow County Courthouse. A second official copy of the deed and letter was kept by Belinda Bailey, who inherited the land and the Sitting Tree in the early 1900s. Belinda got married and moved to North Carolina. She never attempted to sell the property.

Creekites had come to consider it public property, and Belinda didn't mind. Until last year, there was even a grave under the Sitting Tree. Etta Howell was buried there by her husband, Ben, in 1947. Ben and his second wife, Sadie, visited Etta's grave faithfully for decades. A year ago, after Ben died, Sadie moved Etta's body to rest beside Ben's in the cemetery at Mossy Creek Presbyterian Church.

When Belinda died, the property went to her children — Farley and his younger sister, Amarosa. Now Farley is long-dead, too, and Amarosa, who turned 85 last fall, spends her time playing golf and poker at an upscale assisted-care community in Asheville. Amarosa is still pretty sharp, but not sharp enough to recall that there's a dusty old legal reason why she can't sell her mother's Mossy Creek property without first giving the Hamilton heir — that would be yours truly — a purchase option.

So when Reverend James showed up on Amarosa's doorstep with money in hand and a slick story about developing the land as an amusement park for God's purposes (where does the Bible say that churches should own water slides and roller coasters?), Amarosa took the bait.

I didn't find out about her deal with the reverend until I rushed to the Sitting Tree last fall to block Whoopee Arcades' bulldozers. I got spitting mad but felt confident I could squash him like a gnat just by producing the letter.

I hustled down to the Bigelow County courthouse. There, to my astonishment, I discovered that the deed was on file but the amendment letter could not be found. Not even a copy. Not even on microfilm.

Someone had made that century-old handwritten letter *disappear*.

I fumed, searched, got my lawyers involved, and even instructed the intrepid Katie Bell, Mossy Creek's super sleuth, to dig around for hints about the culprit who'd stolen the letter from the courthouse, but found no evidence. Nada. Zippo. Amarosa was horrified when I explained the reverend's deception but could not offer even one clue as to where her late brother, Farley, might have tucked their copy of the deed and letter.

"That letter exists," I argued loudly in court. "I intend to find out who stole it, and I intend to find the copy my Bailey relatives received, and as soon as I do, I'll buy the land from my cousin Amarosa. In the meantime I insist that the Reverend James' contract be declared null, void, and a violation of the Ten Commandments. Personally, I'd like to see the reverend beset by a plague of locusts."

Judge Blakely, aka "Judge Doom," my nemesis, who's never forgiven me for turning his court-ordered anger management class into a hotbed of civil disobedience (you may recall that the class spawned the Foo Club, introduced me to Del, and led to us kidnapping Ham's 'Welcome to Mossy Creek' sign,) anyway, Judge Blakely has never forgiven me, and so he used the "Case of the Lost Sitting Tree Letter" to extract a little revenge.

"Sorry, Mayor Rebel-Without-a-Pause," he ruled last fall, "but unless you can find the letter — a letter that's only a convenient memory, a half-baked *rumor*, in your high strung family — unless you can actually produce that *supposed* letter or the legitimate copy of the letter you claim the Bailey family received, then you're up Mossy Creek without a paddle. All I'll grant you is a ninety-day restraining order against Whoopee Arcades, Incorporated. If you don't find the *alleged* letter by, hmmm, let's take a look-see at my calendar, here, ninety days, hmmm, yes, indeedy, produce the *purported* letter of agreement between your family and the Bailey ancestors by ninety days from today, that deadline being January 10, why, then, the reverend's bulldozers roll on January 11." He rapped his gavel. "Bye-bye, Sitting Tree."

I wanted to call him a tree-hating old bastard, but I knew he'd love the excuse to charge me with contempt. Since I didn't want to suffer through another anger management course, I kept quiet. I guess his anger management class *did* teach me something: Don't get mad, get revenge.

Just in time. Today was January 10. As my grandmother, Big Ida, liked to say for emphasis, *I hope to shout* ...

"Well, heeeeello, my dear nephew," I said now, strolling unannounced into Ham's ornate office at the Governor's Mansion. "And heeeello, Reverend James. My, my, this brisk winter weather makes me feel righteous and *energized*, you know? Or maybe it's simply that I enjoy a good, victorious *gloat*."

Ham popped from his massive gubernatorial desk quicker than a chipmunk sighting a snake. Tall, middle-aged and handsome in a smirky way, he was dressed in corduroys and a brown leather pilot's jacket over a custom-made flannel shirt that had never seen any rugged outdoor use. His schedule for later that day called for an overnight duck-hunting trip to the state's southern end courtesy of a wealthy campaign donor. To quote my hip-hop granddaughter, Ham enjoyed blasting a cap up the tail feathers of unsuspecting mallards.

"Aunt Ida, who let you in? Your appointment isn't for an hour. And what are you talking about? I thought you just wanted to negotiate a truce —"

"I never negotiate. Not with you, dear nephew." I held up the yellowed letter. "I have here, in my hand, an official handwritten letter. A duly notarized, authentic, read-it-and-weep, verifiable letter stating that no Bailey can sell the Sitting Tree property without first giving the Hamilton family — represented by yours truly — an opportunity to buy it."

Ham's jaw went slack. "That can't be. It was only rumor that there was a letter at all, much less an official copy. Just ... gossip."

"Really? Why don't you admit that you and the reverend conspired to steal the original letter from the courthouse?"

"Ridiculous!"

"I'm not going to stand for this accusation!" the reverend said. He lurched to his feet from a deeply cushioned leather armchair, scowling at me like a tubby blond hamster with a bad comb-over. Since he was scheduled to accompany Ham on the sitting-duck trip, the reverend was dressed in a fuzzy mohair sweater and glossy leather pants. I kid you not. Leather pants.

"You're standing for this," I pointed out. "Looking like a designer sausage."

"I own that land! I bought it!"

"Not anymore." I grinned at him. "My cousin Amarosa sold it to me this morning, right after I told her I'd found the letter. I have a legal claim. So bye-bye, Reverend James. Sorry you didn't get to con my elderly cousin out of her land and defraud me and my family." I switched my glare to Ham. "It's a nice day for a gubernatorial butt-kicking, Ham, wouldn't you say? Bend over."

Ham waved his arms wildly. "I've done nothing wrong, as usual!"

"Oh, please, spare me your fake indignation. Admit it. You had some governmental flunky steal the original letter from the county courthouse, didn't you? You assumed I'd never be able to unearth the copy owned by the Bailey heirs."

"The Bigelow County courthouse loses one old, obscure document and you blame me?"

"I know your track record. Every time I forget that you're a scheming worm I look at the empty field where you promised to rebuild Mossy Creek High School."

"I told you, I'm working on it. Even though I'm governor I can't just demand that the state allocate three million dollars for a high school in my aunt's home town."

"You promised. Two years ago."

"What does that have to do with the subject at hand?"

"You have no intention of keeping your word about *anything*. No intention of empowering the people of Mossy Creek. Instead you're trying to infiltrate my town. Stage a power grab so you'll never have to do my bidding again. You hope to smooth the way for your sycophants and Bigelow kin —" I cut my eyes at the reverend "—because once you circle my town with a loyal tribe of your toadies, you'll take over."

He rolled his eyes. "You've always been high-strung, but now you're getting paranoid. Aunt Ida, please. Get some help. Everyone's worried about you. My mother suggests you have your hormone levels checked. As she keeps saying, you're over fifty, now. You need to calm down."

I snorted. Ardaleen pointed out my fiftieth birthday at every opportunity. Mainly to distract people from the fact that she was sixteen years older than I. "Where my sister's concerned I have a simple philosophy. Never mud wrestle with a pig. You get dirty, and the pig *likes* it."

"You're calling Mother a pig?"

"She oinks at the scent of a truffle." I pivoted toward the reverend. "Speaking of pork —"

He sputtered. "You think you're very funny, don't you, Mayor Walker?"

I fanned myself with the antique letter and batted my eyelashes. "Why, yes. How kind of you to notice."

"I intended to build a wholesome theme park in your godforsaken part of the county. Whoopee Arcades, Incorporated is dedicated to promoting quality development, to helping the unfortunate underprivileged —"

"Dedicated to making a buck, you mean. Dedicated to bulldozing the foothills of a pristine mountain to build a crappy amusement park. Dedicated to replacing a historic tree with a parking lot."

Ham held up both hands. "I have to insist that you not slander the reverend this way. He is my cousin's husband, after all. And a faithful supporter of mine."

"Yes, Ham, I know you hate it when one of your campaign donors steps in a big pile of Bigelow nepotism and cronyism. It continually amazes me that you and I came out of the same gene pool. Somebody should have added more chlorine to the Bigelow end." I swiveled my attention back to the reverend. "It doesn't help when Bigelow women marry despotic little scam artists like you. If they keep this up we'll have to drain the whole gene pool and scrub its walls."

The reverend turned more colors of red than a Russian May Day celebration. "You're nothing but a ... tree-hugging heathen! The Lord won't fail to notice your attack on me! And He won't fail to notice that you value the fate of an old tree over a family-friendly entertainment for our precious children, who are desperate for clean-spirited fun in this age of debauchery and Britney Spears! Jesus wants that amusement park built!"

"What would Jesus do? *What would Jesus do*?" I poked a fingertip at a pendant swinging from a gold chain on the reverend's chest. W. W. J. D. was set in tiny diamonds. "Well, for one thing, I doubt He'd dress like a plus-sized L.L. Bean model and spend his time lying to little old ladies so he could buy more diamond trinkets."

"I prayed with your cousin Amarosa! I helped her understand that God wanted her to sell that land to my amusement park company!"

"Prayed with her? Don't you mean *preyed on her*?"

"Jezebel!" He shoved me.

You can call me a Jezebel all you like, but *nobody* shoves me.

So I punched him. Right in the mouth. Proof that Judge Blakely's anger management course didn't take.

After that, things got a little chaotic. Reverend James staggered around clutching his bloody lips and shrieking like a Girl Scout who's just had her cookies crushed. Ham yelled at me in between trying to herd the wobbly reverend toward a chair and bellowing at his speaker phone for help. Several state troopers burst into the office.

"Reverend James tripped over his Jesus jewelry," I deadpanned. "Jesus didn't intend for obnoxious little men to wear a lot of diamond bling around their necks."

"She talks like a rap singer on MTV!" the reverend squealed, flopping against a wall full of Ham's glorious photos with other politicians. Ham and the President did a belly flop into a wicker trash can.

"Get the President out of the garbage!" Ham yelled at the state troopers.

They headed to the rescue, but that's when Regal Von Doggin raced into the office, still being chased by Bob. Regal ran between the reverend's feet, completing Whoopee Arcade's new attraction, the Whirl-And-Crash Preacher Ride. The reverend fell on the trash can. Ham and the President parted ways with a crunch of tempered photo glass and polished teak frame.

"Not the President!" Ham moaned.

"Regal!" Gloria screamed, joining the fray.

"Bob!" Ingrid bellowed, right behind her.

I stood there smiling in amazement. In all the punking in all the world, this punking had to be the best, ever. I had outdone myself.

"Time to go, Mayor," a deep, familiar male voice said behind me. My smile froze. I whirled around.

"Oh, no." That was all I managed to say, unless you count, "Oooph," which is the noise I made as a result of being bodily lifted and tossed over a broad male shoulder.

Amos Royden's broad, male shoulder.

I hung upside down, cushioned by Amos's brown leather jacket, with a bird's eye view of Amos's lean, handsome, khaki-clad, no-nonsense butt. He headed for the door. Like a good heroine fighting a kidnapper in your average 1930s Western, I fluttered my feet, then balled up a fist and began thumping Amos's thoracic vertebrae. "I'm ordering you to put me down. I'm your boss. I'm the mayor, and you're giving me vertigo ..."

"It's mutual," he answered, and toted me out.

❦❦❦

Disgusted and grim, not to mention under arrest, I sat in the back of Amos's patrol car with my arms crossed over my chest. Ingrid and Hope gaped at us from the sidewalk in front of the governor's mansion. Amos shut my door and locked it, then leaned down and gazed calmly at me through the open window. "Comfortable?"

"I don't need to be rescued."

"This isn't a rescue. I made a deal with the state troopers and the GBI. If I cart you away, they won't charge you with trespassing and assault."

"Fine. But look down at the front gate. That's an Action News satellite van. I told them there'd probably be fireworks during my visit to Ham. You can't haul me back to Mossy Creek without letting me fulfill my obligation to the media. All I'm asking for is five minutes in front of a camera. I'm going to show them the Sitting Tree letter. And my bloody knuckles."

"Not today, Mayor."

"I'm ordering you —"

"I'm all that's standing between you and a night in the Atlanta jail. Trust me, you don't want to go there. They don't have curtains on the windows like we do."

"Drop me off. I can take a night with no curtains."

"Ida, the subject is closed."

I gave him a stare that could flash-freeze a side of beef in July. He didn't even break out in frost. He just smiled and headed around the car to the driver's side. I cupped my hand around my mouth and called to Ingrid and Hope. "All right, Ingrid, you ride with Amos and me. Hope, you take my car."

They looked from me to Amos, feigning uncertainty. Ingrid cradled Bob in her arms and murmured soothing sounds at him. Hope gazed at the blue winter sky. "Hey," I called louder. "Are you women, or are you wussies?"

Amos slid into the driver's seat and swiveled to look back at me. "You think we need a chaperone? I'm flattered."

A lot of complex and disturbing thoughts ran through my mind. Thoughts, feelings, and sensations. Dammit. I just sat there, frowning at him. And he simply stared back, his cocky smile slowly fading to something more serious. Ingrid and Hope wandered closer and gaped at us. Then Ingrid gave up all subtlety and hooted. So did Hope.

"You take her straight home, Amos," Ingrid said primly. "Put her under house arrest. Don't leave until you've tucked her into bed. She's dangerous."

"Yep," Hope added cheerfully. "You might want to handcuff her to her bedpost."

Amos faced forward then, oh, yes. He scowled at my partners in crime then pretended to organize his car keys. I could almost picture his muscles contracting to suppress a blush. I've never seen him blush. But he does a lot of contracting and suppressing. So do I. He hit a button, and my window began to rise.

I glared at the still-giggling Hope and Ingrid. "Traitors," I called over the edge of the window. I raised my bruised fist, knuckles forward. Slowly, wincing, I lifted a finger at them.

The middle one.

Mossy Creek Gazette

VOLUME V, NO. FOUR   **MOSSY CREEK, GEORGIA**

Public Notice
I Declare My House a Public Disaster Area

I, Louise Sawyer, do hereby officially announce that my aged house, until recently the historic hovel of my late aunt, Catherine, is a public (and private) menace. It confounds contractors. It eats decorators. It invites unwelcome visitors of the wild, four-legged variety. And now, as proof of its evil intentions, the house has personally attacked both me and my husband, Charlie.

I urge you, neighbors and fellow Creekites, to keep your distance! Stay safely on the sidewalk, no matter how sweetly the house whispers to you. Don't be lured by nostalgic memories of its nicer days. Trust me, the house can't be trusted. From its rotten floorboards to its crusty ceilings, it has turned bad.

*Renovating an old house is a labor of love, patience
and just a little touch of insanity.*

Louise and the Money Pit
Chapter 9

"Louise!"

I heard Charlie's scream all the way down to the kitchen. I've lived with my dear husband most of my adult life, and I had never before heard him make a sound like that. I went up the front stairs two at a time.

"Where are you?" I shouted.

"Bathroom!"

I raced down the hall, narrowly avoiding the tatters of wallpaper hanging off the walls like banners. The bathroom door was closed, but not locked. As I barreled through it, I had visions of Charlie laid flat out with a stroke, heart attack, concussion, broken bones, blood …

"Stop! Watch your step," Charlie said.

I skidded to a stop just inside the door and gaped. I could see the top half of him sticking up out of a hole in the bathroom floor where there should have been a toilet. He still had the sports section of the morning paper propped against his naked knees, the only other visible portion of his anatomy.

We had spent Friday evening and a good part of Saturday pulling up the ratty old linoleum from the upstairs bathroom floor of the house I inherited from my Aunt Catherine. When I had gone downstairs to microwave some instant coffee and heat up a semi-stale coffee cake, the toilet had sat on the bare wood floor surrounded by piles of broken linoleum.

"How on earth ..." I started.

"Walk over here very carefully, Louise, and pull me out of this hole. Try to walk on the joists."

"How am I supposed to see the joists under the floor-boards?" I tiptoed, expecting to join Charlie in free fall to the main floor of the house.

"It would seem," Charlie said with suspicious calm, "That dry rot has eaten the sub-floor in this part of the bathroom. Apparently, the only thing supporting this toilet is the plumbing stack. As I suspect it is iron and therefore prone to rust, it may crumble at any moment."

"Oh, Lord," I whispered.

Charlie tossed the newspaper at the sink and reached both hands up to me. It was a very small hole, really, not much bigger than the toilet itself. Charlie is six feet two. When the toilet fell through the floor, he had folded into the hole after it like an accordion with his chin on his chest.

I yanked.

He yelped. "Louise, dammit!"

I couldn't budge him. I hauled again.

"You're scraping the skin off my back."

I heaved and heaved until both of us were panting. "No use," I gasped. "Don't move. I'm going to call the police."

"I can't move even if I wanted to!" he shouted after me. "I'll be the laughingstock of Mossy Creek."

"If that floor gives way I'll be the *widow* of Mossy Creek."

I went downstairs and called Amos at the police station. "He's down in Atlanta," Sandy answered wearily, as if she'd given that statement a lot in the past hour. "And I don't think he's gonna be in a good mood when he gets back." But when I explained the situation, she gasped. "Mutt's patrolling near your house. Hold on."

A second later, her brother Mutt came on the line.

I asked him to help me, but to keep as quiet as he could about it.

"Sure." Mutt is never wordy, although I swear I heard the beginnings of a snicker.

"Charlie will kill me if this gets out."

"So long as he doesn't kill himself. Leave the house. The upstairs floor could cave in on you."

"I'm not leaving, Charlie. Besides, it's freezing outside."

"At least stay away from that bathroom."

"But ..."

"Don't go upstairs," Mutt said. "I'll be there in a minute." He hung up. So did I.

"Honey," I called to Charlie in what I hoped was a cheerful voice. "Mutt Bottoms'll be here to help you in just a little minute. Would you like a cup of coffee while we wait?"

He made that sound again.

Aunt Catherine's house had been trying to kill us since summer. Today, on a glorious, cold winter afternoon, it might succeed.

None of this was my fault, although my family would no doubt find some way to blame me.

🐾🐾🐾

For twenty years, Charlie and I lived in a big, rambling, suburban house on the outskirts of Mossy Creek. I always planned to leave the place feet first on my way to the cemetery. After Charlie retired, we talked about moving to someplace smaller, more modern, more efficient, closer to town, but I, for one, never intended to actually do it.

Then my family snookered me.

My daughter Margaret, her husband Bud and their two sons had been living in a small rental house since Bud moved them back to Mossy Creek so that he could take his new job. Since Bud is six-feet-six and the boys seem to be taking after him, they were desperate to buy a larger house, but couldn't find one they could afford without moving south of the north Georgia border. (Once you get south of Atlanta you're officially outside of north Georgia and into south Georgia, land of flat, piney woods, cotton, peanuts, and Jimmy Carter.)

When my Aunt Catherine died two years ago, I inherited her Queen Anne cottage close to downtown Mossy Creek. I offered to rent or sell it to Bud and Margaret, but Margaret said it wasn't big enough and needed too much work. After listening to her carp and whine, one day last June I said "Oh, for pity's sake, you all buy this one, and we'll move to Aunt Catherine's."

I certainly didn't mean it, but before I knew it, Charlie jumped on the idea like a duck on a June bug. "We can do a lot of the renovation work ourselves," he said. "Have to hire somebody to put in new heating, of course, and central air conditioning. Those old window units won't cut it. Have to bring the plumbing and wiring up to code — probably hasn't been updated since the house was built."

"That was 1904," I said. "Did they even wire houses for electricity back then?"

He kept going just as though he didn't hear me. Not surprising. I have a theory that the last words any man hears his wife say are, "I do." Thereafter, he's deaf to that particular range of sound. Besides, Charlie is an engineer.

Those of you who are not actually married to engineers will not understand. For those of you who are, I can already hear your moans. Engineers feel that they can do anything perfectly, and refuse to accept input from any layman. Wives count as laymen. *No* man will ask for directions when he's lost. An *engineer* won't ask for directions when he's building a thermo-nuclear device. If I screw up, it's my fault. If Charlie screws up, something went wrong with the tools he used.

For years, he's had a woodworking shop behind our house that makes Norm Abram's shop look like a lean-to. He built our heart pine kitchen cabinets and the bookshelves that line the walls of our library, repaired the plumbing and the electricity and the well pump and the air-conditioning. He installed the outside lighting and the automatic sprinklers.

Unfortunately, he did those things years ago when he was younger and more manually dexterous than he is now. I knew darned well, however, that if I even mentioned the twinges of arthritis in his fingers or how tired he was after we painted our bedroom last year, he'd climb up on his high horse and I wouldn't be able to talk him down for hours.

Arranging to sell our house to Bud and Margaret and fix up Aunt Catherine's was considerably more complicated than simply calling the mortgage company and the moving van.

I had always loved Aunt Catherine's house. I had spent so much time there when I was growing up. My parents dumped me on her most of the summer every year so they could go fishing. I learned to play chess and bridge in her house.

I fell in love for the first time in her kitchen, and gave up that love on her front porch. She was ninety-two when she died, really my *great* aunt. She left the house to me, and I'd been waffling about what to do with it. The neighborhood was changing with young families and children moving in to replace the old folks, like Aunt Catherine, who could no longer tolerate stairs or big yards.

Several real estate agents had approached me about selling it, but I couldn't see strangers in it. It would have been an invasion.

We all have houses we return to in our dreams. Aunt Catherine's was mine. I could have found my way around in the dark. Every time I had checked it out after her death, I felt her in every room. Not precisely a ghost — more like a friendly presence.

But the first time Charlie and I walked through the front door after we'd decided to renovate the place, I felt as though the house knew we planned to change it and didn't like the prospect one little bit.

The only downstairs bedroom at Aunt Catherine's was miniscule and the closets nearly non-existent. At the moment, both Charlie and I could climb stairs, but in years to come we might not be able to manage the second floor, so we needed a big bedroom on the main floor.

The existing downstairs bathroom was tiny and lined in vomit-green tile that had last been replaced just after World War II when Aunt Catherine updated her kitchen. We needed big closets and a bathroom connected with the bedroom that would be large enough for my exercise bike and Charlie's treadmill.

Aunt Catherine produced family dinners for twenty from her big old kitchen, but I doubted I'd be able to roast a decent chicken in the range that was one step up from a wood stove. The refrigerator was only a couple of generations removed from the sort of ice box that used real ice. No dishwasher.

The entire area would have to be gutted, redesigned, and rebuilt along with the downstairs suite. That necessitated construction loans, building permits from the Mossy Creek Planning Commission *and* approval from the Mossy Creek Historical Preservation Society, an architect to draw plans, and hiring a general contractor.

Charlie and I realized quickly that even with Bud and Margaret's help, we could do some of the *des*truction like stripping wallpaper and linoleum, but we couldn't do much on the *con*struction end except cosmetic stuff like painting.

From the first day Charlie and I climbed Aunt Catherine's attic stairs to the cavernous attic that stretched across the cottage and found boxes and trunks that I had never gotten around to when I had Aunt Catherine's estate sale, the whole operation spiraled out of control. Charlie took one look at that attic and decreed that it would be a perfect television den, home office and a sewing room for me. He peered at the vaulted roof and saw not squirrel damage and cobwebs, but skylights. More plans. A bigger budget. More zoning approvals. More time before we would be finished.

The two small upstairs bedrooms each had fireplaces. That's the way houses were heated in 1904, and although the house had an aging furnace in the basement, the fireplaces were still operational. That lead to the house's first attack on us.

Labor Day weekend, Charlie decided he had to see whether the chimneys required tuck-pointing. He reared back and hit the front of the chimney face in Aunt Catherine's bedroom with a sledgehammer. At first nothing happened. Then slowly, a crack opened across the tile and ran up the plaster toward the ceiling. "See, Louise," he said and turned to me with a grin. "Easy. A couple more whacks and that old plaster will peel right off."

"Um, Charlie," I whispered, as I looked over his shoulder and pointed.

"What?" Then he, too, heard the rumble.

I grabbed his sleeve and yanked him across the room just as the first two-foot-square hunk of plaster hit the floor right where he'd been standing.

Then the first brick fell. Followed by half a dozen more, then a dozen. As we watched in horror, the entire chimney collapsed.

Charlie grabbed me, tossed me into the hall and slammed the bedroom door behind us. "Come on, Louise," he shouted and practically carried me down the stairs and out the front door.

We stood on the front porch listening to the crunch and thud. We were both completely covered in plaster and brick dust.

When the noise finally stopped, I was afraid to open the front door, but Charlie took a deep breath and stepped into the front hall. A cloud of dust still roiled down from the second floor, but the stairs looked to be intact.

"Stay here," he said and crept up those stairs. A moment later, he called, "Okay, come on up. It's all right."

Well, of course it wasn't all right. But miraculously, the bedroom floor had held despite the weight of brick and plaster we had dumped on it. Charlie stood in the middle of the room with his hands on his hips and said, "Obviously, if one little poke can bring that chimney down, it was already on the verge of collapse. Good thing I checked it before it fell on us."

Checked it? It had held up perfectly well since 1904 and would probably have held up until 2104 if he hadn't *bashed* it. We added chimney reconstruction to our list of things that needed to be done by somebody else. Quickly.

We had been living at home — the house I still considered home — while we worked at Aunt Catherine's. Margaret and Bud were helping when they could, but since Bud travels and Margaret has the boys, somehow their assistance wasn't as frequent or as whole-hearted as they'd promised.

The afternoon after Charlie destroyed the chimneys, Margaret and Bud came by unannounced and without the boys. I was praying they'd given up the idea of buying our old house.

No such luck.

"They're raising our rent," Margaret said. "And they want us to sign a new one-year lease. That's ridiculous, since we should be moving before Thanksgiving."

"Which year?" I asked. Margaret just gave me a look.

"Obviously, we'll have to move in here with you sooner than we expected."

"Wait just a darned minute," I said. "We don't have room for four additional people plus two Labrador Retrievers in this house."

"The dogs won't be any trouble," Bud said. "The boys can pick up after them."

"It's only for a couple of months," Margaret said. "It is going to be our house, after all."

"It isn't your house yet," I snapped.

"You could always move into the new house," she continued. "I mean it's not like you couldn't camp out in the upstairs bedroom until your downstairs suite is finished."

Charlie and I had grown fond of our privacy since Margaret moved out. I had never realized what a territorial imperative I had until the four of them moved in. Whenever I wanted to wash a load of clothes, the washer and dryer were invariably already full of their things. The dogs were sweet, but each of them weighed in excess of seventy-five pounds, and they enjoyed stretching full length across any doorway I wanted to get through. The boys played endless video games in the den when they weren't playing soccer in the kitchen. Even quiet, gentle Bud got on my nerves. He was just so big.

And eat? *Lord!*

The morning that Charlie tripped over a pair of Joshua's gym shorts on the back stairs and nearly broke his neck, I decided we would move to Aunt Catherine's even if we had to camp out for another year.

We moved a double bed from our guest room and a

couple of bureaus into Aunt Catherine's upstairs bedroom with its rebuilt chimney and its miniscule closets, bought a new microwave to use until the new kitchen appliances arrived, made certain the new furnace met code, and despite the inconveniences, thanked God for the peace and quiet.

That's how Charlie wound up falling through the bathroom floor.

❦❦❦

Mutt was as good as his word. He pulled up in front of the house in his squad car within two minutes. Unfortunately, he arrived with lights strobing and sirens screaming.

Right behind him came the big Mossy Creek Volunteer Fire Department's pumper truck complete with cherry picker. I hoped they didn't plan to cut a hole in the roof and haul Charlie out that way. I had visions of Charlie rising majestically above the roof with his pajama bottoms around his ankles. I didn't like to think of what he'd say.

Then the city ambulance screeched to a halt behind the pumper, and three EMT's piled out, including Mutt's brother, Boo.

Before Mutt reached the front steps, Rob Walker's car careened to a stop behind the EMT's. The mayor's grown son, who runs Hamilton Department Store, moonlights as the volunteer coordinator of local emergency management. Usually, that just involves testing the tornado sirens. Now it included rescuing Charlie.

So much for keeping this quiet.

By then the neighbors were pouring out their front doors, standing around stamping their feet in the cold and huddling in their coats wanting to know where the fire was and were Charlie and I all right and who'd had a heart attack and I don't know what all.

I dove back into the house and shut the door on all of them, Rob included. I did not trust myself to explain.

"He's up here," I said.

"Louise, get out of the way," said Mutt. Then he, three firemen in full fire-fighting gear — including Ed Brady's brawny son, Ed, Jr. — and three EMT's — Boo Bottoms, another man and a woman I hadn't met before — followed with their first-aid bags.

I ignored Mutt and trotted right up those stairs behind them.

"Louise!" Charlie bawled as the first fireman reached the bathroom door.

Mutt took a look from the doorway, then ducked into the hall and leaned his face against the wall. I could see his shoulders shaking. I didn't think he was crying.

Charlie and I both have known Bill Bainbridge, the fire chief of Mossy Creek, all our lives. Charlie was in his class, although I was a few years younger. Bill, whose favorite saying is, "When there's trouble, call a fireman," took one look, cleared his throat, and said in a strangled voice, "How in hell did you manage that?"

"Shut up and get me the hell out of here." Charlie saw the female EMT behind the chief and shouted, "Get her out of here too."

Rob Walker smiled. "Now, Charlie, she's a professional."

"I don't give a damn what profession she's in, get her out of here."

"Uh, Chief," said the very pretty young blonde, certainly younger than Margaret, "Maybe I should wait in the truck in case we need to bring up a stretcher."

She passed me in the hall on her way downstairs. She had both hands clapped over her mouth. I didn't think she was trying to avoid throwing up.

"Just pull me up, dammit," Charlie snarled.

"Now, sir, just relax and let us help you," said a fireman who looked about as old as my grandson.

Charlie's reply did not sound in the least relaxed.

I peered under the rim of the fireman's helmet. It was Nail Delgado. A cutie. The girls say he looks like Justin Timberlake, whoever that is. He's one of the mayor's Foo Club cronies. He and Ida met at court-ordered anger management class. Nail had used a cattle prod to save a baby calf from a cruel neighbor. That is, he used the cattle prod on the neighbor. My kind of guy, Nail Delgado. "Hi, Nail," I said. "Got a cattle prod handy?"

Nail shook his head. He couldn't speak. He was too busy trying not to laugh at Charlie.

Then the phone rang. I ran into our bedroom and picked it up.

"Mother? Are you all right? Is the house burning down?"

"No, Margaret, the house is not burning down, and if it were, standing here talking to you while Rome burns is not the finest idea." I hung up on her. I stuck my head around the corner of the bathroom to see how things were progressing.

"Not going to be easy, Charlie," said the chief. "First off, we have to stabilize you so you won't fall through to the downstairs if the plumbing stack collapses." At that point the floor gave an ominous groan, and I caught my breath. They could all wind up in the basement at the rate they were going. After all, the firemen and EMT guys were wearing all that heavy gear to boot.

"Got to get a line around your chest," said Boo. "Lift your arms a little. That's right. Now, if you can just raise your knees so I can slide this line under ... *there*."

The firemen trussed Charlie the same way I truss the Thanksgiving turkey. Since there was no room between Charlie's shoulders and the wall, Ed, Jr., holding the chest rope, had to stand between Charlie and the old claw-footed bathtub, while Nail, holding the rope under Charlie's knees, stood as far back as he could from the edge of the hole.

"Going to have to cut out some of the floor," said the chief. "You're stuck, Charlie."

"I know I'm stuck. Do you think I'd still be here if I wasn't stuck?"

"'Scuse me, ma'am," said the third fireman. My eyes widened when he passed me. He was carrying a cordless electric saw with a blade that looked capable of cutting down a giant redwood.

"Godawlmighty," Charlie whispered when he saw the thing.

As the fireman fired it up, I saw Charlie's eyes grow huge, his mouth open in a desperate "O" as that blade descended perilously close to his groin.

"You better stay very still," Rob advised loudly.

Charlie glared at him. "Don't you have a tornado siren to check, somewhere?"

I don't know about Charlie. I couldn't breathe, much less move. I shut my eyes and prayed.

"All right, men," said the chief. "You got room now. Pull him up."

I opened my eyes just as the ropes tightened and Charlie levitated in a sitting position with his naked rear end hanging out of his pajama bottoms.

"One, two, three," said the firemen on the lines. Nail, Rob and Boo swung Charlie like a deer trussed under a bushman's pole into the waiting arms of the EMT's.

The instant his rump touched the floor, Charlie started struggling out of his ropes, hauling up his britches and trying to scramble to his feet.

"Now, hold on, Charlie," said Mutt. "You've had the circulation to your legs cut off."

"You have some scrapes and bruises, sir, We'll bring the

gurney right up and take you to the emergency room."

"The hell you will!" Charlie snapped, just as his knees buckled. Boo and the female EMT grabbed him under his arms and walked him past me like a drunk in the final stages of delirium tremens.

"Everybody out of this room before the whole floor falls in," Mutt said.

When I turned around Charlie had been unceremoniously bundled onto the stretcher and was being carried down the stairs protesting every step of the way that he was not going to any damned emergency room.

Of course he did. At least his pajama bottoms were secure around his waist, and he was swathed in blankets before they carried him out on the front porch and down the steps to the sidewalk through the audience of neighbors.

Leaving me, of course, to try to explain what had happened. I knew that no matter what I said, the real story would be all over town in an hour.

I was not certain how this incident would become my fault, but I was certain that somehow it would.

During the months we had been working on the house, Charlie had actually spent most of his time in his workshop out at the other house building bookshelves for the dining room, while I'd stayed at Aunt Catherine's and dealt with the workers.

I had also had to clean out both my attic and Aunt Catherine's, organize, cull, pack, and decide which pieces of furniture to take and which either to leave for Margaret or sell. The grand piano would stay with Margaret. Charlie swore he'd buy me a spinet to go in the new keeping room that would be attached to the new kitchen.

Building a new house from scratch would have been preferable by far. Probably cheaper, too. With every problem, every decision, every change necessitated by the age of the place, I grew to hate not only the idea of living in the house, but the house itself. How could I ever have loved it?

I didn't, of course. I loved the people who had lived there, the antiques and photos and sit-arounds with which they surrounded themselves and which came to represent memory to me. Each bit of transformation, each new wall that went up, each new cabinet or appliance ate away at the house as it had been and separated me further and further from my memories. The new additions and renovations made the house habitable for Charlie and me, but less precious somehow. I couldn't share any of my feelings with Margaret, of course. No sense in making her feel guilty.

Nor could I let Charlie know how I felt. He was having a wonderful time. His energy level had risen with his interest level. He'd lost ten pounds and told me he felt better than he had in years.

I, on the other hand, had gained the ten pounds he had lost, and both my energy and emotional state plummeted. Everybody seemed to be having fun but me. I was so tired of eating fast food or microwave dinners, using paper plates because the faucets for the new sink in the kitchen hadn't arrived on time, and the new stove wasn't hooked up yet. I was basically living out of a suitcase because the tiny closet in Aunt Catherine's upstairs bedroom (in which we were still camping out) had been made for the average wardrobe in 1904 when everyone had two outfits for every day if they were lucky and one for Sunday-go-to-meeting.

Thank God the yard could wait until spring for planting, but in the meantime it required clearing and pruning and pre-emerge fertilizing.

After Charlie came back from the emergency room and slunk into the house to avoid the neighbors, I absolutely had to get away from him, the house, and everything about it. Cold as it was, I walked all the way back to the fence that divided the yard from the alley that ran along behind all the houses on the block. I could no longer feel Aunt Catherine's presence anywhere. It was though I had lost her all over again. I wanted to get into my car and drive away from Mossy Creek until I ran out of gas, then fill up and keep driving, God knows where. Just away from Mossy Creek and my family and my responsibilities and my lousy decision to do this insane thing that threatened to destroy my family and even my marriage.

The old slat hurricane fence that divided the back yard from the alley that ran behind the house was scheduled to be replaced by a fancy new one in two days time. I wanted somehow to maintain the old-fashioned Blaze climbing roses. At the moment, they looked pretty sorry. In another month I'd have to prune them back severely. Then I realized I was looking down at pansies. Aunt Catherine's pansies. Most people have to replant pansies every fall, but Aunt Catherine's were some kind of old-fashioned pansies that reseeded themselves and came up as volunteers every year. They weren't the fancy new kind that are all of one color and double-blossomed and fat. They were soft old-fashioned lavender and pale yellow. They looked shriveled and frozen, but they were there.

I sat cross-legged on the grass in front of them and bawled. Those pansies were like the apes of Gibraltar. So long as they were there, Aunt Catherine was there. We couldn't ever strip her completely out of her house.

When I finally pulled myself up and turned to look back up at all the construction, I didn't feel so disheartened. Or so guilty.

I wish I could say things went smoothly thereafter.

I went inside and upstairs. As I opened the bedroom door I could hear Charlie clumping up the stairs behind me.

I am not a screamer. In emergencies I am the one keeping a cool head while everyone around me has hysterics. Ask anyone. They'll tell you.

When I opened the bedroom door, however, I screeched.

"Louise, what on earth?"

I slammed the door and leaned against it. "There's a bear in the bedroom."

"A what?"

"A bear. A fat, brown, furry bear."

He reached for the doorknob. I reached for him.

"No Charlie! Don't go in there! Call Mutt again, call Smokey Lincoln at the Forest Service, call the highway patrol. Call somebody!"

"Louise, for heaven's sake, you're hysterical." He moved me away from the door, none too gently, I might add, opened it and stuck his head in. "Holy Hell!" he yelped, pulled his head back and slammed the door.

"You see, Charlie!"

He gave me a single glance, pulled out his cell phone and pressed the re-dial button for the police station. "Sandy, this is Charlie. We have a problem, again. We need you to send somebody over to the new house right away."

I started to say something, but he held up his hand to stop me. "No, blast it, I have not fallen through the floor again. The floor is fine. Not precisely a burglar. And not just one. It's a gang."

I felt my eyes widen and my jaw drop.

"Yeah, it's a home invasion, just not the kind you're talking about. I don't know how it got in, but at the moment there's a fifty-pound raccoon hanging from the mantelpiece in our bedroom, and he's brought his entire family with him."

"A raccoon?" I yelped. "That's no raccoon." I shoved Charlie aside, opened the door six inches and peered around the jam.

I have seen many raccoons in my life. I had never before seen one the size of Bigfoot or the Abominable Snowman. It had climbed onto the mantelpiece and stood at full height, reaching nearly to the ceiling. It had stretched its arms like King Kong on the Empire State Building, and it positively glared.

At that moment I caught movement from behind the pillows at the head of the bed. Four small bandit faces peered out at me, and a moment later what I assumed was their momma scrambled out from under the bed and joined them. I shut the door on them before they could figure out they outnumbered us significantly and risk an attack.

"I saw four," Charlie said into his cell phone.

I shook my head and held up six fingers. His eyes widened. "Make that six. I am well aware that raccoons are dangerous, Sandy," Charlie said. "I am not about to face down an adult male raccoon or his wife and babies either." He listened for a moment. "Whack them with a broom?"

I grabbed the phone. "I want them, *it*, whatever, *gone*. I don't want them just *whacked*."

"Miss Louise," Sandy said grimly, "I don't know if the moon's full or the winter air's extra frisky or *what*, but we're taking a lot of calls here at the station today, and I just don't have time to come shoo raccoons out of your bedroom. You're on your own."

She hung up.

Charlie and I tiptoed back to the bedroom and looked in. There was no sign of the raccoons.

"Look up here," Charlie said, as he pointed to a hole beside the chimney that I swore had not been there that morning. You could feel the cold air from the attic whistling down into the bedroom.

"That's not big enough for a mouse, much less that bull moose of a raccoon," I said.

"You'd be surprised. Probably got in through a hole in

the attic roof and just clawed their way down here where it's warm."

"How on earth do we keep them out?"

"Need to go up in the attic and find the hole where they're getting in, then nail up some plywood over it." He started for the attic stairs.

"Not me," I said. "I am not about to go anywhere near those things. They could be rabid."

"Haven't had a rabid raccoon in these parts for twenty years. No, they're just hungry and looking for a warm place."

"That is why God gave them fur. I refuse to have them cozy up to my down pillows."

Charlie found the hole with no trouble. The roofers had apparently not done a very good job of installing the new soffits around the eaves, and the raccoons had found a place where they didn't quite meet. Charlie nailed a board over the hole, and then we packed the hole beside the chimney with steel wool.

"They won't try to come back in until after dark," Charlie said. "If you want, I could put some poison bait out for them."

"No, indeed. Thank you, dear."

We went back to the bedroom and looked around. I wailed. "There is raccoon pee and poop on the floor, the walls, the bedclothes, the pillows, and definitely on the mattress."

"I didn't see any poop, but you're right about the mattress. I guess we'll have to call Bud over here to help me haul the thing out to the dumpster. The rest, however, you can wash."

"How many times would you suggest I wash them? Besides, you don't wash goose down pillows. They lump up. No matter how many times I wash and dry those things, or how much bleach I use, I will still smell raccoon on them."

"Now, Louise, be reasonable."

"Reasonable? You call it reasonable to come home from the emergency room to an invasion of the beasts? Thank God we haven't stripped the floors in the upstairs yet. Peeling off a couple of layers of oak ought to get rid of the raccoon pee odor. I don't care what you say, we're deep-sixing the sheets, the blankets, the pillows, the mattress pad, and the mattress. And I refuse to sleep in that room. Ever. I'd lie awake all night long expecting to be jumped on."

"Where would you suggest we sleep? We can't use the new bedroom yet, and the other bedroom upstairs is so full of boxes we couldn't get a camp bed in there. Louise, we simply cannot afford to move into even a cheap motel for the next ten days."

"You can sleep anywhere you damned well please. I am going home. The home where I belong and where I should never have left from." All right, so my syntax was a bit confused. I headed for the front door.

Charlie grabbed my wrist, none too gently either, and swung me to face him. He moved his hands to my shoulders and stared at me as though he were seeing me for the first time. Then he nodded and whispered, "Okay," and pulled me into his arms.

All the hassles, the expenses, the delays, the horror stories we had endured, the arguments over wallpaper and bathroom tile and floor stain and carpet just came flooding out of me. He held me while I wailed and clung to him. Finally I gulped and hiccoughed my way quiet.

"This house is going to kill us or divorce us," I said.

"No, it's not, hon," he whispered into my hair. "It hasn't whipped us yet, has it? Look around you. We're so close to finished. I've been puttering around in my workshop out at the other house, while you've been here alone dealing with everything else. No wonder you're exhausted."

"So are you."

"Time to take a break. The house'll be here tomorrow. Come on." He pulled me outside toward the car.

"Where are we going? We've got all that mess to clean upstairs."

"Screw it. First we're going to buy one of those blow-up beds, then we're going to buy all new bedding— sheets, towels, pillows, everything. Then we're going out to dinner. Someplace where they don't eat microwave pizza off paper plates."

As we drove away, I shook a fist at the house.

I'll be back.

Mossy Creek Gazette

VOLUME V, NO. FIVE   MOSSY CREEK, GEORGIA

The Bell Ringer

I Quilt, Therefore I Am

by Katie Bell

Yes, I'm obsessing about the estate sale and the quilt I lost to Patty Campbell. Nothing brings out the best, or the *beast*, in a Southern woman like a patchwork quilt. Heirloom "Wedding Rings" and "Log Cabins" and "Grandmother's Flower Gardens" have been the cause of more Southern feuds than the Hatfields and McCoys combined. Long before Martha Stewart told us how to turn ordinary home decorating into an art, legions of Southern women — from all races, creeds, classes and places of Southern origin — have turned scraps, rags, and old flour sacks into quilted masterpieces.

It's something about the tedious thrill of it all. You sit, and you cut out tiny pieces of fabric, and you piece those tiny pieces together, and you stitch. Tiny stitches. Perfection, thy name is stitchery. Quilters know that one hundred years from now some stranger will look at their work and go, "How did she ever make such tiny, perfect stitches by hand?" Now that, friends, is the secret to eternal life. Your stitches live on.

Quilters know that. And they know this, too: Quilts talk. Quilts remember.

They remind you that your mother once wore a gingham apron with a poodle embroidered on it. They bookmark the day you took your granddaughters to a fabric store for the first time. They whisper your memories back to you, held in bits of cloth.

My husband looked so young and handsome in this plaid shirt.

I wore this satin dress to my son's graduation party.

My grandmother saved this handkerchief from her mother's college trunk.

To quilters, and to women who aren't quilters but love quilts just the same, an heirloom quilt isn't a thing, it's a *being*. A cotton soul full of history. Look at a quilt, and you see your great grandmother's hands at work.

(continued on page 168)

MOSSY CREEK GAZETTE   VOLUME V, NO. FIVE

I Quilt, Therefore I Am
(continued from page 167)

Touch the stitches and hear the voices of your ancestors as they sewed by lamplight. Pull the quilt around your shoulders, and you'll stay safe inside your family's heart. It has warmed your ancestors just as it warms you, now. Touch the quilt, and you touch them.

See how just *talking* about quilts makes me get poetic and philosophical? But let's get back to grim reality, here.

Don't mess with a Southern woman's quilt. She'll come after you with her pinking shears. She'll hurt you. *Bad.*

Just ask Addie Lou Hamilton Womack and her sister, Inez.

Solomon never had to decide who gets Mama's heirloom quilt.

Sandy Is Caught Up In An Alteration

Chapter 10

I'm just going to have to get me one of those portable sirens for Jess's old Ford pickup— the ones they used to use in *Starsky & Hutch*. Trying to get to a burglary in progress in a vehicle that will barely crack fifty miles per hour just won't cut it. Maybe one day Amos'll let me have my own cruiser.

Like I kept telling everyone, Amos was down in Atlanta for the afternoon. I wasn't telling anybody *why* he'd gone to Atlanta, or who'd tipped him off about Ida's scheme to confront the governor. Let's just say I didn't fall off the turnip truck yesterday, and I have my sources.

It was a crazy Saturday all around, what with that escapade at Orville Gene's place, Amos going after Ida, Miss Irene running amuck on her scooter, Pearl and Spiva at war over some brownies, the Sawyers at war with toilets and raccoons —I didn't need any more calls to answer. Neither did Mutt. He'd taken this one not ten minutes ago, when I was on another line. He looked serious at first, but then he started squinching up his face, which started turning all shades of purple and red. Since he'd spent most of the past two hours laughing himself sick over Charlie Sawyer's predicament, I thought I was fixing to have to do CPR on my own brother. (I trained for that with the paramedics and got the highest score in the state that month on the written part.)

Anyway, it turned out he was trying real hard not to laugh anymore. I finally figured that out when he started making little snorting sounds, like a pig at a trough. He covered the receiver and hissed, "Miss Addie Lou Womack says her big sister Inez has busted into her house to steal a quilt. She says she's holding her until we get there — *at cane point.*" He did bust out laughing, then, and it sounded like a jackass braying. It is no wonder that Sugar Jean Milford keeps stalling every time he asks her to marry him.

Personally, I don't think burglary is any laughing matter. Especially when somebody's accusing their own flesh and blood of doing the burgling. I doubted that Miss Addie Lou would run Miss Inez through with the cane, but you can't ever be too careful. Family feuds could be tricky. Goodness knows nobody understands that better than us Creekites. You know what I'm talking about.

Besides, not only was this a burglary, it was also a domestic matter, what with Miss Addie Lou and Miss Inez being sisters and all. Everybody knows that a domestic call can be one of the most dangerous an officer of the law has to make. I wondered if Miss Addie Lou was using her everyday adjustable aluminum cane or her Sunday-go-to-meeting polished wood cane.

Another complication was that Miss Inez's granddaughter, Lucy Belle, (distant kin to Katie Bell,) was a friend of mine. She's a few years older than me. In fact she used to babysit me and Mutt and Boo summers from the time we were ankle-biters until we graduated to yard apes. She used to pull us into town for ice cream in a Radio Flyer and tell us stories. I owed it to Lucy Belle to make sure Miss Inez and Miss Addie Lou (Lucy Belle's great aunt, of course) didn't assault and batter each other too awful bad before Lucy Belle could get there to referee.

Being a referee was something that Lucy Belle had gotten good at over the years. Why, she could be the zebra at the girls' basketball games if she wanted to, I expect. That grandmother of hers — Miss Inez — is what we call a sight, a mess, a caution. Take your pick. She came from a long line of formidable women, which included her and Miss Addie Lou's first cousin, Big Ida Hamilton, the grandma and namesake of our mayor, Ida Hamilton Walker. And she loved to fuss with people, just for the fun of it, I reckon. It kept Lucy Belle on her toes just trying to keep her out of trouble.

Sometimes she isn't as successful at keeping her grandmother out of trouble as she'd like to be. And sometimes she mires up in it neck-deep, herself. There was that incident back in the summer at Ham Bigelow's political fundraising event that like to have got the both of them arrested— or at least wrestled to the ground— by Ham's state patrol bodyguards.

But as I understand it, Ham's mother's silk suit was saved and she never could prove who stole those rare chili peppers anyway. And the shih tzu recovered too, physically, at least, if not his pride, which was pretty much shot to hell to begin with on account of Ham's mother naming him *Pierre* and having his toenails painted. But that's a whole 'nother story. And don't even get me started on what happened to that Bigelow Mercedes with the trunk full of fireworks. Lord have mercy.

❧❧❧

I called Lucy Belle on my cell phone as I was peeling out of the parking lot at the police station. "Lucy Belle," I'd said, "You better get over to your Aunt Addie Lou's. Her and Miss Inez are mixing it up."

I can't rightly tell you what Lucy Belle said. But I *can* tell you that if she'd said it on the street I'd have had to arrest her for public indecency, old friend or not. I'm sure there must be a law against such language in public. If there's not, there ought to be. She thanked me, told me she'd meet me there and hung up.

Lucy Belle and Inez's chow-chow business had taken off so well that Lucy Belle had been able to quit her job as a computer programmer and help her grandmother run the business full time. In fact, she lived with Miss Inez a few blocks from Miss Addie Lou's.

Lucy Belle never really liked her computer job that much anyway. Her manager — a man — had just passed her over for a promotion, giving the job instead to an individual — another man — who was very nice but had only a fraction of Lucy Belle's experience. Lucy Belle knew this because she had trained him herself.

When Lucy Belle finished the business plan for the chow-chow operation and figured out that she could make a living working in her grandma's kitchen, she walked into her manager's office, told him that not only did he not *know* anything about computers, but she was quite sure he didn't even *suspect* anything. She further told him that not only could he not "manage" computer programmers, but that he also could not "manage" to find his own behind with both hands, a road map, and a flashlight.

I must say I was right proud of her. And I will tell you straight out, if you do not want to hear the truth of a thing, do not ask Lucy Belle.

When I pulled up in front of Miss Addie Lou's house, Lucy Belle was just crossing the yard toward the front door at a dead run. She was wearing a faded cotton apron spackled with what looked like chow-chow stains over jeans and a tee shirt. Even though it was cold, she hadn't even taken time to grab a sweater on her way out. She paused right outside the door to get her breath and to let me catch up with her.

"I don't know what's got into her this time," Lucy Belle

said. "She told me she was going to take a nap and waddled off toward her bedroom. She must have snuck out the back door when I wasn't looking. That old woman can walk as quiet as an Indian scout when she's up to something. I should have known something wasn't right because she always manages to stay awake for her stories."

I'd reached the porch by then and stood beside Lucy Belle. "I thought she was still tethered to that oxygen machine. How did she make it all the way over here on foot?"

"She's doing a lot better since they changed her medication and she started taking Tai Chi at the senior center," explained Lucy Belle. "Her portable oxygen tank was gone, so I guess she took it with her and hoofed it on over here."

We heard a crash from behind the door and the sound of old-lady cussing.

"You'd better let me go in first," I said. I really wanted to draw my gun just to get their attention, but that's against regulations.

"I'm not going to fight you for *that* privilege," Lucy Belle said, raising her palms. "In fact, if you have a flak jacket in the truck, I suggest you use it."

"Aw, it won't get that bad." I thought about drawing the gun again.

"Maybe not. But just keep in mind that they're both a lot more spry than they let on. Remember that incident when old man Dexter next door climbed up in that pecan tree not long ago to try and pull some vines out? It turned out he was on Aunt Addie Lou's property and she thought he was a peeping Tom. She whacked him upside the ribs a few times with that cane before she realized who he was."

I nodded. "I remember that. He said she had a swing like Chipper Jones. Came at him from both sides."

"Yeah, she's a switch hitter. Anyway, old man Dexter, who can't see two feet in front of his face, didn't know what had got after him. He just climbed higher and higher up that tree."

"Boo told me about having to get him down out. It was real hard. The boys had to use a cherry picker. Didn't he have to go to the hospital?"

"Yeah, but not from the beating, or else I expect the old coot would have sued her garters off. Turned out the vines were mostly poison ivy, which he couldn't identify what with the nearsightedness and all."

I winced. "Weeee doggies!" I exclaimed sympathetically. "You hate to see that. Why didn't he ever get him some glasses?"

"Vanity, I reckon. Aunt Addie Lou said he was done in by his own vanity."

"Of course, her beating him with a stick didn't help him none."

"That is a fact in this world if I ever heard one," agreed Lucy Belle.

We both flinched in unison at the sound of something shattering and some more cussing. "I expect we ought to go on in. She seems to be hurling something breakable. I hope she can't pitch as good as she can hit ..."

Lucy Belle finished my thought. "Or else I'll be picking pottery shards of out of Grandma's tough old hide for a week."

"What do you reckon she's throwing in there?"

"She keeps her collection of Precious Memories figurines in a case by the front door. That would be my guess."

"That's a shame."

"Yeah, what with them being collectable and all." Lucy Belle shook her head sadly.

"Well, here goes nothing." I cleared my throat and hollered, "This is Officer Sandy Crane. I'm coming in!" I opened the door, expecting to get beaned by a porcelain cherub.

I must say the scene that greeted me and Lucy Belle was somewhat surreal. Miss Addie Lou was decked out in a house dress, fuzzy slippers, and polyester duster, the kind with snaps all the way up the front and a Peter Pan collar. She had her aluminum cane raised in one hand and pointed at her sister, Inez. In the other she held a porcelain bell with two sad-eyed, ceramic angels perched on the top.

Miss Inez wore pull-on stretch jeans, a tee shirt, and slip-on tennis shoes. She had on a hooded fleecy sweater open over the tee shirt, which read, "Cooking Philosophy: A little cat hair never hurt anybody." I thought about all her chow-chow I'd eaten and my mouth went a little dry. One of these days after eating a wiener slathered in Miss Inez's chili concoction, I expect I'd be harking up a hair ball. But I swear it'd be worth it. The stuff is just that good.

"It's about time you got here, Sandy," Miss Addie Lou said. "This old heifer was trying to make off with my Mama's best quilt, what she gave to me right before she died."

A shock of Miss Inez's snow-white hair had escaped the fleece hood and was standing on end, due probably to the static electricity that seems to be everywhere in the winter. It made the tall, formidable woman look even wilder than usual. Her oxygen tank was stuffed into the backpack she had strapped behind her back. She gripped the handles of her aluminum walker with both hands.

The whole effect of Miss Inez's getup was pretty impressive, but I think it was mostly the hood, the oxygen tank, and the competitive gleam in her rheumy eyes that made her look the most like an octogenarian mountain climber getting ready to shuffle up the side of Mount Everest.

"If my Mama gave you that quilt, I'm a suck-egg mule," declared Miss Inez. "I'm the oldest. That quilt should have gone to me, and you know it."

"You're as stubborn as a mule, all right. I done told you

175

she gave it to me. Are you calling me a liar?" Miss Addie Lou brandished the cane again, looking like a bad actor in a swashbuckling movie.

"If the shoe fits," sniffed Miss Inez, adjusting the plastic tubing that went from underneath her nose on each side, beneath the hood, to hook behind both ears. "And put down that tacky dime store gewgaw before you hurt somebody."

Miss Addie Lou hoisted her ceramic cherubs higher and gasped in indignation. "It's *collectable*."

Lucy Belle and me exchanged glances. Neither of us liked where this was going.

"Collectable my hind end," Miss Inez said. "I'll bet they're the same ones as they got at the Dollar Store in Bigelow. Them what was made in China."

I expect that was about the last straw as far as Miss Addie Lou was concerned. You just don't defame a Southern woman's choice of ceramics. Not and expect to ever be given a good name by the offended party. Taste in decorating is too close to one's heart. My mother was once taken to task for her choice of curtain material by one of her own sisters.

I'll admit the print she'd picked out at Aunt Effie's Fine Fabrics Shop was unfortunate, but it was on sale, and besides, Mama just loves daffodils. My baby brother, Boo, was a baby then, and Aunt Janey Sue blamed his stubborn colic on being surrounded by the jaundiced shade of yellow in the giant jonquils.

Mama retaliated by saying that she'd never much cared for Janey Sue's living room couch on account of the cheap vinyl upholstery which always made you sweat like a hog when you sat on it, even in the winter.

Janey Sue said that the couch was genuine Naugahyde and cost a pretty penny. Mama came back with how she didn't care whose hide it was or how much it cost, it was a fire trap and tacky besides, and if it was her couch, she'd leave it on the side of the road until some poor broke bastard took it off her hands.

Long story short, those two didn't speak to each other for a year. No sir, you should never criticize what a woman chooses to surround herself with in her own home. In fact, I do believe you would cause less of a fuss if you criticized a husband than if you criticized the couch he sat on.

Miss Addie Lou, pushed to the brink, eyed Miss Inez's oxygen tank darkly. "Why, I ought to light a match and watch you go up like a torch."

"Yeah, well, I ought to take that cane away from you and beat you like a rented mule!" Miss Inez growled.

Lucy Belle stepped between them and said, "I ought to take the both of you and knock your heads together until you see stars, you pair of old battle axes!"

I got out my brand new police whistle that Jess bought me when I was promoted to officer and blew it until all three of them covered their ears and my lips were turning numb. When I had their attention, I quit blowing and said, "Now, listen here to me, all y'all. Nobody's going to knock heads or kick asses or set anybody afire while I'm here. Everybody just simmer down, now."

Miss Inez continued to rant as if I hadn't said a thing. "I had wondered what happened to that quilt all these years. The last time I saw it, it was on my dear Mama's deathbed. And then lo and behold, when I was over here t'other day, I saw it on the spare bed in yonder."

"So rather than asking me about it," Miss Addie Lou hissed, "you sneaked back in here through the back door while my stories was on and you knew I wouldn't be paying attention — on account of how this is the week that Dawn finds out who the father of her baby is on the Saturday re-runs of *The Young And The Restless* — and tried to steal it."

Lucy Belle turned to me. "It's Victor's. I'll bet you anything."

"I'd put my money on Juan-Carlos, but that's just me," Addie Lou said.

"You're both wrong." Miss Inez picked up her walker and pounded it back onto the floor. "It's gonna turn out to be Joaquin's. It looks like him around the eyes."

Lucy Belle rolled her own eyes. "Grandma, that's not his real baby. That's an acting baby."

"Oh, yeah." Miss Inez looked a little embarrassed before getting back onto the main subject. "I don't care whose baby it is. I deserve that quilt if for no other reason than Addie Lou tried to *poison me* with rancid rabbit here awhile back."

Me and Lucy Belle exchanged a look at this point. I couldn't have heard that right. Maybe "Rancid Rabbit" was a Native American character in one of Miss Addie Lou's soap operas. "Will somebody tell me what's going on? I thought we were talking about a quilt." I said.

Miss Inez inclined her head toward her younger sister. "Ask her. It makes me right bilious every time I think about it. I'm getting all sour even now."

Lucy Belle, who stands about a head taller than me, bent down to whisper in my ear. "She's as sour as a green persimmon most of the time, in actual fact." She shook her head wearily with a long-suffering expression that you might have seen on the face of Job himself right about the time he was beset by all the sores. "It sounds like this situation has been simmering for quite a little while," she said.

"Yeah," I agreed. "Miss Addie Lou, why don't you just put down the cane and the figurine and start at the beginning. How did all this get started?"

"Very well," Miss Addie Lou said, lowering the cane and leaning on it. She'd been waving it around so much I had to wonder if she ever needed it to begin with. "It all started the other day when I asked my sister here to come over and have dinner. I had fried up a rabbit and made some biscuits and white pepper gravy to go with it." She turned her attention back to Inez. "And you can't say it wasn't good."

"Yeah, it was pretty good eatin'," Miss Inez admitted. "But then I wondered to myself where you got that rabbit. I mean, it had been a coon's age since I'd had any rabbit or seen any for sale at the butcher's department at the *Piggly Wiggly*. So I asked you. I said, 'Where'd you get this here rabbit, anyway?'" Miss Inez turned to us with an indignant look. "And do you know what she said? She said, 'Enloe Crump found it on the side of the road.' Why, I like to have upchucked right then and there. My own sister was feeding me road kill!"

"There weren't nothing wrong with that rabbit!" Miss Addie Lou shot back. "Enloe said he'd seen it get hit by that car and it just had a glancin' blow to the head. It would have been a shame to have let a perfectly good rabbit go to waste."

"Well, then why didn't *he* eat it?" Miss Inez demanded. "He's a deacon of the First Baptist church and makes plenty of money. Is it his idea of Christian charity to pick up road kill and take it to old widow women just like they don't have anything better to eat?"

Lucy Belle lost it. She bent from the waist, propping herself by one hand on the back of one of Miss Addie Lou's matching, overstuffed wing chairs. She laughed until tears rolled down her cheeks. I must admit it was all I could do to keep a straight face. Lucy Belle finally looked up at her grandma, who was glaring at her, and then started laughing again.

She started to wipe her eyes on the tail of her apron but must've remembered the hot chili pepper juice it was soaked in and went for the crocheted doily on the back of Miss Addie Lou's chair instead. "Ahhh ... " she groaned, like you will whenever you pull yourself together after a good giggling fit. Then she hiccoughed and started laughing again. I could tell she wasn't going to be any help for a while.

"It's not funny," Miss Addie Lou and Miss Inez said in unison.

"Like I said," Miss Inez complained. "My stomach's not over it 'til yet."

"If there's anything wrong with your digestion, it's because the acid of those chili peppers has done et through your stomach lining. Or maybe it's because of the rot-gut 'secret ingredient' that ain't quite as secret as you seem to think it is," Miss Addie Lou jeered.

Miss Inez started getting dangerously red in the face, and Lucy Belle patted her on the shoulder to try and calm her down. What Miss Addie Lou said was true. The fact that the chow-chow contained moonshine was the worst-kept secret in the county. You know that TV chef who talks about 'kicking it up a notch?' That moonshine gives that chow-chow a kick like a mule. 'Bam,' indeed. Miss Inez can show you 'bam!'

I cleared by throat and tried to get them back on the subject of quilt-napping. "So what happened then?"

"I beat it to the bathroom because I was afraid I was going to be sick," Miss Inez said. "And that's when I saw that quilt on the bed in the spare room. The chenille spread she usually keeps on top of there to hide that quilt was out flapping in the breeze on the clothesline. She'd forgot to bring it in and put it back on that bed to hide that ..." Here Miss Inez paused for effect. "Stolen property."

"You've got some nerve talking about stolen property! You took advantage of my hospitality to come in and case my home." Miss Addie Lou turned to me. "If you shook her down right now, there's no telling what else you might find that she may have took. Why, she might have my VCR in that backpack for all I know."

"I might as well," Miss Inez huffed. "You ain't got sense enough to use it. It's been flashing twelve for the past ten years. At least I can program mine."

I looked wonderingly at Lucy Belle. She muttered under her breath just loud enough for me to hear. "No she can't. Every time she tries to tape *Matlock* reruns, she winds up with *Judge Judy.*"

"I heard that," growled Miss Inez.

"Grandma loves that Andy Griffith," Lucy Bell said to me. "He reminds her of Grandpa."

"Your grandpa was a handsome man," I said.

"Wasn't he, though?" Lucy Belle said.

"Pat her down, I say," railed Miss Addie Lou. "She might be armed."

"With what?" Lucy Belle demanded.

"She used to carry Daddy's pocket knife. The one with the hula girls on it." Miss Addie Lou stamped her slipper-clad foot.

I had a feeling that if I tried to 'pat down' Miss Inez, I'd have to call for backup. I looked at Lucy Belle, who was massaging her temples. "Damn, I wish I had some of that moonshine right about now," she said.

"I don't want to have to arrest you too," I said. "Try to get them back on the subject."

"Now, Aunt Addie Lou, you know it's not necessary to search Grandma for weapons, not with you yourself letting fly with statuettes right and left. Let's get back to that quilt. Tell us again when it was you say that Great Grandma said you could have it?"

Miss Addie Lou paused to stoop down and pull up her thin Buster Brown socks. "She was on her deathbed with consumption when she was ninety-six. That's when she gave it to me."

"Ha!" Miss Inez said. "Her mind had done gone bad right before that. You could have talked her out of anything. Why, she tried to give her teeth to the preacher the last time he came."

"Huh?" Lucy Belle asked.

Miss Inez waved her hand dismissively. "She knew she was on her way out. I guess she figured she'd just gum her grits from then on and some poor person might need her teeth more than she did."

"She was generous to a fault." Miss Addie Lou agreed. She produced a faded handkerchief from her cleavage and dabbed at her eyes. "But she knew just what she was doing when she gave me that quilt."

"What's so special about this quilt anyway?" Lucy Belle asked.

Miss Inez smiled a bit. "It was made from the scraps of my little baby dresses, and a lot of the dresses I wore when I was growing up, all the way into my teenage years until I stopped growing."

"And my little baby dresses and all the dresses I wore," Miss Addie Lou put in.

"Which I take it were one in the same since you, Miss Addie Lou, would have worn Miss Inez's hand-me-downs." I said. I was starting to think that the old ladies' problems with each other were more than quilt deep.

Lucy Belle looked at me with one eyebrow raised. She was thinking the same thing I was. "So, it's no wonder the quilt is so special to both of you," she said soothingly. "Can Sandy and I see it?"

Miss Addie Lou looked at each of us suspiciously, but finally agreed. Lucy Belle and I followed her into a back bedroom with Miss Inez clomping along behind with her walker. When we got there, Miss Addie Lou peeled back the chenille bedspread to reveal an ancient-looking quilt whose squares consisted of Sunbonnet Sue appliqués clothed in many different fabrics.

Lucy Belle ran her fingers over the surface of the quilt. "Granny made this?"

"Uh-huh," Miss Inez said. "She did some of these appliqués back when you ironed back the seam allowances with a flat iron you had to heat over an open fire."

"It was a labor of love," put in Miss Addie Lou with another dab at her eyes. She blew her nose real good and stuffed the hanky back down her lengthy cleavage.

"The batting is real cotton. Not the polyester stuff you buy in the craft stores nowadays that comes in a roll," continued Miss Inez.

"She carded the cotton herself to get it smooth and even," Miss Addie Lou said. "After she'd gotten the top and the batting and the backing put together and put in the quilt frame, she had her sisters and aunts and cousins like old Big Ida over to help her quilt it. They sat around all sides of it and worked at once. When you got one row of squares done, you'd roll the quilt up and re-hang it and start right in on the next row."

"We helped, too. By that time we were expert quilters ourselves. I still remember that quilting bee, with all our womenfolk gathered around the fire. We quilted in winter when the planting and the gathering and the canning was over." Miss Inez said.

"And after the hog killing in the fall," Miss Addie Lou added. "In the winter we quilted and did needlework and sewing. That quilting bee was special because it was the last quilting that our own grandma did before she died. We had a big time then. Our mama had baked a caramel cake and a devil's food cake with buttermilk icing."

"And a coconut cake with divinity icing that was crunchy with fresh coconut when it cooled just right," Miss

Inez said. She closed her eyes and breathed deeply as if she could still smell the fruits of her long-dead mother's oven.

The two old ladies exchanged brief but tender looks, remembering better times, I reckon. Times when they didn't need canes and oxygen tanks and youth was forever and the world was safe and secure with warm cozy fires and doting females.

Miss Inez pointed to a piece of fabric that formed one of the sunbonnets. "That red piece was from a Christmas dress I wore when I was five. I tore it when I went out with Daddy to help him cut down a little cedar for our Christmas tree. I just hated to tear that dress."

"But Mama fixed it and the next year I wore it," Miss Addie Lou said.

Miss Inez pointed to a different square, a pretty print of tiny blue flowers. "I wore that dress when I first met the man I would marry. It was at a church barbecue and I spilled some of Daddy's Brunswick stew on it. He always made the Brunswick stew at the barbecues, you know. You can still see the stain if you look real close."

"I reckon y'all's family makes the best Brunswick stew in the county," I said, and all three women beamed. I was actually just trying to be diplomatic. (That's important in crisis negotiations.) Their Brunswick stew was good, but my own family, the Bottoms, made the best Brunswick stew in the county. Not that it was all that different from the Brunswick stew in the Hamilton family. Among Creekite cooks, Brunswick stew is always red and tomatoey. No potatoes for us, not on your life. When you see pale stew, you've got potatoes. Just so you know what to watch out for when you're evaluating stew.

To be fair, wherever you go in the South, everybody thinks their Brunswick stew is the best there is anywhere. It's just one of those things. But my family's stew is really the best. When it comes to stew, you can't get better than a Bottom's.

Lucy Belle pointed to a beige colored piece with tattered embroidery. "Mama embroidered flowers on this muslin. They're almost all worn off."

"That's not muslin. That's a flour sack," Miss Inez said. "We wore plenty of flour sack dresses in the old days. Everybody did. Mama embroidered on them so they wouldn't look so plain. She used those old iron-on embroidery patterns over and over again. When they got so pale she could hardly see the transfer, she's go over them with a lead pencil."

I had always thought all the Hamiltons were wealthy, but after hearing the old ladies talk about wearing flour sacks, I remembered Lucy Belle telling me once a long time ago that their branch of the family were the church-mouse variety of Hamilton.

In fact, now that I think about it, she used to tell me about standing in line for government cheese with her grandmother one time back in the seventies. It was the processed kind that melted real good, like Velveeta, and made extra fine macaroni and cheese and grilled sandwiches. Those Hamiltons had land but not a lot of cash, so Miss Inez qualified.

Lucy Belle told me that when her father found out his mother-in-law was seen standing in line for a five-pound block of welfare cheese, he like to have hit the roof, it embarrassed him so bad. But like I've said, nobody's ever been able to reason with Miss Inez. But I'm getting off the subject again.

"Well, I can certainly see why this quilt is so special to both of you," I said.

"I guess it's too much to ask for one of you to back down and just let the other one have it," Lucy Belle stated, a complete waste of breath if I ever heard one, knowing both

Miss Addie Lou and Miss Inez the way I do. After a considerable pause, in which both old ladies pooched out their lower lips in identical pouts, Lucy Belle sighed and looked at me with a shrug. "Well, Sandy, you're the law. I guess it's up to you to decide. Do you take Grandma to the jail house for larceny or do you take Aunt Addie Lou for fraud?"

I paused just a moment to savor the mind picture of both of those fractious old ladies behind bars and almost had to laugh. But the situation was too serious, and besides, if they were in the jail, I'd have to take care of them and I'd wind up being sorely tempted to shoot them both in the leg with my service revolver so Bigelow Regional Hospital would have to take them off my hands.

Miss Addie Lou had a heart condition and Miss Inez, thanks to using up her lung tissue on unfiltered Camels, wasn't in very good shape either. Why, one of them might have a stroke over this feud if I didn't handle it carefully, and I couldn't let Lucy Belle down like that. My gaze fell upon the Bible on the night stand by the bed, and I got an idea.

"All right, ladies, here's the situation as I see it. Miss Addie Lou here says that her mama told her she could have this quilt. But I take it the old lady never put that in writing."

"Are you calling me a liar?" Miss Addie Lou demanded, her bristly chin thrust forward.

"No, ma'am," I said.

"I am," Miss Inez said.

"Grandma!" Lucy Belle warned.

I continued. "On the other hand, Miss Inez is the oldest, so you could make a case for the quilt going to her."

Miss Addie Lou started to protest, but I held up my hand for silence. "The way I see it, there's only one fair way to settle this. Lucy Belle, go get your aunt Addie Lou's scissors."

The two old ladies were stunned speechless (probably the first time in eighty-something years that had ever happened, at once anyway) and stood with their mouths gaping open. Lucy Belle winked at me and went back to the living room.

"You can't mean ..." Miss Addie Lou trailed off, looking mighty like she was on the verge of a spell of the vapors.

"Surely not," Miss Inez said. She pressed the oxygen hose to her nose and look a deep breath.

"Do you want regular sewing scissors or pinking shears?" Lucy Belle called from the other room.

"I don't know, ladies, would pinking shears keep the batting from falling out as bad?" I asked innocently, looking back and forth between them. Lucy Belle appeared from the living room then, a pair of large scissors in each hand, working them open and shut vigorously and with a vicious clicking sound.

The two old ladies continued to look horrified. "You can't do this," Miss Inez said. "Not to Mama's quilt."

With a flourish, Lucy Belle handed me the huge shears handle first, like I was a surgeon and she was my trusty assistant. "Sure I can," I said. "I have a pair of big scissors and the opposable thumbs to use them."

Lucy Belle and I pushed past the old women to the foot of the bed, where we sized up the quilt. "I'd say the middle was right between these two rows here," Lucy Belle said, indicating the proposed cut with the side of her hand, as if she was getting ready to deal a death blow via Karate chop.

"Here goes nothing, then," I said, and opened up the huge shears, guiding the quilt binding between the shining blades.

"Stop!" Miss Addie Lou and Miss Inez hollered in unison.

Lucy Belle and I looked up at them. Two pairs of little dark eyes stared back at us as round as saucers. I felt kind of ashamed of myself then, for scaring them. Of course, I'd never intended to cut into the fruit of their dear mother's labor of love for them.

"Don't cut it," Miss Inez said, wringing her hands. "Addie Lou can have it. Just as long as I know it's safe and sound and I can see it now and then."

"No, no. You can have it," Miss Addie Lou whimpered. "Mama never really gave it to me. I just wanted it so bad. I didn't think it meant as much to you as it did to me, but now I see that it does. I've had it all these years, so now I want you to have it."

"Aw," I said, genuinely touched. "Ain't that nice?" I asked Lucy Belle.

Lucy Belle looked at me and a strange expression came over her face. "Actually," she said, "I think you *should* cut it up."

"Child, have you lost your mind?" her grandmother Miss Inez demanded. Miss Addie Lou and I just stared.

"Hear me out," Lucy Belle said. "This quilt is a precious family heirloom, so why not spread it around? Aunt Addie Lou, you know those beautiful patchwork pillows with the layers of lace edging that you make and sell at the church auction every year?"

Miss Addie Lou nodded. I was beginning to get an inkling of what Lucy Belle was driving at.

"Why not take the quilt apart, carefully, a block at a time. I can help you. Then you can put on a new binding on each square and use the blocks to make a pillow for you and Grandma and me and your two daughters and their girls and Mama and aunt Jody and her girls. That way all the women in the family will have a little piece of Granny's love for her girls." Lucy Belle looked at the two old women hopefully.

The hard line of Miss Inez's mouth began to soften, "You are the best seamstress in the family, Addie Lou. Hell, you're the best seamstress in the county. You'd make those pillows look real nice."

"Do you really think so?" Miss Addie Lou's cheeks pinkened and suddenly I could see just a glimpse of the girl she used to be.

"Sure as shootin'," Miss Inez declared.

Lucy Belle had been counting the quilt squares. "There's enough for all of us, with two left over," she said. "I suggest we frame one and put it on display at the local history room of the library."

Both old ladies grinned from ear to ear. "I know what to do with the last extra one," Miss Inez said.

Lucy Belle nodded and gave me a wink. "I think we're on the same track."

"Yeah," Miss Addie Lou said. "We give the last pillow to Sandy."

I do declare I was touched. Really touched. Being raised with a couple of brothers, like I was, I would have loved to have had a sister. I was glad that Miss Addie Lou and Miss Inez were back on good terms. It would have been a tragedy if, at their advanced ages, something had happened to one of them while they were still feuding over a quilt. "Do you mean it?" I asked.

"Of course," Lucy Belle said. "Who better to give it to than Mossy Creek's newest police officer? The one with the wisdom of Solomon."

I gave Lucy Belle and Miss Inez a ride back to their house, and before I left, Miss Inez loaded me up with free jars of chow-chow. I was glad to get them, cat hair and all. I'm going to make a batch of Brunswick stew pretty soon. (There's nothing like a dollop of that chow-chow to fire up soups and stews.)

You know, Brunswick stew really hits the spot on a cold January day. I'll use my Grandma's recipe, (the one I told you about) that has been handed down from generation to generation, and cook it nice and slow in a iron pot over an open fire. Just like the women in my family have always done. Beef, pork, and chicken — it takes all three. Always has, always will.

I reckon you could say we cherish our traditions here in Mossy Creek, most especially our women's ways — whether they're likely to produce a quilt that represents the love and care a mother gives to her daughters or a good stew recipe. My feeling is that when we get crossways with each other, especially if we're kin, we need to just do whatever we have to do to patch things up and get along.

Mayor Ida and Governor Ham, are you listening?

WMOS
R A D I O
"The Voice Of The Creek"

Good afternoon, radio listeners! This is Bert Lyman again, welcoming you to a second hour of your musical favorites. First, let me mention again that Honey and I really appreciate all your kindnesses and sympathy concerning the death of Honey's sister. Honey will be flying back here this afternoon with her sisters' babies. We know everybody in Mossy Creek will welcome these two sweet children and help us start them on their new lives.

Well, that's enough about that. You can tell I get choked up whenever I talk about it.

Okay! Here's my regular Saturday afternoon "shout-out" — as the kids say — to Miz Eula Mae Whit, who says to tell all of her fellow Creekites, as usual, "I'm still alive, dammit."

Miz Eula, here's something that's guaranteed to keep you with us for another week, at least. Lena Horne, singing one of her classics.

Stormy Weather.

After you hit one hundred, you got a right to cause trouble.

Eula Mae
Turns Another Year
Chapter 11

My name is Eula Mae Whit, and last fall I celebrated my hundred-first birthday. To say I'm disappointed is an understatement.

Now, don't get me wrong. I like living and breathing just like the next senior citizen, but I feel slighted. God done already called home my sisters and brothers, cousin Chicken and other relatives, but He left me here with my great-granddaughter, Estelle, and my granddaughter, Clara.

Clara gives me the hives somethin' awful. She cain't stop fussin'. I think that's her callin' in life. Fuss until her relatives drop dead.

The way she goes on, sometimes, I take my own pulse to see if I checked out by surprise.

Still ticking. I sigh. See, all the Whits die by their hundredth birthday. It's a family tradition. I been working on dying for the better part of a year, so that's why I'm taking short, shallow breaths and holding them as the sun warms my cheek.

Still, nothin'.

Just like that vacuum salesman got from me one time, after he vacuumed my whole house.

"Great Gran, you awake?"

I put on my glasses and sit up straight. I had been taking my early afternoon nap, worn out after protesting in the scooter parade, enjoying Lena Horne on the radio. It was a bit chilly in my bedroom in January, even with two space heaters and an electric blanket. I poke my left hand with my right forefinger. Cold as a corpse.

"Great Gran?"

My great granddaughter hates to enter my room without my answering. Every time, she's scared I'm dead. She's got a thing against dead bodies. I figure they ain't never bit me and so far, none has come back alive, so we ain't got a problem.

After she knocks, I always tell her she's safe. But you know how thirty-four-year olds are. They are sometimes very much like children.

"Come in," I say.

Estelle is my only great grandchild under thirty-five. The product of my daughter, Alma, God rest her soul, who birthed my granddaughter, Clara, the snorer in the other room, who birthed this beautiful gal.

She's got a full head of black hair, rich brown skin married from Georgia clay and New Jersey topsoil. I forgive her for her heritage problem. I'm not big on Northerners.

"How'd you sleep?" Estelle asks me.

"Well enough to stay alive."

Her stricken expression reminds me of someone captured in a picture when they've been asked to be a substitute teacher at the middle school. It's obvious they'd rather donate ten pints of blood.

"Great Gran, you know what you need? A job."

I focus my keen eyes on Estelle. "Have you been in my homemade soap again? That lye can be a very persuasive mind-altering drug. I'm a hundred-one. Not eighty-five. Working ain't really an option."

She laughs like I used to, all tinkly and sweet. "I learned my lesson about the soap, believe me. I just think, instead of you waiting for death every day, you might think about focusing your attention on something else. Something you can do in the community that will be of service to others."

"It's not enough that I used to ask Al Louis to take me to the grocery. Now that's community service! Retarded boys need jobs too."

"He's not retarded. He's just a little slow."

"That's the way I like my men," I say and smile.

"*Great Gran*," she admonishes, as if we don't know where babies come from. Younguns are the strangest creatures. They think they invented everything. Kissing, huggin', fornicating. My mama used to say all the good stuff's been done so you'd better take a lesson and enjoy yourself. I happen to agree.

Estelle is looking at me like I had a passel of men callers who didn't leave my house before 8:00 p.m. Now I believe in a lot of things, but it better happen before bedtime. I didn't live over a hundred years without getting my beauty rest.

"Estelle, if I have to tell you about the birds and the bees again, I'll make a flip chart."

Her lips shake like they do on people with too much coffee in their system. I recommend decaf, but she doesn't say anything. Her eyes flutter, and she waves her hands in the air.

"Great Gran, I was just thinking that maybe if you volunteered, you'd feel more fulfilled."

It was as if an alarm clock went off because my bladder started croaking like a Christmas goose. God bless Depends.

"I'll be right back. While I'm getting cleaned up and dressed, will you make sure my funeral dress is pressed? I can't go home to Jesus with it looking like a used brown paper bag. No, suh. I've got to be right. *Cain't nobody do me like Jesus, can't nobody do me like the Lord.*" I sing as I hurry.

A half hour later I'm washed, dressed and ready to meet Jesus, but nothin' happens, so I go to the kitchen to find me a snack.

Clara looks cross as I enter the kitchen on my walker with the two green tennis balls attached to the bottom. I love those darned things. Cousin Chicken and me used to have fun stealing them from the woods behind the high school. The old-timey tennis balls were wonderful toys but great missiles at the head of anyone who tried to hurt us. Those were the days. I sigh.

"What's this idea about you volunteering, Grandmama?" Clara says to me. "It's foolhardy. You simply cannot do it."

Now Clara is the hoity-toity one of our family. She wasn't raised in Mossy Creek like the other five generations of Whits. She was born here, but dragged up North when her mother found a teaching job in the capital of H-E-double-hockey-sticks, New Jersey.

Clara has a warped sense of the South and our lovely town, and everyday she's been here, I've tried to change that perception.

"Since when am I too old to help somebody?" I ask. "I suppose a life should only be fulfilling if you're eighty and under?"

Sometimes she gets on my nerves with her two-inch heels and sixty-six year old legs. I'd kill for those darned things. She's got all her real teeth, too. It's downright sickening that she doesn't show them off more instead of that salty look she always has on her face.

"No, Grandmama. That's not what I'm saying," Clara says with exaggerated patience. "You're old." She gags on the word, and I don't even try to stop her. "I just meant, what would you do?"

"There's lots of things," Estelle chimes in, sitting some cookies in front of me. "Great Gran could work at the Wal-Mart down in Bigelow."

"I've been there," I say, getting excited until I remember something. "'Cept, sometimes they play their announcements too loud, and when I complained to the manager, he told me to turn down my hearing aid. I should have caned him, but I didn't have my cane. And I don't have a hearing aid. 'Sides that, I didn't like that the senior center thinks it's funny to take us seniors to the Wal-Mart on a field trip on the first Tuesday of the month and leave us there. The last time I went, we were stuck there for an hour listenin' to some boogaloo music. 'Bout drove me crazy. I ain't never been so happy to leave a place. And I'm not going back."

"There's nothing for seniors to do in Mossy Creek on a regular basis," Clara points out. "So, I guess you're stuck with us."

That's a scary thought, considering I don't much care for her company. "I'll make you a bet, Clara."

"What is it?"

"I'll get a job if you get a job."

"What kind of bet is that?"

"One you'll lose if you don't find something to do besides make an old woman's life miserable with your boring self."

Clara flinches, but sometimes the truth hurts.

"You can't work," she says, "End of subject."

She ain't that hurt, I think as she walks outside. Frankly, I'm relieved. Estelle and I have more like minds than my Clara and me.

Estelle looks at me with her serious eyes. "I think we should get her a boyfriend. She's bored, that's all. I'll go get her."

"No. Let her find her own way, Estelle. She's searching for something and it has nothing to do with us. But that won't stop me from finding my own gig."

For the first time in a long time, I'm energized. Getting old in Mossy Creek has meant the world to me. I know this place like the back of my hand, and I've loved every second of being here. "Bring me a pen and paper," I say.

Estelle grabs them and sits across from me.

"Number the paper one through three."

"I thought you were going to do the writing," she says, a sly look on her face.

"Why should I when you're here and not at the coffee shop working?" Estelle works at the Naked Bean.

"Jayne gave me the day off. So, if you could pick a job, what would you like to do?"

"I'd be a cop like Amos. That's the number one job on my list. Put that down."

"Are you kidding?" Estelle asks, her eyes wide.

Now she sounds like Clara. I think over what I just said and give her a definitive nod. "Yes, I want to be a cop in Mossy Creek. In fact, after we make the list, I think I'll give Amos a call and have a chat with that man about some changes that need to be made around here. Number two, I'd be a street-sign maker." The pen teeters in Estelle's hand and I point. "That's an important job. Yes, suh!"

"Great Gran, I don't know about that. You have to have some experience in the area you're trying to work in."

I lick my last real tooth and smile. "The only people that need to have experience are doctors and people who pave roads. The rest is up for grabs."

I think of all the signs I'd make. "I'd make a sign for the boys that were smokin' behind the Piggly Wiggly last month. I was coming from JoRay Cummings' funeral in Bigelow, and Clara had to stop at the store. I told her we didn't need to park in the handicap parking space, but she pulled in anyway. I guess it was divine intervention, because I see these boys behind the store smokin'."

"What's wrong with that?"

"Nothin' 'cept they was sharing a cigarette. Passin' it back and forth. I just shook my head. If you can't afford to kill yourself by buying your own pack of cigarettes, you can't afford to smoke. Don't share with your friends. That's just plain unsanitary. Besides, the only decent tobacco is peach snuff. I don't care what I said at New Year's, I'm not giving up my snuff. And the next time Katie Bell writes something about my snuff, I'm gonna spit on her. Spit peach snuff."

Estelle's eyes tear and she starts gasping, then coughing uncontrollably.

"Chil', let me get you some water. It wouldn't be fair if you died before me."

She sips the water I give her, and that's when I notice there's nothing on the paper. Although my body is fragile, my mind is sharp as a shark fin. But sometimes I forget. I guess it's a by-product of being on earth long enough to know everybody's business.

"Estelle, write this down. Cop, sign-maker and last but not least, mayor."

This time she spits water all over the table. I give her the evil eye. "You're too old for that nonsense. Spitting your water out like you're a child."

"Great Gran." She mops the table, not looking at me. "None of these jobs are suited for you."

"And why in the Sam Hill not?"

"Who's Sam Hill?" Estelle asks.

This girl has the attention span of a gnat. I need to get her ginkgo biloba.

"A man with a job, I'm sure. Explain yourself, young lady."

"Great Gran, these jobs are very physical. Very demanding. And they require you to meet certain standards."

"You were the one with the big idea that I needed a job.

Now I'm excited, and I thought you'd be excited, too. But if you're not, you can join Clara down the road. I've got to get dressed for work."

"I'm with you, Great Gran," she assures me. "All the way."

"Good. Now get dressed, we're headin' to town."

❦ ❦ ❦

In my room, I dial the phone, hoping Amos will pick up over at the police station. Ever since my granddaughter moved in here with me, she's modernized things. We now have a computer and a printer. Between the loud motor on the printer and Clara's snoring, you get the impression that she has to get oxygen from New Mexico.

But worse than that is the confounded phone. When I'm mayor, I'm going to pass a law that says everybody in Mossy Creek has to have at least one rotary phone in the home. That way, senior citizens are covered. Clara insisted on a push-button thing, but I don't like it. My fingers always press the wrong button and I end up calling someone I don't know. After I talk to them for a half hour, I can't ever remember who I was calling and why.

I finally had Estelle dig up my old rotary phone, and it's in my room with old me. We're perfect together. I dial and get it right the first time.

"Mossy Creek Police Department, how can I assist you?"

"Amos?"

"No, Miz Whit. This is Sandy."

"I don't want to talk to you, I want to talk to Amos."

"He's on his way back from Atlanta. He had to go down there to ... hmmm ... nevermind. He's not here right now, Miz Whit."

"Get him on the phone. I know he's got one of them cell

phones. I called him in his car once, by accident."

"All right, Miz Whit. Hold on. I'll transfer you."

I smile. When you get to be over a hundred years old, the police don't even try to argue with you. They just give you what you want. I hear a beep. Amos says, real polite, "Hello, Miz Eula." I hear road sounds in the background. He's driving.

"Hello, Amos. How you today?"

"I'm having an ... interesting day, Miz Eula. How are you?"

"I'm not dead yet, so I guess I'm fair to middlin".

I don't hear him for a moment, then he says, "Good. What can I do for you?"

"Amos, I need a job. And I decided that being a police officer is right up my alley. When can I start?"

Amos must have swallowed down the wrong pipe, just like Estelle, because he starts coughing like a hound dog during huntin' season. He manages to grouse, "Just a minute," and the phone hits something. Poor young folk. They eat too fast and the food gets stuck. Old people know better.

Finally Amos comes back. "Hello?"

"Are you all right? You shouldn't eat while you drive."

"Yes, ma'am. Now, about —"

"Estelle had the same coughing fit a while ago too. I hope you two don't have an adult version of the whooping cough. That would be terrible."

"Miz Eula, why do you want to work?"

I figure this is the interview phase of the job. "I been sittin' around in retirement for twenty-one years waiting for Jesus to call me home, but so far, nothin'. So I'm thinkin' maybe He has something else for me to do. I'm especially excited about carrying a gun."

Another round of coughing hits the police chief, and

he finally regains his composure. "Miz Eula, I hate to tell you this, but there are certain requirements to being a police officer. And I'm afraid you exceed those require- ments in so many areas, we wouldn't be able to afford your services."

My hopes deflate like a three-day-old birthday bal- loon.

"I'm too old?"

"Yes," Amos says honestly, "But you're smart and wise, Miz Eula, and that's what every police department needs. The other thing is, we have to apprehend criminals. Those criminals want to get away, and they'll do anything to escape arrest, including hurt officers. Nobody wants to see you hurt."

The idea of getting hurt didn't occur to me. Frankly, I just don't think about crime in Mossy Creek as being seri- ous.

"Amos, when was the last time you had to use your gun?"

"Well, that's not the point —"

"And when was the last time you were in a fist fight?"

"Does throwing an angry woman over my shoulder count?"

"When? What'd I miss? Do tell!"

"Forget I mentioned that. You win, Miz Eula. I admit it: I haven't ever had a fist fight on the job in Mossy Creek."

"So what do you do all day?" I say, so far unimpressed with his ability to protect and serve.

"I'm busy day and night stopping people from com- mitting crimes. As a matter-of-fact, I'd better get back to work. I have a criminal in the back seat of my patrol car, right now."

I hear a high-pitched voice in the background. Sounds like somebody saying bad words.

"That a woman?" I ask Amos. "Did you arrest her for talkin' that way?"

"I have to go. Bye, Miz Eula."

"Bye, Amos."

I get up off my bed, change clothes and go to the living room where Estelle is reading the paper.

"You ready?"

"What did Amos say?" Estelle asks me.

"Not what I hoped, but there's another good job out there for me. Let's go to the bank. I drop in occasionally to make sure they still have all my money safe and sound."

"Great Gran, it's a bank, that's what they do."

"You obviously don't watch *Cops*. Sometimes, bad guys can be very sneaky."

❦❦❦

As Estelle and I drive through Mossy Creek, I love the pretty browns and grays of wintertime.

Even though a hundred years has passed since I first laid eyes on this town, it's still beautiful to me.

People stop and wave as we drive by the courthouse, the center of town and the square, where the Methodists are selling food and knickknacks to heathens. Even there, everybody stops long enough to wave.

I'm the oldest soul in Mossy Creek. I feel honored by the tradition and the show of respect.

"Drive over to the bank, and afterwards, we'll go to the sign store. They make copies there, too," I tell Estelle, who's been unusually quiet since we left home. "I could run a copy machine."

We park next to the blue-lined handicap space at Mossy Creek Savings and Loan, which is appropriate since I'm feeling quite spry for an old gal. I get my seat belt unbuckled, and try to untangle myself from the contraption. "I should work for the car builders. This thing is like a prison."

"Great Gran, don't get your hopes up about a bank job."

I regard my great granddaughter. "Would you recommend I get my hopes down or have no hope at all?"

"I just don't want you to be disappointed or sad."

"Estelle, you use those words about things that have so little significance. Sad is when your children die before you and you have to live on without them. Disappointed is when you live a life and don't find joy in the precious moments it gives you. If I don't get a job, then so be it, but I'll never feel sad about it. Now, let's go check on my money. Get my cane. I might have to stand in line."

Estelle and I make our way to the door of the bank, when a young man hurries toward us from the inside. He opens the door and as we start to pass through, so does he. Doesn't even take down the hood on his jacket. After having people be respectful during my drive to the bank, I'm not about to let him ruin that record.

"Excuse me, son," I say to the hooded fella. "You can be on your way as soon as you open that other door for me. I'm not as strong as I used to be, and I can't manage the cane and the door at the same time."

I look him in the eye and wait for an answer. He hops from foot to foot like he's considering my request or has to go to the bathroom.

"Great Gran," Estelle says from behind me, "I'll get it."

Just as I'm about to launch into my being a good steward speech, he reaches for the door handle.

I smile at him, victorious. I knew there was good in this young man. "No, thank you, Estelle, this young man has proven there is community service in every person alive. Thank you very kindly."

It takes a few minutes, as I'm not as fast as I used to be.

When we finally get inside, every eye is on us. Nobody in the bank is moving. I nod hello to the tellers and the head finance man, Rick Ramsey.

The young man hurries down the sidewalk outside, and I go sit down to wait my turn.

Rick rushes to the door and locks it.

Suddenly Mutt Bottoms is outside and he has the young man with his face smashed against the glass, putting handcuffs on him!

"What happened?" I ask, mortified.

Estelle grips my hand as the president comes over and sits down. "You just caught a criminal, Ms. Eula. That man had just robbed the bank. You slowed him down until Officer Bottoms could catch him. You're a hero."

Estelle applauds. "Great Gran! I can't believe it."

I'm so shocked, I don't know what to say. Suddenly there's clapping and lots of it. I begin to clap myself, I'm so excited. This was better than watching *Cops*, because I was a real, live, criminal catcher.

That's just dandy, in my eyes.

"So I guess this means you're giving me a job," I tell Rick.

After a wide-eyed second, he gives up and smiles. "I'm making you an honorary bank guard," he says.

I look at Estelle. And stick out my tongue.

I got me a job.

VOLUME V, NO. SIX   **MOSSY CREEK, GEORGIA**

Meetings & Announcements

The Mossy Creek Garden Club invites everyone to a winter gardening seminar at the Hamilton Inn. Main speaker: Peggy Caldwell, retired English professor, fan of murder mysteries, and creator of an award-winning specialty garden.

Topic: Plants To Die For. Beautiful But Deadly Perennials.

Tickets still available. Open bar. Non-toxic buffet courtesy of Bubba Rice Catering.

*You can always count on cats and grandchildren
to surprise you.*

Peggy and the Wildflowers
Chapter 12

My garden problem started in October, but I wasn't aware of the ramifications until January.

I was stretched out in my outside lounger under the big tree halfway down my backyard, when I caught sight of my granddaughter headed for trouble.

"Josie, no!" I yelped. I struggled up— those things invariably attempt to trap me in a supine position forever— ran down the hill and caught the waistband of my granddaughter's jeans just as she reached the top of the gate to my walled garden. She wriggled like a greased pig.

"No, Grammie!" she howled as I hauled her off and set her down. "It's my secret place. I want to play in there."

"No, you don't, Miss Josephine Margaret. We have talked and talked about my garden. It's Gram's special garden, and it's not a place for little girls."

I could tell by the set of her jaw that she wasn't buying it. Josie has a special way of dealing with 'no.' She seems to accept, but a minute later, she'll come back with, "But, Grammie, if we ... then can I ... " Another no. Another acceptance, and then another two minutes later another convoluted plan that will allow her to have her way. She doesn't fight. She simply manipulates circumstances until she hits on a set that will work for whatever adult she's conning at the time.

I knew darned well that she'd keep on bugging me about my garden until I let her in. If I didn't, then she'd climb over the gate when I was distracted. Next time I might not catch her before she managed it.

As my garden stood at the moment, I couldn't possibly allow her inside.

I am not a born gardener. As a matter of fact, my thumb is as black as basalt. If plants actually react to human beings, mine must shriek when they see me coming. I am a retired English professor whose husband plumped the two of us down in a 1940s English Tudor house set on slightly less than two acres in Mossy Creek, and promptly died on me. I haven't forgiven him.

The little walled garden at the back of the yard had been the pride and joy of the old lady, Astrid Ogilvie, who lived in the house before we bought it. Astrid had been a leading light of the local garden club. After she died at ninety-six and we bought the house, they recruited me out of desperation. I warned them I make Rappacini's daughter look like the Goddess of the Bountiful Harvest. All I really wanted to do was to sit in my paneled library with my grumpy old cat Dashiell and read murder mysteries, preferably British.

Instead, I was co-opted to join the local garden rivalry between Mossy Creek and Bigelow. I thought and thought about what sort of garden to plant. Then it came to me. I had read stories in which the victim was dispatched by a distillation of foxglove or henbane or hemlock, but I had no idea what those plants actually looked like. So I planted my poison garden. All of my plants would make you very sick. A number would kill you.

We won the contest that year, not precisely because of my unusual garden, but because the governor's mother-in-law was disqualified for growing opium poppies on the lawn of the governor's mansion. Somehow she blamed me, though Lord only knows why.

In the next few years, the garden club coached me

so that I could actually keep a small stand of Shasta daisies living outside my back door. Not thriving precisely, although Shasta daisies have been known to overrun an entire community. They not only riot through a garden, they commit rapine and pillage among less hardy plants. Mine were anemic, but alive. A distinct improvement over my excursion into philodendron, which shriveled and gave up the ghost no matter how often I watered and fed it. I've since been told that feeding philodendron is like feeding goldfish. Too little and it dies. Too much and it dies. My philodendron wound up in the garbage can and not in the toilet floating on its back like a dead goldfish. The end result, however, was the same.

The plants in my poison garden, however, were positively thriving. They seemed to realize that both they and I were the pariahs of the gardening world. I had become quite fond of them. Foxglove and autumn crocus are beautiful, if deadly.

You can see why I didn't dare allow Josie, my one and only grandchild, to crawl over the gate to the poison garden and wander amongst the oleander and castor beans. Children that age eat anything they can stuff into their mouths. They do not understand the concept of toxicity.

I spent the rest of the afternoon reading to Josie and keeping a weather eye on her to make certain she didn't attempt to climb my gate again. When her mother, my daughter, Marilee Bigelow, came to pick her up, I didn't mention the incident. Neither did Josie.

The moment I waved Marilee's car out of my driveway, I went to the garage for my big, wheeled garbage can, grabbed a hoe, a spade and my gardening gloves, and headed for the poison garden. The key to the gate hung from a wrought iron hook high on the stone wall just inside gate where I could reach it easily, but I didn't think small hands could locate it. Obviously, that wasn't sufficient to insure Josie's safety. My hemlock and wolfsbane and autumn crocus had to go.

In a way it was an execution. I certainly felt like an executioner. The plants were condemned for their very natures. I actually felt tears sting my eyes as I ripped and tore and rooted the poor things from their beds. By the time I finished I was drenched with perspiration, bitten by mosquitoes and midges, and aching as though I had lifted weights. I was also sobbing. Like the wicked witch in The *Wizard of Oz*, I kept chanting, "All my beautiful evil." The dying plants seemed to reproach me from the depths of the trash can.

I wheeled it up to the road where the garbage men would collect it. I certainly didn't want to burn the plants. The fumes would probably fell half of Mossy Creek.

Of course, it wasn't that easy. It never is with plants.

The following Friday when Josie came to spend the day with me, I took her by the hand, walked down to the garden, unlocked the gate and let us both in. I had no intention of allowing her to stay or to play there unsupervised, of course, but maybe if I demystified the place for her, she wouldn't push so hard to make it her own secret place.

I was astounded to see green shoots springing up in the raised flower beds I had built around all four sides of the garden. I had thought the cool nights of October would finish the job I had started. Evidently not.

I had coaxed and cajoled my poison plants into thriving. They did not intend to stay dead. Even more worrisome, at their immature stage I couldn't differentiate the mildly toxic from the deadly.

I hadn't been able to cut down the castor bean tree by myself. In October, the bean pods were falling. Josie was fascinated by them, but swore she wouldn't go near them under any circumstances. I cajoled her into leaving the garden with a promise of milk and cookies.

That tree had to go, and quickly. I co-opted my son-in-law Claude Bigelow, a stuffy Bigelow but better than most of them, to do the job for me. For some reason, he has decided I am in the final stages of decrepitude and falls all over himself trying to be helpful. I seldom let him, but that day he truly was a lifesaver. He cut down and hauled the dead tree away with him and treated the stump so that it wouldn't reemerge on its own— something I would never have thought to do. He promised to find someone to grind it out of the ground for me after it dried out.

Now, if I can just get him to call me plain ol' Peggy instead of "Mother Margaret." Makes me sound as if I run a nunnery.

Next, I had to find a way to keep my nasty little beauties from reemerging.

I didn't want to salt the earth the way the Romans did at Carthage. I wanted my garden to grow again, but wholesomely. If Josie wanted her secret garden, then she must have it. Somehow.

I am not by nature a grandmother any more than I ever was a mother or a gardener. For one thing, I came to both late. I am not one of those women who has a child at eighteen, then becomes a grandmother at thirty-six when *her* child has a child at eighteen in her turn. I finished my Ph.D. dissertation before I got pregnant, and I worked as an English instructor at one of the local community colleges while my daughter matured. She and her husband waited until she was thirty-one to produce Josie.

I was afraid I wouldn't be able to keep up with Josie as she grew up and I grew older, so I had recently taken up bicycling and doing Pilates twice a week at the gym in Mossy Creek. I was in better shape physically than I had been in twenty years. As a matter of fact, the present day *me* could probably have beaten the stew out of the me I had been at thirty.

Still, redoing that garden was going to be more than I could handle alone.

So I called in the troops. I assembled the "gardeneers" of the Mossy Creek Garden club in my den by promising them frozen daiquiris.

"Herbs," Eleanor Abercrombie said. Eleanor grows superb roses. Obviously she thought they were beyond my capability. She says each one is like having another child because they require so much work. "Definitely herbs."

"*Some* herbs," Mimsy said. Since Mimsy grows a magnificent herb garden, I had every intention of following her lead. "No pennyroyal or valerian or laurel."

"Or feverfew," Erma said. "I think you're safe with basil and oregano."

"And garlic." That from Mimsy.

"*Some* kinds of garlic. Wild garlic is terribly toxic."

"The best thing would be to grow vegetables," said Eustene Oscar. "Simple things a child can enjoy watching grow and then can eat. Carrots, radishes, zucchini— they're all simple."

"Josie would consider those completely inedible," I said.

"If she grows them, she'll eat them, I guarantee it," Eustene said. She should know. She has plenty of grandchildren. "You can grow tomatoes. All children love tomatoes and they are relatively foolproof even for you. Maybe even a watermelon vine on the sunny side."

The ladies of the club did not wear hats with flowers or lace collars or liberty print dresses or wear white cotton gloves. They wore serviceable duck shorts or jeans and t-shirts with such slogans as "Gardeners do it with flowers," and "Beer is for slugs, not people."

Throughout the meeting, all eighteen pounds of my grumpy old cat, Dashiell, glared at us from the top of one of my bookshelves. He is a Maine Coon cat who does not like visitors. He prefers solitude and silence. The only noise he enjoys is the sound of the can opener.

Josie adored him. He tolerated her. Her parents did not approve of mixing pets with young children, so he was the only pet she had access to. Somehow, even at three she understood that she must be gentle with Dashiell. She never rubbed his fur the wrong way or pulled his ears or tail. In return he rewarded her by curling up on the foot of her little trundle bed when she napped or slept over.

Josie realized even before I did that our happy relationship necessitated keeping as much as possible from her parents. When my daughter gave me detailed instructions about Josie's regimen, I generally nodded agreement, then Josie and I did what we liked. Chocolate cake at lunch didn't seem to bother either of us.

Josie never told on me, and I never revealed the havoc she'd created when she knocked an entire canister of flour onto the kitchen floor and poured a glass of milk on top of it, or had a temper tantrum and screamed herself blue in the face when I refused to give her Rocky Road ice cream as her entire dinner. That happened when she was two. When I ignored her, she gave up in disgust and never tried that again.

This *tacit entente* between us, however, made it incumbent upon me to see that so long as she was under my care, she was safe.

I thanked the garden club ladies, accepted gratefully the books on growing herbs they lent me, sat down to read up on things like black cohosh, and promptly fell asleep. Later that evening, Ida, the mayor, called me. "Herbs are okay, Peggy, but what you really need to plant are wildflowers. They're so easy, even you can do it."

"Thank you very much."

"You know what I mean. You buy packets of wildflowers — lots of packets. Then you mix up the seeds in a coffee can — two parts sand to one part wildflowers. Then you broadcast them. Josie will love that. If they don't wind up in the flower beds, who cares?"

"I'd have to wait until spring."

"No, you wouldn't. Wild flowers do best if planted in the fall. They winter over through snow, ice, and weather that would kill most plants, then come spring and summer they emerge happy and healthy as all get out."

"So I could plant them now?"

"You should also plant some bulbs — jonquil and wild iris, for example. I would suggest you take Josie down to Tom Anglin's store and let her pick out packets of seed. Eustene says she'll volunteer one of her boys to cultivate your beds and mulch them. Then you just mix and toss. How does that sound?"

"Perfect." Surely wildflowers would crowd out any noxious seedlings that tried to rear their ugly little heads. So that Saturday, Josie and I went to Mossy Creek Hardware and Gardening to choose our packets.

Josie loved the idea so much she went hog wild. With the help of Tom's assistant, Mr. Rufus, she nearly filled one of the baskets they keep down there. While I selected some bulbs that looked fairly standard, she gaily flung in packets of anemones, ageratum, bachelor's buttons — on down the alphabet.

Even at three she could read Dr. Seuss and most of the Sunday comics with a bit of help, but she wasn't up to big words like "coreopsis," so she chose by the photos on the packets. I didn't want to disabuse her of the notion that any plant I cared for would look remotely like the photos. Time enough for that come spring.

Josie was running around like a chicken with its head cut off. It was all I could do to keep up with her. I couldn't yell at her. All her squeals were happy ones.

Finally, however, I had to say, "Josie, that's enough!"

She gave me two sets of 'but Grammie's,' and I saw her surreptitiously grab a couple more packets of seeds, but by and large, she took it well.

She wanted to plant immediately, of course, but I explained that we had to rake and hoe (and incidentally, yank out any remaining bits and pieces of my poison garden), and that we'd plant on the following Saturday.

By the time I put her down for her nap, I needed one considerably more than she did. I knew she was disappointed, because from her bedroom, I heard her very quietly singing "Twinkle, twinkle, little star," to herself over and over again. The song was Josie's combination mantra and teddy bear. She sang it to herself when she was tired, or bored, or frightened.

Eventually her singing petered out, and I knew she was asleep. I also knew when Dashiell deserted my lap and meandered into Josie's room to snuggle up the crook of her knees.

The following Saturday, we planted. Josie had a high old time flinging sand and seeds as hard and as far as she could into the raised beds on all four sides of my walled garden. I tried to remember to call it "the wildflower garden" instead of "the poison garden," but old habits die hard.

At the center of the garden was a large square brick patio on which sat a wrought iron table and four wrought iron chairs. From the tossing Josie did, I suspected we'd have plenty of wildflowers growing in the spaces between the bricks come May, but I didn't really care, so long as Josie could play there safely.

We didn't actually have to water the garden. As a matter of fact, the heavens attempted to float the darned thing away. Whenever Josie came over, the first place she wanted to go was to the garden to check on the progress of her wildflowers. I told her that the shoots would die in the first hard freeze, but that they'd come back in the spring.

We had a remarkably warm autumn, so the little shoots really got going. About a month after we broadcast them, I noticed something odd about Dashiell. At first I didn't pay much attention, but as the days went by, I came to the conclusion that at his age, he might be experiencing a nervous breakdown.

Dashiell has always been an indoor cat. Even if Dr. Blackshear and I didn't both believe that the outdoors is dangerous for cats, Dashiell has no front claws, so he couldn't climb a tree or defend himself against a Rottweiler, and he's so fat that he couldn't outrun a turtle. He has always been completely content in his indoor domain.

The closest he has ever come to considering the outside as a remote possibility happened last year when a demented male cardinal insisted on banging its head into my French door over and over. I'm not certain whether Dashiell wanted to kill and eat him simply because he was a bird, or because the continuing bonk disturbed his nap. In any case, he sat just inside the French door and chittered at the bird in impotent fury. I hope the poor thing didn't breed, because no doubt his offspring will be brain-damaged. Eventually, after mating and fighting season, he left, and Dashiell settled back into his somnolent existence.

Now every evening, he took to sitting beside the French door with his tail thrashing, gurgling and chattering with impotent rage. Maine Coons have long fur, and Dashiell's tail puffed up to the size of a feather duster. Several times I peered out, but could see nothing. The one time I took a flashlight and opened the door, Dashiell actually tried to edge past me to get outside. The door bopped him on the nose, and he was furious at me for the rest of the evening.

I decided there must be a possum or a raccoon or even a couple of squirrels invading what he considered his territory.

Then one evening, I heard a bloodcurdling shriek and ran in from my kitchen to find Dashiell nose-to-nose with a yellow cat that made Dashiell look like a kitten. Only the glass separated them. Thank God it was safety glass, because both combatants launched themselves at one another with a thud.

I hesitated to grab Dashiell. He's been known to attack anything that touches him when he's concentrating, which he definitely was.

The minute I banged on the door and shouted 'shoo,' the semi-lion ran away into the dusk. For a solid hour Dashiell stalked around the house with his fur fluffed out and his tail high.

Over the next few days, I began to notice that Dashiell spent most of his time at that window, and all too often, his tail was lashing. I took to taking extra care when I went out onto the back porch because Dashiell had developed a mania to get outside.

Several times when I did go outside I caught small shapes either gliding or pelting across my yard.

One evening I called Hank Blackshear and said, "Doc, I have a problem."

"Dashiell all right?" he asked. Dashiell barely tolerated him, but he was fast and experienced. Dashiell had never managed to connect with either teeth or claws.

"He's having a nervous breakdown," I said, and explained the circumstances. "I have lived in this house over four years, and I have never had a problem with feral cats, but that's what they are. Wild as March hares. They slink or bolt or tear off the moment I crack the back door a smidgen. Dashiell is desperately trying to get outside and at them. Lord knows what a wild cat with claws would do to him."

"Any idea why they showed up now?"

"None in the world. I don't know whether to start to feed them, and therefore turn them into a permanent problem, or to try to trap them and bring them to you for shots and neutering."

"That would cost a fortune, Peg, and you'd never catch all of them."

"My granddaughter, Josie, plays over here at least once or twice a week. I can't have her bitten or scratched. What if they're rabid?"

"No rabies in this part of the world, but there are other nasties. Listeria, for one, or cat-scratch fever. She's unlikely to get close enough to any of them for disease to be a problem for *her*."

"What about Dashiell? What about me, for that matter?"

"Dashiell's had every shot known to man, and so long as you keep him inside, he's not going to come in contact with his feral buddies." He hesitated. "There's always poison, you know, if they become a real hazard."

"Are you nuts? I just got rid of my poison plants because of Josie. How do you think I could put poison bait out? Even if I could, I wouldn't. That's a terrible idea! I'm ashamed of you."

He laughed. "I thought you'd say that. Look, they don't seem to be starving, so they must be existing on mice and snakes ..."

"And song birds."

"Yes, and song birds. I would suggest leaving them alone for now. Maybe once the females are in kit, they'll go find somewhere else to raise their babies."

"But don't count on it?"

"Right, don't count on it. Keep me posted."

That's where we left it. I hung up the telephone and hauled Dashiell, who was at present in one of his somnolent modes, into my lap and stroked him. "Nature really is red of tooth and claw, old guy. We have to make certain none of the blood is yours, mine, or Josie's."

Next I noticed that the cats that frequented my yard weren't invariably feral. My neighbors don't necessarily agree with me that all family cats should be kept indoors, but even though the Persian (neutered) from a block over, and the Johnson's two Siamese females came and went as they saw fit, they had never seen fit to come within spitting distance of Dashiell.

Now nearly every afternoon I found them lolling on my back deck. Oddly enough, Dashiell didn't seem to have a problem with them, as though he knew they were people cats and therefore entitled to some slack.

He still chittered, however, every time the humongous yellow tom came around. I finally gave in and started putting feed out for them all under the back porch.

Of course, Josie wanted to play with them. I told her that the feral cats were wild. She soon discovered that on her own. One afternoon she chased a small black cat who looked as though she were pregnant and entirely too young to be having babies. Even in her advanced stage of pregnancy, the little mama easily outdistanced Josie.

We had taken to spending every pleasant afternoon down in Josie's secret garden. I had tried to ride herd on Josie's selection of seed packets, but she had gotten away from me. Several of the shoots I couldn't identify.

They shriveled during December, and even Josie forgot her garden in the joys of Christmas. We had a rare snowy yuletide, and Dashiell was happy to be indoors. He even settled down, and the feral cats seemed to have abandoned us. I worried about them in the cold weather, but there wasn't much I could do.

Wouldn't you know, the weekend that I agreed to keep Josie from Friday through Sunday so that Marilee and Claude could go off to Lake Lanier to a house party, we had a major storm front slide in. The weather was cold and clear, but forecasters said we might get rain and possibly sleet before the weekend was out. The best thing to do in weather like that is to stay indoors, keep the television set going and flashlights close by, in case the power goes out.

I had taught Marilee not to fear either the dark or storms. In my day, before weather reporting began to be so accurate, we could enjoy a good ice or thunderstorm without worrying so much about whether there was a tornado on the ground in the next block.

Now I was teaching Josie. We always spoke together of 'the friendly dark.' Although I kept a night light on in the hall and the bathroom, Josie had resolutely refused one in her room. I suspect watching *Monsters,Inc.*, about a hundred times helped many children get over their night fears. As a matter of fact, they probably slipped into their closets in hopes of finding something cuddly.

Late Saturday afternoon, however, darkness had closed us in early, and the temperature dropped even further. Josie crept into my lap and leaned her head back against me while she watched cartoons — something I seldom allowed — and I read the storm crawl across the bottom of the screen. We began to have lightning — a rare occurrence in the winter.

I had taught her to count the seconds from the flash to the boom so that she could tell how far away the lightning was from us. Under her breath I could hear her counting, "One-one-thousand — two-one-thousand — three-one-thousand. Oooh!" As she heard the crack. Several times she sang under her breath, "Twinkle, twinkle little star, how I wonder what you are." That was a sure sign that she was nervous.

Dashiell was also more nervous than usual, although I saw no sign of his buddies on the back porch outside the French window.

I had decided that this would be a good night for pizza, Josie's absolutely favorite meal. I buy a pizza at Piggly Wiggly, then fix it up with extra mozzarella and pepperoni. I left Josie watching some Japanese cartoon with a big-eyed child who could fly, while I fixed the pizza.

I had just put it into the oven, when Josie came flying into the kitchen.

"Grammie, Grammie, come quick!" She grabbed my hand and pulled me into the den.

"What's the matter, baby?"

"It's Dashiell, Grammie!" Her face looked stricken. Her eyes were enormous. "He got out."

"He what?"

She shrank from me. "The little black cat came up on the porch. I wanted to pet her." She shuffled her feet and whispered, "I just opened the door a tee-ninesy bit."

"Stay here," I snapped. I opened the door to the back porch. The wind cut through me. The trees were flapping in the wind, and I could smell ice on the way. I called "Dashiell!" over and over again. I ran down the back steps and almost tripped in the dark. If he'd been chasing the black cat, Dashiell could be halfway to downtown Mossy Creek in two minutes. He's old, but he can still run when he wants to.

Josie tried to come after me. "Don't you move!" I snapped at her.

Dashiell wouldn't be able to hear me above the sound of the wind. Although it was barely five o'clock, the light was already fading. I ran through the yard calling for him. He must be terrified. Once outside, he'd have no idea how to shelter from the wind he'd never felt before.

He knew nothing about streets and cars. I ran around the house and up and down the street praying I wouldn't find his little body. Then I ran back all the way to the alley fence line. I checked the hidden garden too. I called again and again, but neither saw nor heard him.

I even crawled under the back porch in the mud hoping

he'd taken shelter there. Again nothing. I hadn't stopped to pick up a jacket, so by the time I climbed the stairs to the pack porch I was shaking.

Oh, Dashiell! He'd never survive a night like this alone and afraid.

Then I saw Josie standing just inside the door. I had never been truly angry with her before. I didn't touch her. I don't believe in using violence against children. In my heart I knew she hadn't intended to cause harm, but she had willfully disobeyed me, and in doing so she might well have caused injury or even death to Dashiell.

Her thoughtless action could have terrible consequences.

I think she was expecting me to scream or rant or cry. That's what Marilee does when she gets upset, and she upsets easily. I, on the other hand, almost never become angry, but when I do, it is a cold anger.

"I'm sorry, Grammie, I'm sorry," she wailed.

I didn't dare speak to her, but went to the telephone and called my neighbors. Their cats were all safe indoors. They promised to keep an eye out for Dashiell. "I'm afraid he'll be run over in the street," I said to Mrs. Johnson. "Or be torn to bits by that blasted yellow tomcat."

She tried to reassure me that he'd find his way home. If he didn't, we'd put up posters in the morning. "It's all we can do," she said.

When I hung up, I realized I could smell the pizza. It was more than due to come out of the oven.

Josie ate two bites of her pizza. I didn't manage that much. She kept jumping up and running to the door to look out. She didn't ask me to read her a book. I helped her bathe, put on her pj's and tucked her in early. We both knew this was no ordinary night.

As I closed the door of her room, I could hear her sobs.

To: Honey Lyman

From: Katie

Honey —

I agree with you wholeheartedly.
Something was in the air
on Saturday. It was a day
for ... changes of heart.
Transformations. Fresh starts.
Okay. I'll just say it.

Miracles.

I've read the story you sent
me. The one about what happened
to you and Bert and the kids.
You asked me to give my honest
opinion of it, so here you go:

Yes. Yes. Yes. Your sister's
children will love it. When
they're old enough, sit them down
in a quiet spot, and read it to
them. Tell them it's your words,
but their mother's spirit. Yes, I

think our loved ones can speak
to us after they've passed
from this world. Maybe not in
voices we always recognizes,
but they do send messages. I
believe your sister wanted you
to write this story for her.
I believe she whispered it in
your ear.

And I believe you'll be
speaking for her, speaking her
heart, when you share it with
her twins.

Darn it, Honey, reading this
story made me cry. Me. A tough
gossip columnist. Crying.

Keep this up, and you
could ruin my journalistic
reputation.

Your friend,
Katie

Love lives on.

Gone, But Not Forgetting
Chapter 13

I should have gone back to Mossy Creek for a visit sooner. Like maybe before I died. Then my twin baby girls would have met their aunt and uncle, Bert and Honey Lyman, while Cam and I were still around to ease them into the relationship. And maybe now they wouldn't be screaming at Honey while she laid them into car carriers in the back of her beat-up '92 Pontiac Lemans.

Shoot, my sister Honey hadn't even met their daddy. And no, it's not what you're thinking — it wasn't my husband who'd kept me from going back to see my sister for five years. From the time I met Cameron Ross, an executive at the San Francisco movie studio where I did voice-over work for cartoons and commercials, to the day we had the twins, he'd wanted to meet my family.

They would have liked him, too, if only because of how he'd taken to me. Just as an example, my specialty at the studio was a Southern accent. I know, I know, but hey, a woman born and raised in Mossy Creek whose accent was thicker than syrup had to start somewhere. Even so, I always worried about it sounding too countrified, but Cam thought it was "sultry." Go figure. He found everything I did "warm" or "cute" or "adorable." You've gotta love a man like that.

Anyway, it wasn't Cam's fault I didn't go back. Or Honey's either, for that matter. Honey and I were close, even if we did live on opposite coasts. We weren't the kind of sisters who called each other up once a year to exchange stilted "how are you's" and excuses about why we had no time to write. We were the in-your-face kind, always intruding on each other's lives.

She'd send me articles torn out of *Ladies Home Journal* about how to make a Thanksgiving centerpiece with just a burlap sack, some chickpea hulls, and pumpkin-orange ribbon, and I'd send her a cappuccino machine. Even though I knew she could be at the Naked Bean in five minutes to get her own cappuccino.

It was easier than sending myself.

But I was here now, and not exactly by choice. All because me and Cam hadn't made a will. We kept putting it off until we had time. After that freaking bus hit us on the one night we hired a babysitter so we could go to the movies, the time factor became pretty much irrelevant.

After the accident, Cam had floated right on up the tunnel and into the light — he was sensible that way. You don't get to be an executive, even in the movie business, by breaking the rules.

But me, Miss Ever-Loving Rule Breaker, I was still here. I couldn't let go of Amy and Anna, especially when I knew where they were going. To be raised by our only living kin, Honey and Bert, in the same house as the Demon Child: Jeremy Albert Lyman.

Where was Jeremy anyway on this uncharacteristically icy Georgia afternoon? Why hadn't he gone with Bert to the airport to pick up Honey and the babies? Had she finally come to her senses and sent my severely autistic nephew to an institution? Or at least placed him in a group home?

"How was your flight?" Bert asked Honey from the driver's seat.

She flashed him a crooked smile. "How do you think? I had two babies with me."

"Couldn't have been worse than flying with Jeremy."

"Want to bet?" She smiled. "Actually, they weren't too bad. At least they only screamed at takeoff."

"So the other passengers weren't cheering when you got off the plane?"

She laughed weakly. "No, thank heaven. I hope I never have to go through that again. Although with the way Jeremy has improved, these days I think he might actually behave well on a plane."

I snorted. That was Honey's latest tall tale — how much better Jeremy had gotten since my last visit. I didn't believe it for one minute.

"You look tired," Bert said.

Honey pulled down the car visor to examine her face in the inset mirror. "I guess I do."

She should have tromped on the fool's foot. A man ought to know better than to say something like that to his wife. Especially a sweet guy like Bert, who bought Honey roses whenever she cooked him a roast because "roast is a lot of trouble to make."

Maybe that's why she didn't deck him for his comment. Because one thing you knew about Honey — she loved Bert. I guess I understood why, even if he did tell corny jokes and run a radio and TV station out of the renovated barn next to their house.

Honey sat back. "It's been a wild week, I tell you — dealing with the custody thing, talking to lawyers and pediatricians, arranging the funeral —" She crumpled in the seat. "Oh, Bert, I should have flown out there before. After Jeremy got better, I should have gone to see Sunny. Now it's too late."

With a scowl, Bert reached over to take her hand. "Don't you dare feel bad about that. It was a lot easier for her to come here, and she wouldn't."

Just as the old familiar guilt grabbed me, Honey said, "Can you blame her? On her last visit, Jeremy put on a real show for her — that was all she remembered."

Oh, yeah, definitely. Five years ago, I'd visited them for three days of hell. Jeremy had slapped Honey a couple of times for trying to keep him from racing down the path to Hank and Casey Blackshear's homestead next door so he could jump in the pond on their property. Whenever he escaped the house, he made a beeline for that scummy pond. And since he drank the water when he took a swim, Honey wasn't about to let him "fill his belly with germs."

For all her maternal trouble, she practically got beat up. And that wasn't the first time either. Nor did he limit his "challenging behaviors" (isn't that a nice euphemism for "beating people up"?) to Honey. He knocked Bert in the back once, and even took a swing at me.

Not that I blamed Jeremy for being mad about his lot in life. He couldn't talk or even sign. His weird obsessions compelled him to patrol the house closing doors and toilet lids and putting the caps on things. Every time you walked through, he had to come behind shutting everything. And if you moved the books or videos he kept in some bizarre order only he understood, he went ballistic.

Jeremy went ballistic a lot.

No, it wasn't his fault he was autistic, and yes, I should have been more understanding, but it's hard to be understanding after hearing your sister's head crack against tile when your nephew pushed her into the tub because she'd tried to make him bathe — apparently, ponds were fun but bathing wasn't. Only the grace of God — and a hard head — kept her from splitting her skull open on the ceramic soap dish that day.

The truth was, the boy terrified me. I made a resolution then and there. No visits to Mossy Creek as long as the Demon Child lived in that house.

Yet here I was heading to Mossy Creek again anyway. Funny how fate messes with your life. Or death, as the case may be.

Honey sighed. "Sunny never gave Jeremy a chance, no matter what I said."

How could I? I knew my sister— she always put a good face on everything. Like those god-awful outfits she wore. She claimed it was because she liked it that way, but I knew better. In grade school, I used to bask in the reflected glow of my older sister Honey. As the high school homecoming queen, she was considered the prettiest and most fashionable girl in Mossy Creek.

Now look at her, dressed from head to toe in khaki. Jeremy always pitched a fit if her clothes weren't the same color — he liked brown or a nice olive green. God forbid she should wear a purple skirt with a goldenrod blouse like the one she'd worn to my junior high graduation. Jeremy would howl for days.

With a sigh, Honey twisted around to look at Amy and Anna where they were dozing in the car seats. "I miss Sunny already."

When she brushed away tears, a lump filled my throat. Well, a lump *would* have filled my throat if not for my being dead.

She settled back in her seat. "And what on earth are we going to do with these babies? It's been fifteen years since I had to deal with bottles and diapers and all that crap."

"No pun intended," he quipped.

Honey rolled her eyes.

He glanced over into the back. "We made it through puberty with Jeremy, so we can sure make it through bottles with a couple of rugrats. He's better about helping out now, too. Maybe we can teach him to change diapers."

Over my dead body. Pun intended. So much for hoping that Bert and Honey had come to their senses. But now they were pulling into the long driveway that led to our old family farmhouse just outside Mossy Creek. Somewhere back there, the Demon Child still lurked, waiting to pounce on my babies.

By the time we pulled up in back by the barn/TV station, I was practically sitting in little Amy's lap, trying to figure out what to do. I peered out at the rambling house where I was raised, the familiar rub of memory stirring up old feelings. Bert and Honey had inherited it from Mom when she died, and I had been more than happy to let them have it.

What if I hadn't? How would my life have been different if I'd stayed right here? Where nothing changed. Where the same old red brick chimneys and same old white clap-board siding graced the family-worn place.

If I'd stayed, I would never have known Cam and never had my girls. And I wouldn't be floating around in the ether, watching for some sign of the boy who would surely be the death of my babies.

"You want me to go over to Hank's and get Jeremy?" Bert asked. "Casey said she'd keep him as long as we needed."

Casey had to be nuts. How could she defend herself in a wheelchair with a boy like that running around? I don't care if she had been an Olympic contender in softball — Jeremy was dangerous.

"I'll call her and tell her to have Hank bring him over. We should get these girls inside." Honey opened the door and shivered, pulling her flimsy coat tighter around her as she got out. "Geez, it's cold out here. I go away for a week, and suddenly the Deep South becomes the Midwest?"

"Knock, knock," Bert retorted.

I rolled my eyes. Bert and his stupid "knock, knock" jokes. Why Honey put up with them, I'll never know.

She just shook her head. "Who's there?" she asked as she opened the back door of the car.

"Oldman."

"Oldman who?"

"Oldman Winter came down to Georgia."

She groaned. "Very funny." She bent into the car. "Now come on, Old Man Lyman, and take a baby, will you?"

They each took one, which was a lot easier than taking one in each arm like I always had to do when Cam wasn't around. You get used to it after a while, but it's hard juggling two babies, especially at feeding time.

Feeding time! I floated over to glance at Bert's watch. Uh oh, almost time for their bottles. The girls knew it, too, because as soon as their bare little faces hit the frosty air, they woke up on a wail.

Amazing what a motivator those tiny lungs can be — Bert and Honey got up those stairs faster than you could say, "bottle." At the top, Honey shifted Amy to one arm so she could open the door with the other. "The way these girls cry sometimes breaks my heart."

Mine, too. In more ways than one. The crying was why I was still around.

You see, when you die, you feel this strong compulsion to go after that great light shining at the end of the tunnel. Especially when you've got a guy like Cam at the other end waiting for you to show up.

But the babies' cries dragged at me worse than the undertow at San Francisco's Baker Beach. I couldn't leave my girls. I just couldn't abandon them.

So here I was, tethered to them like a balloon. The minute I wandered off, they'd cry, and it would be like jerking the balloon close. I'd bob up next to them and want to wrap my arms around them so badly I could practically smell the talcum on their skin.

Practically. I couldn't actually smell. It seems that ghosts can't smell — I'd discovered that early on. Hearing and seeing seemed to be about it — kind of like watching television, only you're in the picture.

Which can be pretty maddening. I could get right up close, but I could only watch as somebody else picked them up and cuddled them and fed them. Then after they fell asleep, the big light would beckon me and before I knew it, I'd be wandering off toward the tunnel. Until they cried again, and the tether jerked me back.

Today, the tether was shorter than a shoelace as we came into the farmhouse. I got sloppily sentimental when I saw our old kitchen table, complete with a half-gnawed leg from the one time we'd had a pet, a Jack Russell terrier with a hankering for cheap pine.

But it didn't distract me for long. While they cater-wauled away in stereo, Bert settled into a chair and let Honey put Amy in his arms, so she could get the girls' bottles made. And I was right there, with one ghostly hand on Amy and the other on Anna.

Meanwhile, Honey made her call to Casey, then scurried about the kitchen, putting stuff together. "Thank goodness Sunny's nanny had a brain. You should see the instructions she sent along for everything from feeding times to bathing. You just add babies and stir. Although I don't imagine it'll be that easy. Did you get the formula?"

"It's in the first grocery bag on the counter." Bert raised his voice to be heard over the babies. "Didn't have a chance to unload anything but the perishables. Jeremy and I had just got back from the grocery when you called from the airport."

"Who's handling the station?"

"Win. Said he could handle it for today as long as Clifford the Clown stayed out of his way." Bert jiggled the sobbing babies. "It's coming, sweet peas, it's coming. Auntie Honey is getting it for you right now."

"Shoot," Honey said, "the special bottle nipples for Amy are in the diaper bag, and I left it in the car. Be right back." She hurried out the kitchen door.

That's when the Demon Child chose to make his grand entrance. He strolled in through the front door big as you please and headed through the house to the kitchen. If I could have wrapped my ghostly body around my babies when he walked through the kitchen door, I would have. Because Jeremy was even bigger than I expected — five foot ten and two-hundred pounds at least. And he frowned as he lumbered up to tower over Bert.

"Hey there, sport," Bert said. "Meet your new cousins, Amy and Anna."

"Amy and Anna," Jeremy echoed.

The boy was what they call "echolalic." He couldn't say "I'm hungry," but he could repeat whatever you say, or at least the last part of it.

Right now, however, he was more interested in scowling at the wailing twins. Oh, right, the Demon Child didn't like loud noises. Of any kind. Turning on the vacuum cleaner could send him screaming into the room to jerk the plug out of the socket. Well, he'd better not even think about pulling any plugs on my babies.

He walked closer to Anna and Amy, and I screamed, *Stay away from them!* For all the good it did. I might as well have been blowing kisses.

Luckily, just then Honey returned with the diaper bag. She saw Jeremy and broke into a grin. "Hi, sweetie."

His gaze swung to his mama. "Hi, sweetie."

"Jeremy, go out to the car and get the suitcase. I opened the trunk for you, okay?"

"Okay?" he echoed and stared at her.

Are you nuts? I thought. That boy can no more understand about getting a suitcase than —

"Outside, Jeremy," she said. "Car. Suitcase. Bring to Mama."

"Bring to Mama," he repeated, then lumbered out the door.

I was sorely torn. Should I leave the twins? Or follow Jeremy? Curiosity got the better of me. I floated on out to the car. Shoot, Jeremy was actually lifting the suitcase out of the car. I could hardly believe it.

But then he didn't do anything with it, just stood there like a porter at a hotel, protecting the luggage.

Honey poked her head out the door. "Bring the suitcase in, sweetie. Bring it to Mama."

"Mama," Jeremy echoed. He lifted the suitcase and carried it right up the stairs and inside.

I could hardly believe it. The last time I saw the boy, if you handed him a grocery bag full of potato chips to carry, he dropped it on the ground and looked at you like you'd asked him to eat rats.

Maybe Honey hadn't been exaggerating when she'd said Jeremy had improved. But as far as I was concerned, lugging one suitcase did not erase Jeremy's Demon Child status. Not yet. I'd seen him compliant before. It lasted about ten minutes. Maybe this was his ten minutes for today.

"Take It upstairs," Honey ordered the boy as he entered the kitchen where she and Bert now sat holding one baby apiece. Casting the babies a wary glance, he trudged right to the stairs. At least he wasn't frowning at them anymore, probably because they weren't crying. They were happily sucking down formula in the arms of their aunt and uncle.

As he disappeared up the stairs, Honey turned to Bert. "Did you fix up the room for the twins?"

"Did it last night. I moved the rocking chair from Jeremy's room into the babies', and I brought his old baby bed down from the attic. Until we can get an extra crib, they'll have to sleep in the same one."

Honey stared down at Anna, who bore her usual Ah-the-joys-of-the-bottle expression. Honey's eyes grew suspiciously moist. "I never thought we'd get to use that old baby bed again."

"Me either."

The wealth of emotion in those two words brought me up short. Honey had once told me that she and Bert had decided not to have more children after Jeremy was diagnosed, because Jeremy was all they could handle. Bert had even gotten himself fixed.

It had never occurred to me that the choice had been hard. Or that maybe they had even come to regret it. They sure did seem happy to have my darling girls in their home.

"Do you think they'll be okay sleeping upstairs in the guest room?" Bert asked.

No way! I shouted. Jeremy's room was upstairs, and Honey's and Bert's was downstairs. So who was going to protect my darlings from the Demon Child?

"They'll be all right for one night," Honey said.

"Sorry I didn't have enough time to get that extra room down here cleared out," Bert said. "With the weather turning so cold, the furnace started acting up again. I had to work on it half the morning."

The scowl crossing Honey's genial features looked surprisingly like her son's. "I told you to hire Arturo to fix it."

"I've got it figured out this time. It wasn't that hard, really."

"Now, Bert —"

"Knock, knock."

Honey frowned, but still said, "Who's there?"

"Don."

"Don who?"

"Don'cha know I love you?"

A laugh sputtered out of Honey. "That has to be the worst one you ever told."

He grinned. "It made you laugh."

"I'm so tired right now, I'd laugh at a monkey picking its nose."

"What a visual."

"It's all your fault — you're the one who taught me that gross-out humor is better than none at all."

"And knock-knock jokes."

She snorted. "Did you get that baby monitor from Jayne?"

"Sure did."

"Then the babies will be all right upstairs tonight. We'll clean out the downstairs room tomorrow."

Amy was fighting the bottle and Bert stared at her in typical male confusion. "The girl hasn't drunk very much for sounding so hungry."

"She needs to be burped." Honey arched one blond eyebrow. "Think you remember how to do that?"

Bert lifted the baby to his shoulder with a sigh. "This will take some getting used to, won't it?"

"Oh, yeah," Honey said as she hefted her own baby up to burp her.

Bert looked thoughtful as he patted the baby's back. "Do you think we made a mistake, offering to take them? Do you think we can handle them?"

I tensed, not sure what answer I was hoping for. If Honey and Bert didn't keep the babies, I wouldn't have to worry about Jeremy. On the other hand, my husband had been an orphan, and whenever he talked about what that had been like, I knew I didn't want that for my children.

Besides, how many people would be willing to adopt twins? An adoption agency might have to separate the babies — would I really want that over having them grow up with Honey and Bert?

"It's like you said," Honey replied after a moment, "if we could handle Jeremy, the twins will be a piece of cake."

Yes, but could they handle both Jeremy and the twins? That's what worried me.

I was just starting to relax and drift off, half-consciously, toward the white light, when I heard heavy footsteps on the stairs. Jeremy was back. Oh, no. That jerked my tether tight.

The boy entered the kitchen and stood waiting until he got his mother's attention. When she looked at him, he flicked his hand toward the refrigerator.

Honey glanced at the clock. "Oh, sweetie, I'm sorry. It's way past your dinner time, isn't it?"

"Dinner time," Jeremy said solemnly, and flicked his hand again, with more urgency.

"Sit down. I think Anna's done eating anyway." Honey looked over at Bert, but Amy, the slower eater, was still sucking on her bottle. So Honey took Anna and headed over to where Jeremy had dropped into one of the ancient kitchen chairs once belonging to our mother.

"Would you like to hold the baby?" she asked Jeremy.

No! I screamed, so loudly I nearly splattered my ethereal self on the ceiling.

Jeremy merely repeated, "hold the baby," which was just as likely to mean, "Go fix my dinner, woman," as "I'd love to hold my cousin, thank you."

But Honey, who should have known better, still bent and pressed Anna up against Jeremy's chest, then placed his arms in position around the baby. "Hold tight now, sweetie," she ordered him, and he squeezed the baby hard enough to startle her into a cry.

"Not that hard," Honey said hastily. "Gently. Gently."

Meanwhile, I was doing the dance of the dead — hopping from one ghostly foot to the other while trying not to go insane over the prospect of my sweet darling being squeezed lifeless by the Demon Child.

He relaxed his grip, but leveled a severe frown on the crying Anna. For some reason, she found that humorous. Anna always did have fun with faces. She not only stopped crying, but started patting his cheek.

"Good job," Honey told Jeremy as she went off to make dinner.

Jeremy looked skeptical, however. As Anna's little fingers batted at his mouth, he inched his head back farther and farther until he was bending his neck at an unnatural angle to avoid the baby's touch.

I laughed in spite of everything. Maybe Jeremy was just as wary of Anna as I was of him. The twins were a lot like him, after all. They couldn't talk, they expressed their emotions at an obnoxious volume, and they flailed about and put their hands where they didn't belong without rhyme or reason.

But they couldn't hurt him. And he could sure hurt them. In fact, Anna now had her tiny grip on his lip and was yanking it like she yanked the arm of her Ernie doll. When Jeremy opened his mouth and I saw those teeth of his, I threw myself at him, screaming. Then flew right through him, which did no good whatsoever.

Before I could even come back around to try again, however, Honey had returned to whisk the baby from Jeremy, apparently not even noticing that her deadly son had been about to make a meal out of my poor child's fingers.

"Okay, your pizza pockets are in the oven," she told him cheerily. Jeremy's diet consisted of two things — pizza pockets and burgers. And probably baby fingers. "I'll be back to get them out in a minute. Your dad and I are taking the babies upstairs to bed."

I went with them. Not that I had much choice. I could wander a little away from the babies, but not very far, not if I didn't want to get sucked into the light. I'd figured that out pretty quickly. And going to the light just wasn't an option right now, not until I'd figured out a way to alert Honey to the dangers of Jeremy.

Yes, that's what I needed to do — send her a message. My Baptist sister would never attend a séance, but maybe I could spell out a message in refrigerator magnets or something.

What I needed was advice from other ghosts about how to haunt the living. Too bad I hadn't run into any other ghosts. I wish I had. We could have formed a support group — Dead People Anonymous. I wouldn't even have minded being the first to stand up in the front and say, "My name is Sunny Ross, and I'm a dead person."

But I was on my own.

*Just when you think it's safe to go home
at the end of the day.*

Nightfall:
Ida and Amos
Chapter 14

Ingrid is a rebel when it comes to doing what I say. She thinks her crone-hood gives her the right to piss people off for their own good. She's the only person in Mossy Creek who gets in my face and tells me I don't belong with Del Jackson.

"That man still has one foot in his marriage," she lectures. "When a man puts his foot into something, the rest of him eventually follows."

Her argument is bolstered by the fact that Del's ex-wife, Sheila, moved from Tennessee to Bigelow two months ago, right before Thanksgiving. She's living in a condo five minutes from their son and two grandchildren. Her son and grandkids don't just love her, they actually like her. They want her and Del to re-marry, despite the fact that the marriage ended in amicable divorce a good twenty years ago.

Okey dokey. I may not enjoy the situation, but I'll never try to come between Sheila and her family. I have a perfectly pleasant relationship with them. Del and I took his grandkids and Little Ida to Disney World last summer, and we had a great time. All very civilized.

Until Sheila slithered back into Del's life. She seems to be a competent person, so why has she been crying on

Del's shoulder at every opportunity? Okay, so she had her savings hijacked by a bad investment counselor, and the Memphis technology company she worked for sent her job to Bombay, and she has to start over in a new career as a real estate agent in Bigelow, and her rich boyfriend has left her for a younger woman, and so...

So Del feels sorry for her. Go figure. He's a protective man. A military man. Apparently, he finds Sheila's needy girlishness more appealing than not. Unlike yours truly, she wants a man for personal security, the kind of man who clubs mice and shoots garden snakes. Me, I *like* mice and garden snakes.

Not that I feel threatened. Even if she is tiny and blonde and looks a good ten years younger than 45, meaning that even though I look a good ten years younger than 52, she is still younger than me, in dog years, or something. Anyway, she's small and I can take her in a fight. If I slug her just right, I bet Botox will shoot out her nose.

So I'm not worried, no. Not worried, just ... disappointed. I guess deep down I still want a soul mate, another Jeb, a man who has saved himself just for me — metaphorically, at least — a man who won't ever look over his shoulder at an old flame.

A man who will only look over his shoulder at me, even if that means he has to peer through the steel bars between the front and back seat of his patrol car.

"Home, sweet home," Amos deadpanned, as we drove up the lane at Hamilton Farm.

I swept a gaze over my house and yard. The cold afternoon sun had just sunk below the horizon. Shadows slanted across the trees and shrubs, casting lonely, blue hues under the veranda. Night was falling quickly, with a hard freeze predicted. There were no visiting cars, and no lights in the windows. June, my housekeeper, must be gone for the day. Amos and I were all alone.

I shivered but put on my best air of nonchalant sophistication. "Just slow down enough for me to jump out at the front gate. You know, the way chain gang convicts used to leap off the county's old flatbed truck on their way back to the prison camp. I'll make my escape."

Amos chuckled darkly. He parked the patrol car directly in front of my wrought-iron garden gate and fieldstone walkway. "Go ahead. Make a break for it. I'll give you thirty minutes before I bring in the bloodhounds."

"There's not a bloodhound in this county that can track me down. The scent of Chanel throws them off, every time."

Amos got out, popped the locks, then opened my door. He gave me a bow, complete with a sardonic smile. "Then I'll bring in trackers with French poodles."

I swept out of the patrol car like a starlet on a red carpet, gauging my effect and playing the drama to the hilt. My shoulder brushed his hand on the door frame. An errant lock of my upswept hair feathered across his chin as I stood. He straightened as if burned, but when I looked up at him he gave back only the tight, cool smile I knew so well. I returned it with an arched brow and a taunting attitude, daring him, reckless. "Amos, I'd hop an oil tanker to China before I'd let you and your French poodles catch me."

"All right, then, I'll go after you with swimming *Chinese* poodles."

"Because you're the kind of police chief who always gets his man?"

He bent his head toward me. The smile remained but his eyes went darker, more serious. "*Because I'm the kind of man who intends to get his woman.*"

I stopping breathing. "How can you be so certain?"

"Ida, the only question is, How can you not be?"

One, two, three. Heartbeats. I took a deep breath. "I have these dreams — these nightmares, where you tell me to jump down from a high limb of the Sitting Tree, you tell me you'll catch me, but when I let go and fall ... I never find out if you're really there. I can't see what happens to me."

"I'll always be there. I always have been."

We traded the kind of look that slips between each pulse of blood in the veins. "Maybe I've been all wrong," I whispered. "You're not rescuing me. I'm rescuing you."

He nodded.

That did it. I can never resist a man who needs me.

I kissed him. He kissed me back. He wasn't a teenager anymore, and I wasn't a freshly grieving widow. We were equals. And we could burn each other up. I held him. I leaned into him. He pulled me up on my toes. That kiss lasted forever; it was a diamond, and every facet caught the light a different way. Sweet, sad, tender, profane, sacred, taking, giving, wanting. Wanting. *Wanting.* We gleamed, together.

"I hope you read Ida her rights, first."

Del's voice.

We froze.

Del.

I give Amos credit for more composure than I managed. He slowly released me, turned smoothly, and looked up at my veranda. I shut my eyes for a second, gritted my teeth, then stepped around Amos and followed his gaze.

Del stood at the top of my veranda steps, a look on his face like ice on stone. He was dressed in khakis, flannel, and a heavy jacket, all spattered with mud. I hadn't told him my plans for the day. Why should I? He was on a camping trip high in the mountains with his grandkids, his son — and maybe with Sheila, too. I had wanted to ask, but restrained myself. I trusted him. He trusted me.

Oh, the irony.

I took a slow, shamed breath, then stiffened my spine.

"Del, there's no excuse for what just happened. But Amos and I didn't plan it, I promise you."

Amos shifted to stand just slightly in front of me, a position of territorial claim. He never took his eyes off Del. Del returned the favor. It's fair to say their staring match resembled two large dogs facing off over a bone. At that point, I needed a calcium injection. My legs felt weak.

"I provoked her, Del," Amos announced flatly, a gallant lie.

I couldn't let it stand. "No, Del, he didn't. I kissed him. I take full responsibility. I apologize to you from the bottom of my heart. Until today I've never been unfaithful to the man in my life. Not in word or deed. Not to my husband, and not to you. I'm ashamed of what I did. But the truth remains. I kissed Amos." I looked at Amos. "It's over. And it won't happen again."

Amos didn't blink. Didn't register any emotion. Always a bad sign. It's fair to say I know him better than anyone else in the world. Patience and determination are two of his strongest traits. Along with pure, stubborn pride. When he's absolutely fixed on getting what he wants, he doesn't blink. "It's not over," he said.

After a stony second, Del slid his fists into his front trouser pockets, then ambled down the veranda steps with the deceptive calm of the air before a tornado. He walked up to us slowly, halting a few feet away, still staring at Amos. Ignoring me. Prickly anger began to sidle alongside my general shame and misery. Apparently, when two big, ballsy dogs face off over a bone, the bone is supposed is supposed to flutter its eyelashes and keep quiet.

"I'll walk you to your car," Del said to Amos.

Amos smiled thinly. "I'll walk you to yours."

I grabbed my coat and purse from the patrol car. "I've got a better idea. You two big dogs stand here and give each other the laser eyeball until you're both reduced to charred piles of furry hackles and male ego. In the meantime, your girlie little bone is walking herself indoors. Alone."

I strode up my front walk without looking back, slammed my stained glass doors behind me, locking them with loud, emphatic rattles of the chain and deadbolt. Then I hurried to a discreet window in the dining room and peeked through the Irish lace of my curtains.

Del walked stiffly to his Range Rover, and Amos got into his squad car. Del edged into the lane, then stopped, waiting. Amos edged into the lane, then stopped. I swear, I think I heard him gun the patrol car's engine, and I think I heard Del gun his, too. What were they going to do — drag race on my one-lane driveway?

Finally, Del blinked. He led the way. Amos followed. After both vehicles disappeared into the darkness I groaned, shook my head, slapped my forehead, and, in general, gave myself a whup-ass mental paddling. I wanted to crawl under the veranda, in misery.

Now here you go again, you say you want your freedom...

Stevie Nicks. Her song, *Dreams*. My cell phone, playing it. What timing.

I checked the caller's number, then numbly lifted the phone to my ear. "What's up, Sandy?"

"Hi, Mayor. Is the chief there?"

I watched my breath make frosty clouds in the night air. "He just left."

"He's not answering his cell phone."

"Give him five minutes and try again."

"He okay?"

"He's been better."

"You okay?"

"What can I do for you, Officer Crane?"

"Uh oh. I guess the creekwater's really hit the fan, this time."

"Which comes as no surprise to you and your usual

group of snooping, co-conspiring confidantes. You and Jayne Reynolds ratted on me, *didn't you?*"

"Uh, well, uh, Mayor, hmmm —"

"Nevermind. What did I miss today? That is, *after* I left town with the Mossy Creek chapter of the CIA secretly tracking me."

Sandy heaved an audible sigh of relief, no doubt glad I'd changed the subject. Then she launched into a long list of bizarre incidents. Inez and Addie Lou. Charlie and Louise. Pearl and Spiva. Chip and Rory. Eula Mae and the bank robber. To name a few. Finishing with, "And Honey Lyman just got home from the airport with her poor sister's orphaned kids, and Peggy Caldwell is upset 'cause Dashiell's disappeared, and Smokey Lincoln over at the Forestry Service says the temperature's going down to ten degrees tonight, and Charlie and Louise haven't been seen for a couple of hours — for all I know, their house has killed them and hid their bodies — and Miz Eula Mae has called twice asking if Amos is gonna give her a badge to wear since the bank president told her she can be an honorary guard, and I just heard that Chip and Rory are asking girls over for a bonfire, and ... and ... Mayor, I don't often say this, but right now, me and Mutt sure could use a pack of cherry cigarilloes, a six-pack of beer and a bottle of aspirin."

I could use something stronger than that. "Sit tight. I'm on my way. I'll check on Peggy, call the Sawyers, talk to Bert and Honey, drop by to see Eula Mae, and make sure the Browns know what Chip and Rory are up to. After that, I'll be in my office at town hall."

She perked up. "Thank you! And, uh ... where do you figure the chief is heading tonight?"

"Anywhere I'm not," I said dully.

Nightfall:
Chip and Rory

In all the excitement earlier that day, I plumb forgot that Rory had asked Ashley Winthrop and the other girls over for a bonfire that night. As it turned out, my little brother Toby had just come home from his friend's house when a knock sounded at the back door. Since he was closest, he answered it.

"Hi, Toby," came a sweet, girly voice I immediately recognized as Ashley Winthrop's. "Is Rory here? We came for the bonfire."

Before I got a single word out, Toby swung the door wide open and invited the girls into the kitchen. Good Gosh A'mighty! The timing couldn't a been worse. Ashley and the girls stopped dead in their tracks, their chatter breaking off and their eyes going wide.

There stood Rory at the kitchen table, helping my mama make candy for Sunday's church bazaar. He was putting tiny pink roses on chocolate lollipops. And he was wearing Mama's frilly red-checked apron and a hair net. Yep, Rory was *clocking* it.

Blood rushed to my head so fast, it made me dizzy. How would he ever live this down? Word would get around school like a flash fire, and neither he nor I would ever be able to hold our heads up in public again. I stood frozen, like a deer caught in the headlights, staring helplessly at our destruction.

Not Rory, though. He paused in what he was doing, tipped a cordial nod to the girls, and said with his own smooth style, "Evening, ladies. Wish I could join you tonight, but I'll be at my aunt's service for quite some time."

This was, without a doubt, a disaster. The girls burst out into a fit of giggling, and some whispered behind their hands, and Ashley Winthrop sallied on closer, as if she couldn't be sure she was seeing right.

That was when I knew my cousin Rory had well and truly lost his mind. Because he didn't tell those girls that he was being punished for stealing my dad's Harley, which would have gone a long way toward salvaging the situation, in my book. He just grinned. And in that grin, I saw not one whit of embarrassment or regret or awkwardness. He was happy. He was so blasted happy, he was silly with it. His mind was entirely gone.

I mean, how could he ever go back to cool after being seen making lollipops in an apron and hair net?

But you know something? He did. Right then and there, he somehow turned it all around. He gave those girls a wink, then said to Ashley, "I'll see you in school — whether Charles likes it or not."

"In school?" Ashley breathed. "You mean, you're *staying* in Mossy Creek?"

The phone rang. Mama answered it, and I could hear saying, "No, Mayor, I think the bonfire's been cancelled. And guess what? Rory's going to be staying with us from now on."

Rory flashed a wide, white smile. And the girls all squealed and clapped and jumped up and down, while Ashley gazed at Rory like she had stars in her eyes. Now don't that beat all?

There's just no one in this world cooler than my cousin Rory.

Nightfall:
Louise and Charlie

By the time we came home from dinner, darkness had long since fallen. I know the twenty-first of December is supposed to be the shortest day of the year, but they seem to get shorter still in January. I checked our answering machine. Ida's voice curled out.

"Look, House," she said drolly. "I know you're holding Charlie and Louise hostage. Let them go. If I don't hear from them within the next hour, I'm dropping a dime on you. *Habitat for Humanity*. Their volunteers will take you apart like a cheap suit. Use you for construction supplies. The next time I see you, you'll be three little townhouses and a split-level ranch. You're going *down*, baby."

When Charlie and I finished laughing, I called Ida and told her we were safe and the house had promised to get counseling.

Charlie offered to go upstairs and bring down my nightgown and robe, but I said I'd have to brave that room sometime. I did open the door only an inch or so, turn on the light and say 'shoo' a couple of times before I went in. No raccoons.

When I came back downstairs in my nightgown and robe, Charlie had kindled a fire in the living room fireplace, blown up our new mattress and made it up with the new sheets and blankets, and was propped up on the new pillows waving an open bottle of champagne and a pair of crystal flutes at me.

"We've been saving the champagne for when we finished the house," I said from the foot of the stairs.

"We need it now."

I folded my legs under me and sat tailor fashion on the end of the new mattress. Actually, it was very comfortable if a bit tippy. "Where did you unearth those champagne flutes?"

"The box was actually labeled crystal."

"Amazing."

He poured and handed me a glass of champagne. "You and I can survive anything." He clinked his glass with mine.

By the time we had finished the bottle, the fire had burned to embers. I'm not quite sure at which point I lost my nightgown, but I do remember thinking that this would be the first time we'd made love in this house.

Afterwards I snuggled down against him with my head under his chin. The hair on his chest was the silver grey of a fox's pelt, not the dark brown it was when we married, but I didn't care. I was drifting into sleep when I felt a rumble in his chest and heard what sounded like a cough. I sat up on one elbow. "Charlie? Are you all right?"

His eyes were closed, but his lips were curved in a smile. The man was laughing!

"What on earth?"

He shook with laughter. "A bear? You thought a raccoon was a big, brown, furry bear?"

I smacked him. He grabbed me and a moment later we were rolling around on that bed and laughing so hard we fell off on the floor. Thank goodness it was only ten inches or so. That sobered us up a little, but not much.

Suddenly I felt so sleepy I yawned in his face. We climbed back onto our bed, I curled up, and he fitted himself against my back. He felt wonderful, but I knew I couldn't stay spooned for long. Between Charlie's overheated metabolism and my hot flashes, lying against his tummy is like sitting in a Swedish sauna.

As I drifted off, I realized that I felt for the first time as though I had truly come home.

Nightfall:
Peggy

"No, Ida, I don't want to form a posse to hunt for Dashiell. Not yet. But I'll keep you informed. Thanks."

I hung up the phone, then went to the window and stood for a long time. I checked Josie, who was fast asleep. Then I stretched out on my bed with all my clothes on.

Maybe you think I over-reacted. He was just a cat, after all, but he was the only real link to my life before my husband died. I knew some day he would tell me he didn't want to go on living any longer, but I hoped when that time came, I could cradle him in my arms as he went. The thought of finding him dead or badly wounded, or even worse, not finding him at all, was too painful to contemplate.

I went to the kitchen for a glass of water, and on the way back, realized that the door to the back porch wasn't quite latched. As I reached to shut it, a gust of wind thrust it against my chest.

I think I knew then. I rushed to Josie's room. She wasn't there. I checked the bathroom, called for her.

Oh, God! She'd climbed out of bed and gone out into the cold and the dark to find Dashiell! I rushed back to the porch door. Her little boots were gone. So was her yellow jacket.

What had I done?

I dialed nine-one-one and got Sandy. "Josie's gone outside. I don't know how long she's been gone." I didn't wait for her answer. I slammed down the phone, picked up the flashlight from the kitchen table beside the back door, ran out onto the back porch and down the stairs into the yard without even stopping for a jacket.

The cold front had finally gone through. The temperature had dropped thirty degrees, and the wind hinted it would drop even more before morning, but there was no ice.

The night was inky. No moon. I screamed Josie's name.

At the foot of the back steps I slipped in some mud, caught myself on the hand rail, dropped the flashlight and wrenched my shoulder. What did pain matter? If something happened to Josie ...

How could I tell Marilee? How could I endure living?

My first thought was that she'd gone to the street. She knew she was never allowed in the front yard, but she'd disobeyed me once, and she'd heard me talking about Dashiell and cars.

I could barely breathe as I raced around the house to the street. My mouth had gone so dry I could barely whisper her name when I needed to shout it. My pulse raced, and my chest hurt so badly I thought I might be having a heart attack.

There's a street light in front of my house. Between it and my flashlight, I saw that Josie was nowhere to be seen.

I ran back around the house and stumbled through the back yard, catching my hair on drooping branches, scraping my arms on twigs, calling Josie's name, then God's name, then her name again.

I sank onto my knees and covered my face with my icy hands. "Please, God, let me find her safe," I wept, "Do whatever you like to me, but protect that child."

In that instant the wind stilled.

In that moment, I heard a sound.

"Twinkle, twinkle, little star ..."

I ran, I slid, I catapulted down the hill. The gate to the walled garden stood open.

I wanted to shout to her, but I'd already frightened her. I slipped through the gate with the flashlight down by my side. "Josie?" I whispered. "Josie? Baby? It's all right, sweetheart. Grammie's here. Grammie's not angry."

I swung the flashlight around. At first I didn't see her, then I saw a small, yellow bundle scrunched up tight under the wrought iron table.

"Shhh," she whispered. "Don't scare them."

My old knees had already taken a beating, but I got down on them again.

"Come on, baby, let's go home. You're going to freeze out here."

"I found Dashiell, Grammie," she said. "He's all right." She moved, and I saw that she had taken my afghan off the couch and dragged it with her. She held it across her knees. From under one corner a single malevolent eye peeked out at me.

"That's wonderful, baby," I said. Frankly, I wanted to wring Dashiell's neck at that moment. I especially didn't want him to run away into the night again.

I reached down and swept him into my arms very securely. He struggled indignantly. I was, after all, cold and muddy. "Oh, no you don't, you old fool," I said, and took a firmer grip.

"Come on, Josie, sweet pea, we have to get you warm and dry."

"Them too."

"Miz Caldwell?" I heard a voice from my back porch.

"Down here, Sandy!" I called. "I found Josie. We're all right. Can you give me a hand?"

I heard her pelt down the hill toward us. She came into the garden and lit us up with her gigantic flashlight. I nearly let go of Dashiell. "Can you take this idiot cat?" I asked.

"Let me carry your granddaughter," Sandy said.

"I can walk," she protested. "I'm not a baby."

"Of course you're not, Miss Josie," said Sandy, as she reached down for her. "But Amos would have my job if I didn't see you safely home."

"Don't!" she snapped. "You'll hurt them."

That's when the blanket rolled back. Sheltered in her lap were three tiny kittens.

"Dashiell found them, Grammie," she said as Sandy carefully lifted Josie and her brood into her arms. "They don't got no mommy."

Well, if they did before, they certainly didn't now. The mother cat would never find them by scent in this cold wind, and I knew wild mother cats had very little attachment to their offspring at the best of times.

Our little band struggled up the hill and into the kitchen. The minute the back door was firmly shut, I shoved Dashiell into the laundry room where his litter box and food dish were, and shut the door on him. He was cold and muddy, but at the moment, Josie was my greatest concern. He'd have to wait his turn.

She was shaking, and her jacket was muddy, as were her boots. The afghan was downright soggy. Her hair was a fright, and her hands were freezing. "Should we call an ambulance?" I asked Sandy. "Take her to the emergency room? She could be hypothermic."

Josie, who still held the kittens inside her slicker, said, "I don't want to go to no mergen room, Grammie. Me'n the babies aren't very cold."

Sandy grinned. "She doesn't sound hypothermic to me, Miz Carpenter. She must not have been outside long. A hot bath ought to warm her up. How 'bout I make us all some hot chocolate? You're probably colder than she is."

"The babies need milk too," Josie said.

As if on cue, they began to mew in that tiny kitten way. I rolled my eyes at the deputy. They probably wouldn't survive the night. How would I explain that to Josie?

The kittens had been sheltered from the worst of the rain. While Josie's bath ran, I dried them with the hair dryer. They didn't like the sound, but they enjoyed the warmth. I snuggled them down in a nest of towels on the bathroom floor while I got Josie into warm, dry jammies and her bunny slippers.

Then I remembered that I still had Dashiell to attend to.

By the time Josie and I came back into the kitchen, Sandy had cups of hot chocolate for both of us.

"Josie looks pretty good," she said, and shook her head. "But you ..."

"I'm fine," I said, and meant it. When I opened the laundry room door, a bedraggled cat stalked out. He certainly wanted to punish me, but his need for comfort after his terrible ordeal overrode his huffiness, and he climbed into my arms before I got myself sat down good at the kitchen table. I rubbed him down with more towels, and laid my forehead against his broad head. "You old fool," I whispered.

"He's a daddy now," Josie said happily. "He's got three babies. My daddy doesn't have but one." Then she yawned. "I think I'll go back to bed now," she said. She handed her cup to the deputy. "Thank you very much," she said, as graciously as though she were a princess.

I followed her into her room and tucked her in.

"Will you look after the babies?" she asked.

I nodded, and hoped they'd live until I could get them to Hank's vet clinic in the morning or at least find kitten formula for them. "Josie, what you did was very wrong."

She wouldn't look at me. "I didn't mean to let Dashiell out."

"No, I mean slipping out in the cold and the wind that

way. You scared me half out of my wits."

"I'm sorry, Grammie. I thought I'd find him and bring him back before you found out and then you wouldn't be sad."

"You could have been lost or hurt. I love Dashiell, but he's a cat. You're my grandbaby. I love you and I don't want to lose you."

We hugged. As she lay back down, she asked, "Do we got to tell Mommy and Daddy? They'll be mad."

Madder at me than at Josie. "Yes, I'm afraid we do. But we won't make it seem too bad."

As I left her, I heard "*Twinkle, Twinkle, little star.*" A moment later, she was asleep.

Sandy stood in the kitchen with her cell phone to one ear. She was saying, "Yeah, Chief, I'm just making sure you're okay. When I left you had *Andy Griffith* re-runs on the TV in the break room. I know you only watch Andy Griffith when you need a real big mood picker-upper. Okay, okay, okay, I'm sorry I asked. Didn't mean to pry. Well, yeah, okay, I *did* mean to pry, but ... never mind. Catch you later, Chief. Over and out." She snapped the cell phone shut and gazed at me wearily. "Miz Caldwell, you got any cherry cigarillos?" I shook my head. She sighed.

"What do I do about those kittens?" I asked. "I'm afraid cow's milk will kill them."

"Hank's got little bottles of kitten and puppy formula at the clinic."

"I can't leave Josie."

"Shoot, I'll run over to his place and get you some. I need a nice, long, quiet drive right now."

She returned after an hour with two six packs of kitten formula. The minute I opened the bathroom door, I heard the pitiful mews.

So did Dashiell. He came bounding into the bathroom, sat on the edge of the sink and glared at us while Sandy and I fed, cleaned, and snuggled the babies back in their nest. When I tried to shoo Dashiell out, he jumped down, walked into the middle of the nest and curled up protectively around his three charges. They scrabbled against his tummy and began to knead with tiny paws.

Sandy laughed. "You sure that's a male cat you got there?"

"Well, he was," I said. "Last time I checked. Neutered. You don't think he'll hurt them, do you?"

"I'd say he's more likely to hurt *you* if you try to take him away from them." She smiled down at them. "Two tabbies and a gray. Hard to tell the boys from the girls at this age."

As I walked Sandy to the front door, she said, "You know, Miz Carpenter, I got to write this down on my report."

I closed my eyes and sighed. "I know."

"I'll just say you over-reacted when you found Josie out of bed, but she was never lost." Sandy smiled up at me like a little blonde angel dressed in a uniform, a leather bomber jacket and a gun belt. "She wasn't really lost for long. Otherwise she'd a-been colder."

"Thank you."

"Now, you'd best get yourself warmed up."

I must look like a witch. I walked back to my bathroom. When I looked at the kittens and Dashiell, who was purring happily with his new family, I realized I was now the mother of not one, but four, cats.

Ida called back. I told her everything was fine, now.

"I don't want any more cats wandering around my house and causing trouble," I said.

"Well, then, you better pull up the catnip in your garden."

"Catnip? I didn't plant catnip. No way."

"Oh, yes, you did. Take a look. Those brown, freeze-dried stalks by your bird bath? Last summer's catnip. Premium nose candy for cats, Peggy. I noticed it when I stopped by the other afternoon."

Suddenly I remembered the day Josie chose the seeds, and the extra packets she'd tossed in at the last moment. I had never really read the packets. I had simply torn them open, dumped them all into a bucket, and swished them around with the sand before we broadcast them.

No wonder poor Dashiell had been crazy. He's had to watch all the neighborhood cats zone out on major cat drugs while he stayed indoors.

I would pull out all the catnip. Four cats are quite enough, thank you.

Four cats and one beloved granddaughter.

Nightfall:
Eula Mae

Ida came to my house late that night. We sat in the living room sipping hot tea and nibbling on all sorts of baked goodies the Methodists sent over from their fundraiser. Well, Estelle and I nibble. Ida looks kinda sad for some reason and doesn't eat anything. I point out roses in a vase, from Rick at the bank, and a box of candy from the tellers, and a CD of Lena Horne classics Mutt Bottoms gave me, as a thank-you from a fellow law officer. Catching criminals has a lot of perks.

"Well, General," Ida says to me, "You sure know how to liven up a day."

"When you don't know how many days you have left, you have to make each one count, Colonel."

"Well, you did indeed."

"And look here," I say. I pull back the lapel of my sweater and show her a shiny gold star with Mossy Creek Police Department on it. "Amos came by just a little bit ago. He says, 'I'd like to present you with this honorary badge. This is for honor and valor and fearlessness. Even before you met the bank robber, you were willing to serve, and in my business, people like you are rare. It's a pleasure to know you, Miz Eula.'"

I beam with pride. Ida nods. I notice she gets sadder-looking when I mention Amos. But I don't pry. "There's more, Miz Eula," Ida says. "I believe you had a suggestion for a sign to post out back by the dumpster at the Piggly

Wiggly?" She reaches into a big white plastic bag. "What do you think of this?" She holds it up.

If you have to share cigarettes, you shouldn't be smoking.

And printed underneath that is this: *Wisdom from Eula Mae Whit.*

I smile at Ida. "I like this very much."

"There's more," Ida says gently.

"I don't know how much this old heart can take."

"General," Ida says to me, "You've been here longer than anybody. Your heart can handle this, I promise."

"All right. What else," I say, happy.

"I'd like to make this day, from now until forever, Eula Mae Whit Day in Mossy Creek. What do you think of that?"

I'm so overwhelmed, I reach for Estelle's hand. Clara is across from me with her mouth hanging open. I guess that's only appropriate after she's eaten five cookies.

But she's happy, I can tell.

"That's a fine idea. A fine idea, indeed," I say. I reach for the mayor's hand, too. "I'm happy and humbled and excited that God left me here to experience this joyous day," I add.

Everybody stares at me like they don't believe they heard that.

I just smile bigger. When you're a hundred-and-one, you get to change your mind about living and dying, whenever you please.

Nightfall:
Linda and Hannah

"Daddy? You know Mrs. Longstreet is probably gonna fire me for bringin' you down here to the library."

Daddy harumphed. "Well, if she does she's a durn fool. You're a good worker, she oughta be glad to have you around."

I felt my face go hot to my ears. I'd gotten better about talking to boys and people in general since I'd had what Miss Jasmine called "a self-esteem makeover." But I still wasn't used to my daddy givin' me compliments. Whatever Momma had done to him, it sure worked. I took Miss Jasmine's rules to heart, like always saying "thank you" after receiving a compliment.

"Thank you, Daddy."

It was his turn to flush, but he looked pleased just the same.

🌑🌑🌑

Earlier, while Momma and I got supper on the table, I'd told her all about the poetry-loving, book-moving ghost in the library. We were sitting down to eat when I mentioned about Mrs. Longstreet staying all night in the library by herself and how worried I was for her. Daddy didn't say a word about it until we'd said grace and started passing food.

"There's no call to be afraid of no ghost," Daddy said as

he spooned up some mashed potatoes. He pinned me with a sharp eye. "As long as you stay away from their haunts, like the graveyards and such."

"But Daddy —"

"Pass the limas."

I composed myself and tried to find the adult way to explain my fear. I'd watched Momma long enough to learn that sometimes you had to go after something from a different side.

"Hannah — Mrs. Longstreet — wouldn't let me stay with her. Said I shouldn't even ask you."

Chewing, Daddy nodded. "She ought to call the police if she's got trouble."

"Oh, she can't call the police and tell them she's got a ghost, she could lose her job. And people might stop coming to the library at all."

Then I switched sides. "I don't *really* think there's a ghost in the library. And I don't think Mrs. Longstreet believes there is, either. But someone is moving those books, and she's determined to find out who." Just like Momma, I stopped and held out the bread basket to Daddy. He nodded again and took a biscuit.

"I'm afraid of her being all alone there, if something happens — like a book falling off the shelf or the lights flickerin' — she might scare herself into a heart seizure. I'm sure I would if I stayed there locked up all alone."

Daddy stopped chewing and stared at me. Momma was watching me as well but the corners of her mouth were turned up slightly. "This chicken-fried steak is better than Mama's All You Can Eat," I said. She smiled then, knowing I was knee-deep in my persuading.

"Thank you, sweetheart."

Daddy had had a moment to think things over but wasn't ready to make a decision. He wagged his biscuit in Momma's direction. "What do you think about all of this,

Mary Beth?"

Momma ate a fork full of mashed potatoes before answering. "I think if Linda's worried, maybe we ought to go and check on Hannah."

"We?"

"Well, you wouldn't want Linda to go down there alone, would you?"

Daddy thought about that for a minute. I knew he was looking forward to watching wrestlin' on *ESPN* after dinner, so I held my breath.

"No need for all of us to go. I'll go down there."

"I'll go with you, Daddy. So I can explain to Mrs. Longstreet that we just have her safety in mind."

"I'll pack up some dinner for you to take along," Momma offered. "And, Linda, you gather up a couple of quilts and your daddy's sleeping bag he uses for hunting. I hate to think of Mrs. Longstreet sitting up in a chair all night."

I started to stand up but Daddy stopped me. "Finish your dinner, girl. The ghost won't show up without you." So, he'd been on to me after all. Oh well. I sat and ate in my most ladylike manner — even helped Momma clear the table. This getting-what-you-wanted stuff was pretty cool.

🌱🌱🌱

The double glass in the library front door rattled in response to Daddy's heavy knocking. "So Mrs. Longstreet'll know it's humans at the door," Daddy said when I winced. I watched his face but I couldn't be sure if he thought the whole thing was funny, or he was taking it serious. Beyond the glass the library was dark except for a few lights toward the rear of the room. Near the head librarian's office.

I called out for good measure, "Mrs. Longstreet! It's me, Linda!"

A couple of minutes later, the florescent light at the

desk flickered on, and Mrs. Longstreet's face appeared on the other side of the door.

She frowned and her face disappeared. A short time later she was unlocking the door. She pushed it open slightly but didn't invite us in. Daddy took the decision out of her hand, literally, and pulled the door open wider to step inside, me on his heels with arms loaded with quilts.

"Evening, Mrs. Longstreet," Daddy said, before walking past her to set the picnic basket Momma had prepared on the check out counter.

"Good evening," she managed. Then she turned her attention to me.

I confessed again, right on cue. "I'm sorry, Mrs. Longstreet. I know you told me not to come, but I couldn't stand the thought of you here all alone."

Daddy settled his hands on his hips and gazed toward the library shelves. "Now what exactly is goin' on here?"

"Nothing yet," Hannah said with a sigh. "You're my only visitors so far. But then —" she glanced at her watch " — it's only eight o'clock." Then she proceeded to give Daddy the condensed version of our ghost problem. She even showed him the poem that she'd put back up on the wall in case the ghost decided to check his work.

"Where are you plannin' on settin' up camp?" Daddy said, like a general ready to take over the war. Still hard to say what his opinion might be on the ghost subject, but at least he wasn't telling Mrs. Longstreet she needed hormones or something.

"Why, back in my office."

Daddy picked up the picnic basket again and motioned to Mrs. Longstreet. "Lead the way." She pressed her lips together, and the look she gave me could've been either gratitude or a storm warning. It was hard to tell. She moved past us and re-locked the front doors, then marched through the darkened library toward her office.

Daddy and I followed. "Now if we was huntin' deer or ducks," Daddy said, "we'd need to build a blind."

"A what?" Mrs. Longstreet asked, like she hadn't heard him right.

"A blind, you know, a hidey place so the —" he straightened his back like he needed to impress her "—your *quarry* won't be scared away by seein' you."

It took less than fifteen minutes for Daddy to rearrange Hannah's "camp" to his satisfaction. We moved her extra flashlight and disposable camera off the desk and I helped him stack file boxes around and on top leaving a hole on each side so you could look out. Then he pulled a chair up next to Hannah's office chair before going with me to the children's area to get a small chair for me. We were like the three bears in Goldilocks. Daddy in the office chair, Hannah in the regular size chair and me on a shorter version.

Then we commenced to watchin.' Daddy convinced Mrs. Longstreet to eat some of the food that Momma had packed up while he and I kept an eye on the book shelves. When she'd eaten about enough to feed a bird, Daddy rummaged around in what was left and had a second supper of cold biscuits and gravy. Then he sighed and leaned back in his chair. "Well, now, this ain't so bad. Reminds me of camping up on old Colchik in the spring." He patted his stomach. "The food's better, though."

"I can't tell you how much I appreciate what the both of you have done, but I really can't ask you to stay here and watch with me. After all, nothing may happen."

I could see she was still worried about her county supervisor finding out that she thought there was a ghost in the library. She knew my daddy. Unless the library's Casper presented himself in the invisible flesh and asked my daddy to dance, by tomorrow morning when the library opened, it would be all over town about the ghost-watch.

Maybe it had been a bad idea to get Daddy involved.

"You two should go on home," Mrs. Longstreet said. "I can handle this."

"I think we'll stay a bit longer." He checked his watch. "Leave in time to catch the eleven o'clock news." He yawned then crossed his arms.

So there we were, hidden from the world in our box fort.

"Is there anything we can do while we wait?" I whispered to Mrs. Longstreet. I was thinking of some kind of library work since the dimmed lights made reading a threat to our eyes. In answer to my question she slid open her desk drawer and withdrew a pack of cards.

Mrs. Longstreet didn't play poker and Daddy didn't play canasta, so we settled on Go Fish. It didn't take long for Daddy to lose interest since we beat him twice in the first half hour. That and the fact we had to whisper as we played so we wouldn't scare off the ghost.

Hannah and I continued to play for another hour or so. By that time, Daddy had fallen asleep in Hannah's office chair. I tried not to jump at every wayward noise, but I guess my big eyes gave me away.

"Every building or house has its own sounds," Hannah whispered. "That particular thump and wheeze was just the heat kicking on."

"Oh. Okay."

In the middle of the next hand, Daddy let out a snorting snore that made us both jump. With one hand on her heart, Mrs. Longstreet gazed at my daddy for a long moment before adjusting her glasses and looking at me. "Your mother must be a wonderful woman."

I wasn't exactly sure what she meant by that, but it qualified as a compliment so I said, "Thank you, she is."

We played cards until both of us were fished out. Then we settled back to wait.

Wrapped in one of my momma's quilts, I had dozed off

myself when something startled me awake. It took a couple of seconds to remember where I was. I found the library clock on the wall in the dim light and realized it was just after midnight.

Uh-oh. We'd slept through the eleven o'clock news. Daddy would be ...

A sliding sound, like something being dragged, sent a flash of fear from my toes to my hair. I sat up and looked into Mrs. Longstreet's wide eyes. She'd heard it too. "The ghost," I whispered.

I pushed up to my feet and dropped the quilt. Just then, Daddy let out another loud open-mouthed snore, and I had to clap a hand over my own mouth to stop a scream.

"Wake him up so he doesn't chase the ghost away," Hannah ordered in a tense whisper.

Daddy was winding up for another snore, so I removed my hand from my mouth and clapped it over his. He snuffled and turned his head, but I stayed with him — holding in the sound.

There was a thump in the back, near the employee break room, in the hallway leading to the rear door. Then the stomping of feet. Hannah gave me a worried look.

I shook Daddy awake, keeping my hand on his mouth. "Daddy! The ghost is here!" I whispered. He pushed my hand away, and I pressed my finger to my lips to shush him.

The squeaking of a door brought him up straight in the chair. He nodded that he understood, searched around for the flashlight at his feet, then stood.

"Stay here," he said.

Hannah grabbed his arm. "Oh, no, you don't. I'm going with you. I intend to see this with my own eyes." She grabbed the disposable camera and pushed the little button to turn on the flash.

Daddy looked at me.

"I don't want to stay here by myself," I said, and I wasn't kidding. Every scary movie I'd ever seen had some stupid girl who went in the basement or the garage or *anywhere* alone and ended up the next victim. Not me. I guess he could see decision in my eyes.

"All right, let's go, but stay behind me."

We were a lot quieter than the ghost. Once he, or I guess to be fair, she, had shown up, he/she didn't seem to worry about making noise. When the three of us reached the hallway door, where the carpet gave way to linoleum, we stopped. Daddy signaled for us to stay on one side of the door, and he stepped across to wait on the other.

The light was on in the break room and the sounds coming out of there were just like the ones in that movie *Close Encounters* when all the electrical appliances started running on their own. We could hear the microwave and the little radio the staff sometimes used to listen to the Braves games. This was my first experience with a ghost, but already I could tell the movies must have it all wrong.

Then the microwave dinged, the radio changed stations several times before going silent and the overhead light flicked off. Footsteps were coming down the hall toward us, headed for the library shelves. Looks like we'd caught our ghost. I had the fleeting thought that people always assumed ghosts *flew* from place to place. But then Mrs. Longstreet said under her breath, "Now, we've got you." She raised the small camera and, like a mirror image on the other side of the door, my daddy raised the flashlight to use as a club.

I'm sorry to admit I screamed when the dark shadow loomed toward us. The flash of the camera blinded me for a moment, but another sound scared me worse. My daddy had swung the flashlight and caught the edge of the door instead of the ghost, but he let out a howl like he'd been run through with a sword. And now he and the ghost were wrestling on the linoleum, bumpin' the walls in the small space and cussin' a blue streak.

"Hold him!" Mrs. Longstreet said, and took another flash picture.

Unable to stand still any longer, I pushed past her and found the hallway light switch. When the lights flashed on, there was my daddy, red-faced, with his shirt all stained by ectoplasm just like in *Ghostbusters*. Except this ectoplasm smelled like coffee. And the ghost looked exactly like Mr. Foxer Atlas, the elderly man who ran Mossy Creek Woodwork and Signs, out on Trailhead road.

"What in tarnation are you folks doin?" the ghost yelled. "Ya nearly scared me into the great reward."

"Foxer Atlas! What do you mean, what are we doing? What are you doing in my library at this time of night?"

I knew Mrs. Longstreet had to be upset, because normally she wouldn't let anyone know she considered the library hers. I bent down to take Daddy's arm. "Are you all right, Daddy?"

Before he could answer there was a loud metallic tapping coming from the front of the library. I think we all jumped, even Mr. Atlas. Then the beam of an industrial-sized flashlight flashed across the walls.

"Open up, it's the police!" a female voice ordered.

Mrs. Longstreet handed me the keys she carried in her pocket. "Here, go let Sandy in."

Turned out it was Sandy *and* my mother.

Momma decided, after we didn't come back home, that she needed to check on us. When she'd pulled her car into the library parking lot, Sandy was driving by and saw her.

"Mr. Atlas," Sandy said in a firm tone, "the Mossy Creek Police Department, consisting only of the chief, my bubba Mutt, and yours truly, has had a real long day. Mutt's gone home, the chief's sitting over at his office in a foul mood with his door shut, and I was just about to head home, myself. Jess is waiting for me with a cold beer and a cherry cigarillo. Now, I want you to explain to my and to Mrs. Longstreet's satisfaction why you have been breaking and entering the library at night. And make it quick."

"I'm an insomniac," Mr. Atlas said.

"A what?" My Daddy asked as he let my momma fuss over his scorched belly and ruined shirt. You could say he was a little perturbed with Mr. Atlas for a lot of reasons. I think the possibility of a real ghost had given us all a good fright.

"An insomniac," Mr. Atlas repeated. "I can't sleep good."

"Your husband is a true hero," Mrs. Longstreet said to Momma. Then she gave Mr. Atlas a hard look. "Insomniac, my hind foot. Who knows what would have happened if I'd confronted you with a gun instead a camera. I was so afraid, I might have shot you before I recognized you."

"Oh, now Miz Longstreet, I wasn't hurtin' nuthin'," Mr. Atlas said, sounding hurt. "I can't help it if I can't sleep and I like to read. I've had a key to that back door for ten years, since I did some signs for the library. If I hadn't taken to writing poetry you woulda never caught me."

"Well, I think you owe Miz Hannah an apology," Sandy said. "Just for scaring her. And I also think Amos will ask Judge Blakely to order you to do some community service to pay for your crimes. So, unless you want to go to jail, I decree that you are the newest library volunteer. It's up to Miz Longstreet to decide what she wants you to do. Whatever she says, goes."

Then she looked at Hannah. "I think you could use a good janitor around here, couldn't you? Might even need a night watchman. You think about it. If he gives you any trouble, you just call me."

Hannah sniffed and looked down her nose at Atlas,

before saying, "You can start by putting away all the boxes in my office."

"Sure thing." He looked back at her gratefully. "If I'm gonna be a librarian, will you teach me the Dewey Decimal System? I've always had a hankerin' to learn that thing."

Hannah gaped at him, but her surprise slowly turned to affection. How many men actually *want* a librarian to teach them the Dewey Decimal System? "Why, I'd be honored," she said.

Case closed. Although, before Sandy left, Mrs. Longstreet quizzed her on the overdue handwriting book. Sandy mumbled, frowned, then brightened when her walkie-talkie began to beep. "Got a call from the chief," she said, and hurried out the front door. "*Andy Griffith* must be over."

By the time we got home, Daddy had finally found the humor in the night's events. Reluctant or not, he'd come out of the situation a hero and a ghostbuster — with only a ruined shirt.

Nightfall: Sunny's Story

I had spent the last few hours experimenting. While Honey and Bert put the babies to bed, I tried moving the rocking chair. No good. It sat there. When Honey headed back downstairs to get out the pizza pockets, I tried blocking her on the stairs. No dice. I listened in when Mayor Walker called on the phone. I heard Bert tell her the babies were doing great. I tried to shout my opinion to the mayor. Didn't work.

And later, as Honey prepared Jeremy for bed, helping him bathe, drying him off, brushing his teeth, I tried sitting on the toothpaste. If I could only write a word or two in toothpaste ...

Nope, didn't work, either. This being a ghost got more and more annoying by the moment.

Honey put Jeremy to bed, then went back downstairs to join Bert, who was already in bed himself. Thank goodness they were both tired — I didn't know how I'd handle watching my sister and her husband make love. And I would have watched, too, if there was any chance it would make them notice me.

As they drifted off to sleep, I made one last attempt to reach her. If I could somehow appear in Honey's dreams, maybe I could tell her how I felt about Jeremy being around the babies.

But how does somebody appear in another person's dream? I flew through her head a couple of times, I tried whispering in her ear, I even danced in front of the bed like a fool. Honey snored, that's all. Of course, that didn't mean she wasn't dreaming about me. And how could I know if I'd succeeded anyway?

Still, I had to keep trying. I was in the middle of a particularly creative maneuver, sort of a charades for ghosts, when I heard a noise on the baby monitor. The twins were stirring. They didn't usually eat in the middle of the night, but with Cam and me being dead, their schedule was off.

I looked at Bert and Honey. They didn't move. Honey had always been a sound sleeper, but she ought to hear my babies. Soon Amy and Anna were launched into full-fledged wail mode. Bert and Honey roused a little, then turned over and continued to sleep.

That's when Jeremy appeared, apparently bothered by the noise. Thank heaven he hadn't done anything about it, like try to silence the babies. Instead, he approached the bed and nudged his mom. Honey snorted a bit, but didn't wake. Geez, couldn't they hear that racket?

Jeremy frowned, then went to his father's side and nudged him. Nothing. Bert was sleeping like the dead, no pun intended.

I watched in a panic as Jeremy headed back upstairs. I flew after him, praying that he'd go straight back to his room, but oh no, he trudged right into the babies' room. He stared down at them a long moment. Then, to my horror, he picked them up awkwardly, holding one under each arm the way a quarterback would carry footballs, and headed down the stairs.

Torn between flat-out terror and relief that he was bringing them to Honey, I followed along, sobbing ghostly tears. He narrowly missed banging their heads on the banister half a dozen times. By the time we'd reached the bottom, I was one simmering mass of ethereal rage, cursing him, cursing my sister, even cursing God for bringing me to this place where I couldn't even take care of my babies.

When Jeremy didn't go toward Bert and Honey's bedroom and instead headed out the door with the babies, I thought I'd explode all over the porch. I flew back to Honey and Bert and screamed at them. *Get up! Get up!* I yelled. All they did was snore.

By the time I got back to Jeremy, he was halfway to the Blackshears' house, crossing a pasture in the freezing cold, still carrying the weeping babies slung under each arm. Oh, no. He was headed for that blasted pond — he was going to drown my babies!

You have never seen a ghost go so nuts in all your life. I was like a whirling dervish, flying in and out of Jeremy, screaming at God, crying soundless, waterless tears.

Then Jeremy walked past the pond. That brought me up short. What in heaven's name was the boy doing? He reached Hank and Casey's house, then trudged up onto their porch. For half a minute, I thought maybe he was planning to rock the twins in the porch swing. But that was an idiotic idea — if he'd wanted to rock them, there was a rocking chair in their room.

Instead, he plopped them down on the porch on their backs. I gasped. All right, so he hadn't hurt them, but darn, it was cold out here and all they had on was their matching sleep suits. Did he mean to leave them here alone, their little arms flailing at the chill? They'd be dead by morning. Bad as I wanted to hold my babies, I didn't want it to happen like that. No, indeed.

But Jeremy didn't leave. He opened the porch door and tried the door knob to the inner door. When it proved to be locked, he started kicking the door. And banging. And pressing the doorbell with his finger, over and over. I went from terror to relief, then back to terror in seconds. What if nobody was home?

Thankfully, it wasn't long before the porch light came

on. Hank opened the door, his eyes still bleary with sleep. "Jeremy? What are you doing here? It's nearly two in the morning!" Then he heard the crying and spotted the babies laid out on the porch like a pair of turtles knocked on their backs. "Oh, no, Jeremy, you can't carry those babies out here like that. What's got into you, son?"

"Got into you, son," Jeremy repeated dutifully. He watched as Hank rushed out and picked up the babies, one in each arm.

Hank started back toward the door. "Come inside a minute, while I throw some clothes on and tell Casey what's going on. Then we'll call your Mom and Dad —"

Jeremy blocked the door before Hank could go back in. Then he pushed Hank, hard enough to make him stagger back a step.

I screamed. Hank just frowned. "Now stop that, Jeremy. You're only making things worse. We've got to get these babies out of the cold."

Jeremy grunted, an almost primeval sound, then pushed him toward the steps. With his hands full of babies, Hank could only protest and back down the stairs. But Jeremy kept pushing, just enough to move him, but not enough to make him lose his balance. Hank finally gave up.

"Okay, we'll go over there now." Hank grumbled the whole way. "Casey's going to be frantic, wondering what's going on. And couldn't you even let me get a coat? Coldest night in Mossy Creek in a long time, and you've got to drag me out into it without a coat. It's freezing out here."

Not for Jeremy. Honey had told me that the boy once dove into Hank's pond in the dead of winter. When they'd fished him out, he wasn't even shivering.

But maybe he wasn't completely immune to the cold, because now that he had Hank moving in the direction he wanted, he was walking so fast that even long-legged Hank was having trouble keeping up with him. As they approached the house, with the babies sobbing and Jeremy nearly running, Hank swore under his breath.

"Your mother is going to have your hide for leaving the door open on a night like this, son." Hank marched up the stairs behind Jeremy, nearly running into him when the boy stopped short on the threshold.

That's when Hank's expression changed. To my shock, he handed the babies to Jeremy. "Stay here. I'll be right back." He hurried into the kitchen where I heard him pick up the phone.

At first, I was too preoccupied with hovering over my babies to notice what Hank was saying.

Then his conversation filtered in through my fear. "It's not too bad in the front of the house, Chief, but I've got to get to Honey and Bert. Just bring Doc Champion, okay? The gas smells pretty strong the further you get into the house. Thank God Jeremy left the door open."

The truth hit me then. Why Honey and Bert hadn't roused. And Bert had said something about the furnace ... The furnace, of course! It must have a leak.

I began to quiver. Some guardian I was. I couldn't even tell when there was a gas leak, when my babies were about to die. But Jeremy could, bless his heart.

Moments later, Hank came out of the house, carrying Honey, and laid her on the porch. He took a few big breaths, held the last one, then went back in and got Bert. By the time Hank had emerged with my brother-in-law slung over his shoulder, the firemen and paramedics had arrived. I recognized Mr. Bainbridge and Boo Bottoms. As the fire chief rushed inside, Boo stayed behind to work on reviving Bert since Hank had already started on Honey.

For the first time since my death, I paid no attention to my crying babies. I just kept watching the air over Honey and Bert, praying not to see a spirit. Because what would I do without them to watch over Amy and Anna? And what would Jeremy do without his mom and dad?

Jeremy. I looked over at my nephew. The babies were practically screaming in his ears, and he just stood there stoically, his face contorted in a frown, his arms holding the babies tight, but gently, oh so gently. He kept his eyes fixed on Honey, and in them I saw worry.

Suddenly, Honey coughed and sputtered a little and came awake. "What on earth — Hank, what are you —"

"You're very lucky to be awake, let me tell you," Hank told her, "and you can thank your boy for that. He saved your life." Bert roused beside Honey, mumbling about his head hurting, and Hank broke into a grin as he added, "Jeremy saved both your lives."

Chief Royden arrived now, lights flashing, and with him was Doc Champion. As Doc turned to checking out Honey and Bert, Hank retrieved one baby from Jeremy and Chief Royden took the other. Boo grabbed quilts from the house and wrapped the babies snugly. Mayor Walker drove up next. She asked questions of everyone, studied the situation quickly, then walked up to the chief. They looked at each other for a moment. There was sadness between them, even I could see that. She held out her arms, and he handed her the baby. Then he walked away without looking back.

With any worries about his parents soothed, Jeremy turned to stare at the flashing lights. I suddenly remembered Jeremy at four, a bundle of energy running from one lighted ride to another at the carnival, laughing the whole time. Now he was watching the lights flash red and blue, grinning like a circus clown. Like a kid.

And the light dawned on me, too. "You love Amy and Anna already, don't you?" I told him softly. "You love them as much as I do."

Honey had once confided to me that she didn't think Jeremy understood the concept of love. But she was wrong. I knew that now.

"Take care of my babies," I told him. Beyond him shone a different kind of light now, bright and white and beckoning me home.

I could swear he looked straight at me then. But I couldn't be sure because the white light was filling my vision.

Then there was no time to apologize for all the bad things I'd thought about him, no time even for one last glance at my girls. Even though they were crying, it had no more power to hold me. The tether snapped, and next thing I knew, I was soaring up the tunnel toward the light, faster and faster, higher and higher.

But just as I spotted Cam waving to me from the distant end, I heard from behind me Jeremy's monotone voice, faint but distinct, say, "My babies." I wouldn't have to worry about Amy and Anna ever again.

Night's End:
Ida

It was nearly four a.m. when I made my way back to the farm. Honey and Bert and Jeremy and the babies were fine, thank God. Everyone in Mossy Creek was safe and sound for the night.

I wandered into Jeb's study, feeling dazed. I built a fire on the hearth, poured a double bourbon into a monogrammed silver cup I'd given Jeb on our first anniversary, then sat in his leather armchair and stared out his dark, frosted window toward Rose Top, the vineyards, and the Sitting Tree.

"It's been a long day, Jeb," I whispered. "A strange day. A special day. Sad. Happy. Confusing. Enlightening. A lot of people's lives changed today. Some, a little. Some, a lot. Mine included. For better or worse, nothing will ever be the same."

And then I cried.

What a day.

Lady Victoria Salter Stanhope
The Clifts
Seaward Road
St. Ives, Cornwall, TR3 7PJ
United Kingdom

Dear Vick,

You see what I mean, now? It
was no ordinary day, to say the
least. We pretty much ran the
gamut of emotions and events.
Public. Private. Funny. Sad.
Silly. Scary. It's hard to say
which happening has gotten the
most debate and discussion
since then, but Irene's scooter
protest, the Lyman family's brush
with danger, and Eula Mae Whit's
encounter with the bank robber
certainly score high on my gossip
meter.

Of course, there's nothing else
quite like the Ida/Amos news, so
if I had to vote, I'd probably
give that the blue ribbon for
shock value. How did the story
of their private kiss get out in

public, you ask? All it took was
Del Jackson confiding his misery
to Marle Settles, Hope's husband.
Marle told Hope, and Hope told
Ingrid, and then Hope and Ingrid
took Ida down to Atlanta for a
girls' night out, and after a few
cosmopolitan martinis at the bar
of the Buckhead Ritz Carlton, Hope
and Ingrid wheedled the story of
the kiss out of Ida, who swore
them to secrecy.

Which is where the story about the
kiss would have stopped, except
that one of the bartenders at
the Ritz overheard it, and that
bartender is the cousin of a
state patrol officer assigned to
the governor, and the bartender
recognized Ida as the governor's
aunt (Ida gets a lot of TV time
in Atlanta, always battling the
governor in the news.) So the
bartender told the state patrol
officer about the secret romance
between the mayor and the police
chief of Mossy Creek, and the
officer told the governor's
secretary, Gloria, (who's dating
the officer, even though she's
married, but that's a story for
another day,) and Gloria gleefully
told the governor — Ham — and Ham
didn't miss two blinks calling

his mother, Ardaleen, in Bigelow
— Ida's older sister — and telling
her, and since Ardaleen is all too
happy to cause Ida embarrassment,
the story of the kiss was all over
the county by the next day.

The kiss story didn't just have
"legs," as we say in the gossip
business, it had wheels, sirens,
and its own lane on the highway.

Ida and Amos are both fit to be
tied, meaning they're mad as wet
setting hens, they could eat lead
and spit nails, they're ill as
sore-tailed cats ... in plain
English, they're up the creek
without a paddle.

Who knows what'll happen next? I
can promise you this much:
Things are about to get even more
interesting in Mossy Creek.

Hurray!

Your shameless, gossip-loving
friend,

Katie

Recipes from Bubba Rice

Recipes from Bubba Rice

Hello, friends, Creekites, and fellow diners!

I'm Win Allen, aka "Bubba Rice," owner and head chef (well, okay, the only chef) of Bubba Rice Lunch and Catering. My diner is located just off the square, behind Mossy Creek Drugs and Sundries. Drop by for a meal any time you're in town, and don't forget to catch my TV show, *Cooking With Bubba Rice*, produced by Bert Lyman at WMOS Media, ("The Voice of the Creek") on local cable access channel 22.

I've personally tested all the recipes that appear in the Mossy Creek Hometown Series, and I guarantee them with the Bubba Rice Seal of Approval. I take good food — and the philosophy behind good food — very seriously. When you visit the diner you'll see my rules of cooking on the placemats and wall plaques. I've included some of them on the next page, for your reading enjoyment.

Happy Cooking!

Win Allen, aka Bubba Rice

All I Ever Need to Know about Life I Learned from Cooking with Bubba Rice

- Starch is the glue that holds a family reunion together.

- Measuring takes all the fun out of cooking.

- Always write down Mama's recipes so you can sell them later.

- A pinch of this and a pinch of that will get your face slapped.

- Barbeque is pork. Everything else is just grilled.

- Never insult the people who handle your food.

- Never be afraid to eat the last piece of cake.

- Don't plant a garden unless you have lots of friends who'll take tomatoes.

- If you need friends, plant a garden. Everyone wants fresh tomatoes.

- A slow, promising simmer never hurt any relationship.

Bubba's Pecan Crusted Dijon Tuna

OK, you've all heard Jeff Foxworthy's "You Might Be a Redneck if…" jokes, right?

Well, this one goes like this, "If you think that tuna only comes in a can, you might be a redneck." A good piece of yellow fin tuna can be cooked in just about any way that you can cook a rib eye or a filet mignon.

Ingredients:

> 2 - 12 ounce yellow fin tuna steaks about 1-1/2 inches thick.
>
> 1/2 cup chopped pecans
>
> 1/3 cup corn meal
>
> A pinch of cayenne pepper
>
> Dijon or Creole mustard
>
> 2 tbsp peanut oil

Preparation:

Put the pecans, corn meal and cayenne pepper in a food processor and pulse until coarse. Small pieces of pecans are good. Dust is bad. Don't overdo it. Brush both sides of the tuna steaks with the mustard, then dredge in the pecan/corn meal mix. Evenly coat both sides, and don't forget the edges. Pour the peanut oil into a non stick skillet over medium/high heat. Sear the tuna, 3 minutes per side. With a 1-1/2 inch tuna steak, this will result in a medium steak. If you're of a mind that fish must be cooked well done, reread the first couple of lines and then finish it off for another 3-4 minutes in a 375 degree oven.

Serves 2

Roasted Asparagus with Red Pepper & Scallions

OK, I've been sitting here trying to come up with some bit of humor or life wisdom, and there just isn't anything humorous about asparagus. It's really good, it's just not funny. But, pecan crusted Dijon tuna and wasabi mashed potatoes go REALLY well with this dish.

Ingredients:

    1 bundle of fresh asparagus
    1 bundle of fresh scallions or green onions
    1/2 cup of diced red bell pepper
    3 tbsp extra virgin olive oil
    Salt & pepper to taste

Preparation:

Trim the asparagus and the scallions and dice the red pepper. Place the asparagus spears in a baking dish. Add the scallions on top of the asparagus, then sprinkle the diced red pepper evenly over the top. Drizzle the olive oil evenly over the dish. Add salt and pepper and place in a 375 degree oven for 15 — 20 minutes.

Serves 4

Wasabi Mashed Potatoes

Yes, I'm really giving you a mashed potato recipe. For those of you who aren't sushi fans, wasabi paste is that little dollop of green dynamite on the corner of the dish that you mix with soy sauce to "liven" things up. And, no, I haven't lost my mind. This is really good, but you may want to serve it to your less adventurous friends in a dimly lit room, because it does have a slight green tinge to it and every good Southerner knows, "mashed taters ain't green!"

Ingredients:

4 large red potatoes
4 tbsp butter
1/2 cup milk
1 tbsp wasabi paste
Salt & pepper to taste

Preparation:

Peel and slice the potatoes and bring to a boil over medium/ high heat. Cook until fork tender, then drain well. Add the butter, salt & pepper and milk and mash until smooth with your handy dandy potato masher. Add the wasabi paste and blend in well with a hand held mixer (Yes, I'm using a mixer on mashed potatoes. You'll never get the wasabi blended in evenly with a handy dandy potato masher).

Serves 2

The Mossy Creek
Storytelling Club

(In order of appearance)

Ida .... Deborah Smith

Irene and Melvin .... Sandra Chastain

Patty .... Maureen Hardegree

Linda.. Virginia Ellis

Rory...Dee Sterling

Pearl .... Maureen Hardegree

Louise...Carolyn McSparren

Peggy...Carolyn McSparren

Eula Mae .... Carmen Green

Sandy... Susan Goggins

Amos ....Debra Dixon

Sunny..Sabrina Jeffries

Bubba Rice ....Wayne Dixon

Book 1 — Mossy Creek

1. Amos Royden, Police Chief of Mossy Creek, is an extraordinary man. Knowledgeable of the law, he tempers justice with common sense. Discuss both the favorable and unfavorable aspects of his application of the law. Could such a police chief really exist today?

2. The town of Mossy Creek is fictional, but could be similar to many small towns across America. Is it more likely that these small towns would flourish in the South? Could some metropolitan areas, such as the boroughs of New York, have a similar atmosphere?

3. Mossy Creekites are proud of their heritage. They love the intimacy of living in a small town. Is it possible that the ethnic neighborhoods of larger towns possess that same feeling? How are the folks who live in those ethnic neighborhoods similar to Mossy Creekites? How are they different?

4. Miss Ida Hamilton, mayor of Mossy Creek, is a feisty, independent woman. She has a small bronze plaque, given to her by her husband, that says: Tradition, Courage. Love. Can you find evidence in the story "Ida Shoots the Sign" of these qualities in Ida? Is she like other women of this century?

5. Mossy Creek's motto is, "Ain't Going Nowhere. Don't Want To." Discuss what this really means. Do you really think it means that nobody in Mossy Creek wants progress? Or does it have more to do with the atmosphere of friendship and caring that exists there?

6. In "A Day in the Life," Sandy practically attacks the woman peering into Miss Lorna's window. Is her behavior rational? Is this just one more indication of the lengths folks in small towns go to in order to protect their fellow citizens? Would this type of behavior ever happen or be tolerated in larger towns?

7. Is the handling of Casey Blackshear's disability believ-

able? Would the courage this woman shows in "Casey at the Bat" encourage others with disabilities to strive to do more? Does her story typify the way "normal" people react to people with disabilities? Does this story encourage you to examine your own feelings toward people with disabilities?

8. What caused Maggie Hart to return to Mossy Creek? Why has she never married? Are her reasons realistic? Do you believe Maggie is hiding behind her mother's illness as a reason to avoid lasting relationships that develop into something more? Discuss Maggie's relationship with Smokey. Discuss Maggie's developing relationship with Tag. Does this relationship show a glimmer of hope for Maggie and Tag?

9. In "Your Cheatin' Dart," is the rivalry realistic? Discuss why or why not? In such contests, is the outcome more important or the playing of the game? What is Michael Conners' philosophy of life? Do you find him intriguing? Would you enjoy sitting at O'Days and discussing politics with Michael and the regulars?

10. Jayne Reynolds and Ingrid Beechum in "The Naked Bean" are both running from their pasts. How are their lives similar? How are they different? What are each of these women doing to overcome the obstacles life has put before them?

11. Do you know people who share Sue Ora Salter's fascination with death? What is her fascination with the subject? Do you believe it stems from a fear of her own death? Discuss how age affects our interest in dying. The humorous manner in which this story is told draws us into the action. Discuss the use of humor in this story and others in Mossy Creek. Is it an effective device for character development? How?

12. The eccentricities of the characters, like most Mossy Creekites, are typical of people everywhere. Is it true that in small towns, our eccentricities are lovable traits, while in larger cities they cause friction?

Book 2 —
Reunion at Mossy Creek

1. Reunions are a central theme of the book. What are
    your most painful or most joyous high school reunion
    memories? What makes the memories of high school
    so poignant? What unforgettable books did you read
    in high school?
2. Kids often interpret their guilt or innocence far more
    dramatically than reality demands. In Reunion At
    Mossy Creek, Rainey, Rob, and Hank were convinced
    they'd caused the fire that burned down the high school
    20 years ago. Who is your favorite guilt-drive juvenile
    character in fiction? Your favorite guilt-driven adult
    character?
3. Reunion At Mossy Creek reveals the romantic tension
    between Mayor Ida Walker and young-enough-to-be-
    her-son Police Chief Amos Royden. Can you think of
    other novels that have explored the older women/
    younger man theme?
4. "The P Patch" is a story about a grieving widow who
    finds unlikely friends in the bawdy women of the Mossy
    Creek Garden Club. What is it about women's friend-
    ships that is so nurturing and so comforting to explore?
    Name other memorable stories about female friends.
5. Mossy Creek's oldest living resident, Eula Mae Whit,
    gets away with comments and attitudes that would
    make the populace shun any younger resident. Why
    do we thoroughly enjoy stories in which children, the
    elderly, or the outsiders of society give everyone else
    a ringing comeuppance?
6. Ed Brady Sr and his son, Ed Brady, Jr. have a poignant
    reunion of their own in the book. Does literature often
    overlook the emotional complexity of the father/son
    relationship?

7. Governor Ham Bigelow is a fun villain, so deliberately scheming that we can almost picture him twirling a handlebar mustache like the villains in old silent films. Are villains in literature more fun when they're so evil we can't picture them in real life, or so subtle they are disturbingly believable?

Book 3 —
Summer In Mossy Creek

1. Mossy Creek Chief of Police Amos Royden isn't a fan of what he refers to as the "gray zone" of law enforcement. Why does he hate police matters that aren't black and white? For what does he risk stepping into the gray zone? Why?

2. Several stories in this collection explore the darker side of friendship— fights and feuds. What did Grace Peacock and her neighbor Mamie Brown, Inez Hamilton Hilley and her cousin Ardaleen Bigelow, Sara-Beth Connelly and former BFF (Best Friend Forever) Carolee Langford, Lila Spivey and her unwitting nemesis Fryzeen Sneerly feud over? What caused some of these women to make amends? What prevented others from doing so?

3. "Louise and Jack" and "Hope and Marle" deal with lost loves returning to Mossy Creek. What kept Louise and Jack from exploring their feelings in the past? What keeps them apart now? Why are Hope and Marle able to reconcile the past with their present and embrace a future together?

4. In "Louise and Jack," we discover that prejudice against inter-racial relationships existed in the past even in idyllic Mossy Creek. Do you think either Jack or Louise regrets his or her choice to give in to societal and familial pressures? Has the South changed enough that inter-racial relationships and marriages are any easier today? Why, or why not?

5. How death affects friendship is explored in "Sadie and Etta" and in "Laurie and Tweedle Dee." What legacy does Etta leave Sadie? What does Laurie leave Tweedle Dee? What things has a dying relative or friend left you?

What life lessons do you think were embedded in these items?

6. Friendship makes strange bedfellows in a few of the stories. For example, Laurie and her pet canary Tweedle Dee, Opal and her sisters' spirits, Lucy Belle and her grandmother-in-crime Inez Hamilton Hilley. What other unusual friendships were explored in this and other Mossy Creek anthologies? What benefits do people gain from befriending others far different from them and their experience?

7. Relationships between sisters are explored in "Opal and the Suggs Sisters" and "Therese and the Stroud Women." How are the sisters in these stories friends? How are they enemies? Why is the sister bond in Opal's story so strong that it transcends death? What other books or movies have you read or seen that explore sisters' lives? Why do you think authors never seem to tire of exploring the nuances of biological and figurative sisterhood?

8. Several authors use Southern traditions in observing death in their stories' settings. In "Sadie and Etta," we learn that Ben and Sadie buried Etta in her favorite spot, under the Sitting Tree, and that they honor her by putting wildflowers on her grave every year on their anniversary. In "Therese and the Stroud Women," Therese learns from Granny Georgie and the aunts how to care for the graves of her relatives in the Old Baptist Cemetery. In "Louise and Jack," friends and family gather at the deceased person's house for food and comfort. What traditions do you follow when a loved one passes? Which of these traditions are related to your family background; which are related to the part of the country you live in?

9. Sara-Beth Connelly misses the "You too?" moments she shared with estranged friend Carolee Langford. Did you ever have a friendship as strong as the one Sara-Beth and Carolee shared before the betrayal? Describe

one of those "You too?" moments you experienced with your best friend.

10. At ten years old, Therese Taylor follows Mayor Ida's advice to look for Opportunity. In doing so, she accompanies her grandmother and aunts to their monthly clean-up at the Old Baptist Cemetery and discovers who she is. How old were you when you discovered who you are? What special or ordinary event in your life helped you determine your place in the world?

11. In "Laurie and Tweedle Dee," Laurie Grey knew she was dying and set out to spend what remained of her life doing what she'd always wanted to do— writing stories and sharing them with others. If you were given a similar diagnosis, what would you do in the time you had remaining? With whom would you spend your time?

12. In "Amos and Dog," Amos decides to let Ida "draw her own conclusions about if there was or was not a little spark of chemistry" between them. Will Ida ever admit to feeling something other than respect or friendship for Amos? Why, or why not?

READING GUIDE

Book 4 —
Blessings of Mossy Creek

1. In Harry's Unexpected Blessing, roses are a metaphor for love and hope. Discuss the symbolism of this very old and very traditional flower. What do roses mean to you?

2. Argelia Rodriguez, Mossy Creek's dance teacher, is of Latin heritage but, contrary to popular belief, doesn't know how to tango. What is it that makes the classic Latin dances (the tango, the rumba, etc.) so sensual, and so much fun?

3. Young John Wesley McCready, who learns a valuable lesson about good deeds and kindness, typifies the fresh perspective of child characters in literature. Discuss the appeal of these pint-sized narrators in your favorite books, such as Huck Finn, To Kill A Mockingbird, and the Little House On The Prairie novels.

4. In "Home Is Where The Sword Is" pub owner Michael Conners tiptoes around the delicate issue of male-female friendships. Do you believe men and women can really be "just friends?"

5. Sugar Milford discovers unexpected blessings in the form of a small goat named Missy Belle. From the funny (Garfield) to the sublime (Seabiscuit) animal characters enliven our favorite novels. What is it about pets that brings out the best in us?

6. Trisha Peavy Cecil is confronted with an all-too-recognizable problem of small town social life: For good and for bad, everyone knows your business. Is this a blessing or a curse? And can't small town people be just as lonely — and just as mysterious — as those of a big city?

7. Most of us have fond memories of belonging to funny, harmless "girls' clubs," engaging in silly escapades

and innocent capers. Is this a rite of passage in childhood?

8. To children, religion is both a complex mystery and a simple value system. Do you think children benefit from exposure to differing beliefs, or is it better to give them a solid foundation before they begin to explore other ideas of faith and redemption?

9. Childhood can seem like the loneliest time in our lives. Often, children who feel isolated simply don't possess the social skills to reach out to others. Also, children tend to believe their problems and humiliations are strange and unique. How can we use books to connect with a child who needs reassurance and a sense of community?

10. Reverend Mark Phillips, new minister of Mossy Creek Mt. Gilead Methodist, follows in the footsteps of fictional ministers, priests, and rabbis who have delighted readers in many classic books and stories. What is it about the clergy that makes them such a fertile source for great reading?

11. Casey and Hank Blackshear travel to China to adopt a baby girl. In today's world, most of us know someone who's welcomed a foreign-born child into their home. Given the diversity of American backgrounds and the "melting pot" effect, do you see new trends in fiction? Have you been enlightened about other cultures by reading novels about them?

12. Younger men and older women. The topic is surfacing more often than ever, as sassy baby-boomer women defy stereotypes and pursue younger men without embarrassment. And the younger men pursue them in return! Amos and Ida are a perfect example of the sexy friendships that exist in the real world. Do you approve? Do you believe it's possible for women to form the same kind of viable relationships with younger men that men routinely form with younger women?

13. Blessings. We use the word to encompass a broad range of gratitudes, some profound and religious, others simple and worldly. Like prayer, meditation, and other forms of spiritually connecting to God, "counting your blessings" is an uplifting ritual that restores perspective in a chaotic world. How often do you count your blessings, and do you believe in the power of recognizing them every day?

Book 5 — A Day In Mossy Creek

1. The on-going, will-they-won't-they romance between 50-ish Ida and 35-ish Amos heats up in this book. Do you think romances between older women and younger men should be just as accepted as May-December romances involving older men and younger women?

2. As often happens, some of Mossy Creek's senior citizens pull off some outrageous shenanigans. What is it about old people doing deliciously shocking things that delights us so much?

3. Without giving away a plot point—you know which poignant story we mean—do you believe in angels?

4. Patty Campbell and Orville Gene Simpson clash over a bargain table full of goodies at a yard sale. The weekend yard sale is a staple of Southern culture. Some people search the sales like treasure hunters looking for Blackbeard's buried loot. What is it about the challenge—and the lovable tackiness—of these events that makes them so appealing?

5. Louise and Charlie have a lovingly cranky marriage. Why is there so much comfort in knowing you can see your partner as both the most wonderful and the most annoying person on earth?

6. Peggy is a typical grandmother. Josie is a typical granddaughter. Meaning they share all the usual joys and troubles. Grandparents often end up being the most memorable of our sentimental mentors. Explain why grandchildren often have far more forgiving memories of their grandparents than of their parents.

7. Winter in the South is often a snowless experience. There is something about a crisp, cold, blue-sky Southern day in mid-winter, among the quiet of the mountains or the fields, that can feel like the loneliest place in the universe. Discuss your own memories and feelings about a Southern winter.

Also available from BelleBooks

Everyone's Special Children's Series

KASEYBELLE
The Tiniest Fairy in the Kingdom

Sandra Chastain

ASTRONAUT NOODLE
on Planet Velocity

Kenlyn Foster Spence

Other Fine Fiction

CREOLA'S MOONBEAM
Milam
McGraw Propst

ALL GOD'S CREATURES
Carolyn
McSparren

SUNRISE
Jacquelyn
Cook

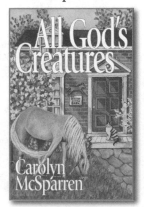
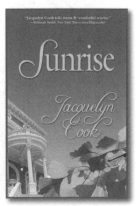

Also available from BelleBooks

Mossy Creek Hometown Series

Welcome to Mossy Creek, where you'll find a friendly face at every window and a heartfelt story behind every door.

Award-winning authors Deborah Smith, Sandra Chastain, Debra Dixon, Virginia Ellis, Nancy Knight and Donna Ball (*Sweet Tea And Jesus Shoes*) now blend their unique voices in a collective novel about the South, a series set in the fictional mountain town of Mossy Creek, Georgia.

So welcome to Mossy Creek, the town that insists it "Ain't goin' nowhere, and don't want to." Welcome Home.

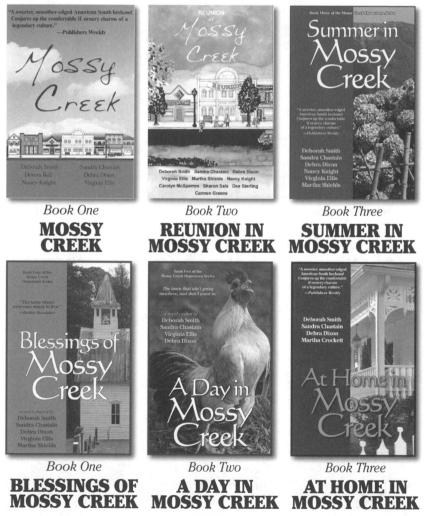

Book One
MOSSY CREEK

Book Two
REUNION IN MOSSY CREEK

Book Three
SUMMER IN MOSSY CREEK

Book One
BLESSINGS OF MOSSY CREEK

Book Two
A DAY IN MOSSY CREEK

Book Three
AT HOME IN MOSSY CREEK

303

The Mossy Creek Hometown Series